Santorini Caesars

A Chief Inspector Andreas Kaldis Mystery

Jeffrey Siger

Poisoned Pen Press

Copyright © 2016 by Jeffrey Siger

First Edition 2016

10 9 8 7 6 5 4 3 2 1

Library of Congress Catalog Card Number: 2016933728

ISBN: 9781464206016   Hardcover
      9781464206030   Trade Paperback

Poisoned Pen Press
6962 E. First Ave., Ste. 103
Scottsdale, AZ 85251
www.poisonedpenpress.com
info@poisonedpenpress.com

Printed in the United States of America

To Azriel Kenyah Siger, Gavriella Tovah Siger, and Rachel Ida McLaughlin.

Acknowledgments

Tranquilina Abad; Panayiotis "Pete" Apostolou; Roz and Mihalis Apostolou; Beth Deveny; Diane DiBiase; Andreas, Aleca, Nikos, Mihalis, and Anna Fiorentinos; Flora and Yanni Katsaounis; Panos Kelaidis; Alexis Komninos; Ioanna Lalaounis; Lila Lalaounis; Linda Marshall; Terrence McLaughlin, Karen Siger-McLaughlin, and Rachel Ida McLaughlin; Renee Pappas; Mihalis Paravalos; Barbara G. Peters and Robert Rosenwald; Frederick and Petros Rakas; Alan and Pat Siger; Jonathan, Jennifer, Azriel, and Gavriella Siger; Mihalis Sigounas and Carsten Stehr; Ed Stackler; Nikola Totuhov; Christos Vlachos; Artemis Voulgaris; Miranda Xafa; Barbara Zilly; Pete Zrioka.

And, of course, Aikaterini Lalaouni.

"*Now in this island of Atlantis there was a great and wonderful empire…But afterwards there occurred violent earthquakes and floods; and in a single day and night of misfortune all your warlike men in a body sank into the earth, and the island of Atlantis in like manner disappeared in the depths of the sea.*"

—Plato, the *Timaeus Dialogue*

Cycladic Islands

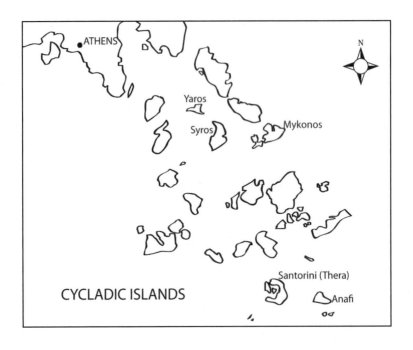

Metro Athens

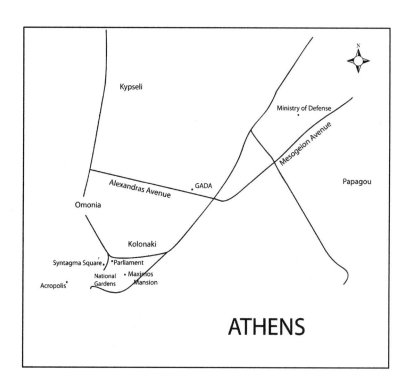

Kypseli

Ministry of Defense

Mesogeion Avenue

Alexandras Avenue

GADA

Papagou

Omonia

Kolonaki

Syntagma Square

Parliament

National Gardens

Maximos Mansion

Acropolis

ATHENS

Santorini

Chapter One

Santorini stands as the southernmost of Greece's Aegean Cycladic islands, one hundred forty-five miles southeast of Athens, eighty-five miles due north of Crete, and slightly smaller than the American island of Manhattan. Its official name is Thera, but Santorini, a contraction of Santa Irini from its Latin Empire days, is how it's known to tourists worldwide. To romantics drawn to legend, it bears yet another name, one tied to a cataclysmic volcanic eruption some 3,600 years ago: Atlantis, the lost island.

Two million years of volcanic activity created a round-top island of lava rock embracing three limestone mountain peaks created eons before the Aegean existed as a sea. Evidence of pottery from approximately six thousand years ago put the first settlers on the island in Neolithic times, and archaeological excavations at the prehistoric city of Akrotiri unearthed a prosperous, developed civilization in residence in the mid-sixteenth century BCE, at the height of the Minoan Civilization.

That's when literally all hell broke loose, destroying everyone who'd not fled a prefatory warning earthquake, in likely the most catastrophic volcanic eruption in recorded history. Catastrophe still haunts the region, but of a different sort. One that threatens to tear apart the fragile fabric of a nation.

The last thing his mother told him when he left for school was,

"Stay away from the demonstrations." She'd been telling him the same thing for a week.

He didn't mind the extra ten minutes the detour added to his walk. He had no interest in watching police in riot gear face down a herd of hooded demonstrators armed with paving stones and Molotov cocktails. He'd seen it all before and knew what tear gas smelled like. After all, he was eleven years old.

The Athens back streets edging around the battleground central square area stood quiet. Businesses stayed tightly shuttered during demonstration hours, at least those that might attract a rock through their windows and a quick grab and snatch by an opportunistic self-proclaimed champion of the long-suffering Greek people.

As the boy approached an intersecting narrow street winding back to the square, a slim figure burst around the corner and ran straight into him. The runner wore the standard demonstrator's uniform of running shoes, jeans, and a loose fitting hooded sweatshirt covering all but the eyes.

The boy stumbled but stayed on his feet until knocked to the ground by two husky men in black charging around the corner close behind the runner, their faces covered in black balaclavas. Like the runner, neither stopped to look after the boy.

Looking up from the pavement, the boy watched the two men hound after the runner around the next corner. He knew where the chase was headed. Everyone in the neighborhood knew. For decades now, whenever demonstrations in the square turned violent, perpetrators fleeing police ran for the university grounds three blocks away, a place of guaranteed sanctuary from arrest under Greece's Constitution.

He stood, wiped his hands on his pants, dusted off his shirt, and resumed his walk to school. It wasn't supposed to be like this anymore. His favorite teachers had told his class that all would be different once the new government was elected and assumed power. There'd no longer be any reason for demonstrations.

He caught a whiff of tear gas and heard spikes of shouting in the distance.

Maybe his grandfather was right. If politicians are involved, there's no hope for change. They're all alike.

The university gates stood open less than a block away. A crowd of hooded onlookers watched from within, rooting the runner home with curses and epithets shouted at the pursuers.

The runner took a quick look back. The men had closed to within ten meters but suddenly stopped. A smile appeared beneath the runner's hood. *They'll never catch me.*

Seconds later the welcoming crowd scattered in panic from a spray of gunshots while the runner lay unmoving a few steps before the gates.

The pursuers jogged over to stare down at the body, glanced toward the gates, holstered their weapons, and trotted off in the direction from which they'd come.

No one tried to follow them.

A phalanx of police cars lined each side of the street leading up to the university gates, while four police motorcycles, two cops on each, stood between the gates and the body in the street. Beyond the body and back up the street, armored police buses discharged cadres of cops in full riot gear in a race to hold back the torrent of demonstrators streaming in from the square.

Smartphones had quickly spread the message that one of their own had been "executed" by police and a swell of angry youth risen up in the square raged through the side streets toward the university gates, shouting "Death to *gourounia*," the Greek epithet for police as pigs.

"This isn't looking good." A lanky motorcycle cop nodded toward the crowd gathering behind them just beyond the gates.

"No shit," said his partner sitting behind him on the motorcycle. "So far they're only calling us names, but once their bomb-tossing buddies get here from the square, this could turn into a hell of a nasty crossfire."

"Whose bright idea do you think it was to flood this place with cops while the body's still lying in the middle of the street?"

"Some newbie political idiot would be my guess. Nobody at GADA seems to be in charge these days."

The lanky one nodded. "For sure, but it's not just at police headquarters. If you ask me, the whole damn government's run by amateurs appointed by their relatives."

"I guess I don't have to ask who you voted for."

"You'd be wrong. Like most of the country, I figured nothing could be worse than the *malakas* we've had in power since before I was born."

"Live and learn."

An ambulance snaked its way around the buses and stopped five meters from the motorcycle cops. The ambulance driver and another man, both wearing surgical scrubs, jumped out of the front seat and headed straight for the body. The driver looked to be in his late twenties, with close-cropped hair and built like a bull. The other man was dark-haired, half a head taller, and looked a dozen years older. The driver immediately began taking photographs as the dark-haired man stood motionless above the body, staring down at a face and torso still covered by an oversized hoodie.

Two more men climbed out of the back of the ambulance, one tall and muscular, in his early twenties and dressed in scrubs, and the second a fifty-year-old wearing a suit and carrying a canvas medical bag. The older man stood by the front of the ambulance while his companion slowly walked in expanding concentric circles staring at the ground, stopping every so often to pick up shell casings with tweezers, drop them into plastic bags, and make an entry in a notebook.

The dark-haired man in scrubs waved for the man in the suit to join him.

"Is that who I think it is?" said the lanky cop, nodding toward the waving man.

"Sure looks like him," said his partner.

"What do you think Andreas Kaldis is doing here dressed like an ambulance attendant?"

"No idea. I thought he'd lost his job when the new government was elected."

"Nah," said the lanky one, "only the political appointment. The old minister of public order resigned because of health problems but convinced the Prime Minister to appoint Kaldis as his successor. When the Prime Minister's party lost the elections, Kaldis was out on his ass like all the other ministers."

"So you think he actually got his old job back?"

The lanky cop nodded. "Sure looks like it, but surprising. Especially since running Special Crimes means he's in charge of investigating official corruption. There must be a real story there."

"I heard he's married to a big-time rich woman from one of Athens' oldest, most prominent families. Maybe that's the answer?"

"Could be. These new politicians talk a big game about being all for the common people, but they still drive around in Mercedes limousines and hang out with the same big power and money crowd as the assholes they replaced."

"Who are the three guys with Kaldis?"

"The one in the suit is from the coroner's office. The driver looks like Kaldis' right hand guy, Yianni Kouros. I don't know the big guy picking up shell casings, but he must be in Kaldis' unit."

"I hear they're tough guys. I wonder what they're thinking."

"I don't know, but whatever they have in mind, they better do something fast." The lanky cop shot a quick glance at the gates. "That crowd's moving closer to us."

"Let's hope they're just curious about what the coroner's doing with the body."

The two cops watched the coroner crouch down and calmly lift the victim's hand. The crowd's cursing faded a bit as he moved his fingers down onto the wrist. An instant later the coroner leaped to his feet, yelling for the big man to bring a stretcher and waving frantically for Yianni to bring the ambulance closer to the body.

The big man thrust the tweezers and plastic bags into his pocket, raced to the back of the ambulance, yanked out a stretcher, and ran with it to Andreas, the coroner, and the fallen runner.

Yianni edged the ambulance past the body, waving the police motorcycles out of his way as he nosed the front bumper in between the gates, forcing the crowd to step back a bit.

The coroner and the big man carefully moved the body onto the stretcher. Andreas watched them lift the stretcher, slide it into the back of the ambulance, and jump inside, closing the doors behind them.

Andreas waded into the crowd in front of the ambulance shouting, "Please move back. We need to get to the hospital. This is the only way out. Please clear a path for the ambulance."

Andreas kept walking ahead of the ambulance repeating his request until the crowd complied. He jumped into the front passenger seat and the ambulance sped across the grounds, siren roaring, toward wide-open gates on the far side, and an empty street beyond.

A moment later the lanky cop and his partner heard new orders come through on their radios.

"All police personnel are to immediately stand down and return to base at once. You are not, repeat not, to engage the demonstrators except as necessary to safely withdraw from the area."

"That Kaldis is one smart *batsos*," said the lanky cop, using another of the many derogatory cop-names tossed at them that morning. "No more martyred body lying in the middle of the street and—*poof*—the demonstrators don't become rioters and turn Athens into flames."

"But the body's dead. Been dead since long before we got here. What's gonna happen once word gets out?"

"That, my friend, is not our problem, because by then you and I, and the rest of us will be safely away from ground zero." He started the engine and pushed off. "And for that I say, 'Thank you, Chief Inspector Andreas Kaldis.'"

Chapter Two

"Turn off the siren, Yianni, there's no more reason to hurry now." Andreas stared out the ambulance's passenger side window at nothing in particular.

"Got to give you credit, Chief," said Yianni shaking his head. "I never thought it would work."

"Yeah, let's see how well it works once the press finds out the truth."

"Who cares at that point?" said Yianni. "You got us in, got the body out, and prevented a guaranteed major riot."

"Plus," added the big cop sitting in the back next to the body, "we collected evidence before the protestors trampled everything to mush."

"As I said, Petro, let's see what happens next. I expect to be reamed out big-time for taking it upon myself to go in and extricate the body."

"Not to mention giving the order pulling our guys out of there once we were clear of the scene," said Yianni.

"Thanks for reminding me."

"Who sent in all the cops in the first place?" said the coroner.

Andreas did a quick upward jerk of his head in the Greek gesture for no. "No idea. Maybe the same idiot who's out there waiting to ream me out. But whoever gave the order obviously forgot the lesson we learned the last time cops killed a demonstrator."

"Or maybe just wanted to see history repeat itself?" said Yianni.

Andreas smiled. "That's rather cynical, even for you."

"Why? If demonstrators go to war against cops it diverts everyone's attention from the unbelievable mess our government's got the country into."

Andreas shook his head. "As I said, cynical."

"How do we know cops did the killing?" asked Petro.

"It's how the report came into GADA," said Yianni. "'Two police killed a demonstrator and ran off, leaving the body in the middle of the street.' Then someone upstairs pushed the panic button and sent every riot cop they could find to the scene."

Andreas drummed his fingers on the dashboard. "Yianni, get the university and anyone else in the area with surveillance cameras to turn over any video that might have caught something on what happened."

"We'll probably see whatever there is running any minute on the news."

Andreas nodded. "Yeah, for sure the media will somehow get its hands on whatever the university has. But check around the neighborhood anyway. I'm sure the reporters won't be as thorough as you."

"Flattery? Wow, your three-month gig as our minister turned you into a politician."

"Don't worry, it won't last and isn't contagious." Andreas turned his head to look back at the coroner. "Doc, what can you tell us about our victim?"

"Once you get me back to my lab I should be able to tell you a lot."

"Just give me what you know about him now."

The coroner frowned. "Well, there's one thing you obviously don't know."

"From the look on your face I'm not sure I want to know. But okay, I'll bite. What is it?"

"Your victim's not a *him* but a *her*."

◇◇◇

Andreas sat outside the autopsy room, waiting to hear what else the coroner might have to tell him. The victim's gender in and of itself was enough to kick the inevitable media firestorm up a quantum level or two, but until Andreas knew what other surprises the coroner might turn up, he wasn't about to get into speculating on details with anyone. That meant staying away from his office in Athens Central Police Headquarters—better known as GADA. At least for now. He'd told his secretary Maggie to cover for him, and she said that from the number of calls she'd already received from folks way above his pay grade screaming for him, she'd have better luck hiding an elephant under a tea towel.

Andreas had taken that to mean, "No problem."

He'd sent Petro off to the ballistics lab to see what it could come up with on the shell casings, and had Yianni looking for video footage and running down their only potential lead to the victim's identity. There were no meaningful labels in any of her clothes and, though her sneakers were expensive, many students wore the same style. As expected, she carried no ID and less than thirty euros in small bills and coins. Demonstrators, especially the rock- and bomb-throwing kind, had long ago learned that losing your ID in the middle of a riot could lead to unexpected visits from the police.

But they did find a possible lead neatly tucked into the bottom of one of her sneakers: a Starbucks customer loyalty card. Slim, but something.

Andreas hoped to identify the girl without turning to the media for help. The press would go wild with the story, some inevitably playing the angle of "police ineptitude" for all it was worth. Still, it was only a matter of time—hours at most—before the victim's friends and family started to wonder where she was, and once they knew, charges of "murder coverup," "conspiracy," "blood on their hands," and every other anti-establishment, firebrand accusation would blister GADA's walls.

Andreas drew in and let out a deep breath. He knew there was nothing he could do about any of that. All he wanted was to let the girl's parents know what had happened to their child before the media made her a *cause célèbre*.

◇◇◇

The coroner charged through the battered pair of swinging doors and headed straight for where Andreas sat.

"You, my friend, are in deep shit," said the coroner, shaking his finger at Andreas.

Andreas stared up at him. "What are you talking about?"

"Because you're a cop and once this gets out, *every* cop's going to be in deep shit. That girl wasn't just shot. She was executed by professional killers."

"Could you run that by me a little slower?"

The coroner dropped onto a chair next to Andreas. "She was approximately twenty years old, well-nourished, well-groomed, athletic, and yes, attractive. She died from multiple gunshot wounds. Four into her heart, three into her spine. If the reports of the shooting are correct, she and her pursuers had been running all-out until the killers stopped at the last instant to take aim at their moving target. That sort of shooting takes terrific marksmanship skills."

"Tell me about the shot groupings."

"All shots within a group were inside a small fist of each other. One grouping came from one gun, one from another."

"You're certain of that?"

He nodded. "It's Ballistics' call, but I've seen enough bullet wounds to tell that the solid point bullets that took out her spine were designed to shatter bone, and the hollow point heart rounds expanded in soft tissue."

"That doesn't sound like a spontaneous, error-in-judgment shooting to me."

The coroner nodded. "Precisely. Her killers had assigned, specific tasks. One shooter brought her to the ground by taking out her spine, the other made certain to end her life by stopping her heart."

Andreas stared at the lab doors. "You know, Doc, I never met a cop who could shoot that well."

"What are you saying?"

"I wish I knew. But if the shooters always meant to kill the girl, why did they wait until she'd reached the gates? They could have done it anywhere, anytime while chasing her, but they didn't start shooting until she was in front of a crowd cheering her on with surveillance cameras filming everything."

The coroner nodded. "Yes, I'm afraid there looks to be another agenda operating here. But the media won't take the time to see it. And the demonstrators won't want to."

Andreas exhaled through his lips. "I know."

"As I said, you're in deep shit."

Andreas' phone rang. He looked at the name of the caller. "Yianni, what's up? Please make it good news."

"Well, Chief, it's news. We have an ID on the victim."

Andreas sat up in the chair. "Terrific."

"I checked out the Starbucks by the university, told them I'd found the card and wanted to make sure it got back to the rightful owner. They looked it up online and lo and behold, she'd actually used her real name, Penelope Sigounas."

"How do you know it's her real name?"

"I did an Internet search and found images of her with her family."

"Do we have an address for the family?"

"Yes, they're from Athens, in Papagou."

"Papagou? By the Pentagon?"

"Yes, her father's in the military. As a matter of fact, he's a Brigadier general in the Army."

Andreas shut his eyes. "Please tell me you didn't just say her father is a general."

The coroner's mouth dropped open.

"Yeah, I know. It's a headline writer's wet dream. 'Daughter of Greek general murdered by police at anti-government demonstration.'"

Andreas rubbed at his eyes with the thumb and forefinger of his free hand. "Pick me up. We've got to get to the family before the press does."

"I'll be there in ten minutes. Bye."

Andreas put the phone back in his pocket, shook his head and looked at the coroner.

"In your professional opinion, Doc, just how much deeper do you think this shit can get?"

The coroner shook his head. "Sorry to tell you, my friend, but I don't think I have a probe that reaches that far."

Andreas stood up, patted the coroner on the shoulder, "Thanks, Doc," he said, and headed toward the front door.

"Penelope, you poor kid," Andreas asked aloud, "what on earth happened to get you killed?"

Chapter Three

The family lived three miles east of the heart of Athens in Papagou, a well-maintained neighborhood of single family homes, tasteful small apartment houses, and wide, tree-lined streets. Named after General Alexandros Papagos, who'd led the Greek Army during World War II and the Greek Civil War, and later all of Greece as its Prime Minister, Papagou was also home to Greece's Pentagon.

This was the part of the job that Andreas disliked most. How do you tell a father and a mother that their child is dead? It was a job for a chaplain or a priest, not a cop. Especially not a cop when the whole world was about to think her killers were cops. He knew this wouldn't be pleasant. But he also knew, as a parent, that he'd want to know. So, here he was.

Andreas and Yianni stood on a street corner in front of an immaculately maintained, white stucco apartment building tucked behind a high stone wall enclosing orange and palm trees. They stared up at the top-floor balcony running the length of the three-story building.

"That's where they live?" asked Andreas. "It looks nice, but even at one apartment per floor it's not a very big apartment."

Yianni nodded. "They've lived there for twenty years."

"You'd think an Army general, even a one-star Brigadier, would live in a bigger place."

"They moved in about the time their daughter was born, and from the family photos I saw they never had any other children. I guess they felt they didn't need a bigger place and so never moved."

"At least there's a lift," said Andreas, walking up to the iron gate separating the street from the building.

"And I bet it works," said Yianni pressing the buzzer marked 3 beneath a camera.

"Who is it?" said a voice with a Filipino accent.

"Police," said Yianni.

"Please show identification."

Each man held his ID in front of the camera. Seconds later the gate buzzed and Yianni pushed it open.

They walked to the elevator and rode up to the third floor in silence.

The first thing Andreas noticed when he stepped off the elevator was white Dionysus marble trimmed in gold inlays covering the floor. Clearly not standard issue apartment house flooring.

"Ready?" said Andreas.

Yianni nodded, and Andreas knocked on the front door.

A half a minute later, the door opened just wide enough for them to see a petite Filipino woman in a pale blue housecoat peeking out at them blank-eyed and silent.

"Uh, are Brigadier or Mrs. Sigounas at home?"

The woman nodded yes.

"Could you please tell them that Chief Inspector Andreas Kaldis and—"

"Lena, who's at the door?" came a shrill woman's voice from down a marble staircase off to the left of the entrance foyer.

So much for living the simple life in a small apartment, thought Andreas. They probably owned the entire building.

"Police, madam," said the housekeeper in a voice not much louder than a whisper.

"What?" came the same loud voice accompanied by the sound of high heels clicking up marble steps. "When will you ever learn to speak up?"

A trim woman in her forties appeared behind the housekeeper. Her blond hair and makeup looked freshly done, and she stood dressed in what looked to be a pink Chanel suit. No matter the designer, she definitely wasn't dressed for hanging around the house, especially with an alligator Chanel handbag slung over her shoulder by a gold tone chain. Andreas made a mental note to ask his wife if she knew Mrs. Sigounas.

"Can I help you gentlemen?"

"Are you Mrs. Sigounas?" said Andreas.

She gave a tight smile. "This is my home, so why don't you first identify yourselves to me."

"Certainly," said Andreas pulling out and showing her his identification card. "Chief Inspector Andreas Kaldis, and this is Detective Kouros."

Yianni showed his ID.

The woman cursorily glanced at their identification. "So, what do you want with my husband and me?"

"Is your husband home?"

"No. He's at work."

"May we come inside?"

Mrs. Sigounas looked at her watch. "I'm already late for an important event."

"It won't take long. And I can assure you what I have to tell you is more important."

She sighed and waved for them to follow her into what most would call a living room, though from its marble appointments, slew of gaudy decorative objects, and gilded red-velvet furniture, a better description might be the sitting room of an upscale brothel. Mrs. Sigounas dropped onto a gold damask Louis XIV settee. She did not invite her two visitors to sit.

Andreas stopped directly in front of her. "Mrs. Sigounas, I think it would be a good idea if you called your husband. He should hear what I'm about to tell you."

"Chief Inspector, neither my husband nor I have time for any of your police dramatics. If it's something about Penelope, just tell us and we'll find a way to work out whatever trouble she's in."

The suggestion of a bribe was obvious from her tone of voice, but Andreas kept his own voice under control. "Your daughter has been in trouble before?"

"My daughter's past is none of your concern. Just tell me what she's done, and what you want to make it go away."

Andreas swallowed hard and sat in the chair across from her.

"I didn't say you could sit."

"Mrs. Sigounas, I'm here on a very serious matter, one that isn't going to go away."

She smirked. "Oh, is that so? My husband is a very important man. It would be unwise to cross him."

"I really think you should call your husband."

"If I call him, it will be to have your head on a platter."

"Please make the call."

"Have it your way." She glared at Andreas as she pulled a mobile phone from her handbag and pressed a speed dial button. She held it to her ear. "Honey, I'm still at home. I've been delayed by a most obnoxious cop sitting uninvited in front of me who's insisting on talking to us together about some tiff Penelope's undoubtedly got herself into. Would you please set him straight?"

She pressed the speaker button and held the phone out in front of Andreas' face.

A voice came roaring into the room. "Who the hell do you think you are to come barging into my home and upset my wife?"

Andreas waited until the man finished his rant. They were an extremely unpleasant couple, but Andreas was about to give them the absolutely worst news a parent could hear, so he kept his temper in check. "I'm sorry to disturb you and your wife, sir, but—"

"I asked for your name," boomed the same voice.

"Andreas Kaldis."

"Well, listen up, Policeman Kaldis, my wife and I won't...." The voice faded for a couple of seconds. "Did you say Kaldis?"

"Yes, Chief Inspector Andreas Kaldis of Special Crimes."

"The former minister of public order?"

"Yes, one and the same."

Mrs. Sigounas jerked to attention. "Lena," she yelled, "please bring our guests some water. Or would you prefer something else?"

Andreas smiled. "No thank you. Brigadier—"

"Sorry to have spoken to you that way, Kaldis. I had no idea it was you."

"No problem."

"What sort of trouble did Penelope get herself into that warrants you showing up at our front door?"

Andreas again swallowed hard and looked straight into Mrs. Sigounas' eyes. "There is no easy way to say this. Your daughter's been killed."

The mother's mouth dropped open, her face drained of color, and her body collapsed back upon the sofa, her hand still clutching the phone. Behind him, Andreas heard the crash of crystal and silver striking a marble floor. Andreas swung his head around and saw the housekeeper standing in the doorway wailing in Tagalog and yanking at her hair.

Yianni stepped over to the maid and gently but firmly pulled her hands away from her hair.

Not a sound came over the phone.

"Brigadier?" said Andreas.

Still not a sound.

Andreas took the phone from the mother's hand. "Brigadier."

"How did she die?"

Andreas cleared his throat. "She'd been participating in a demonstration several blocks from the university, and was chased by two as yet unidentified men to the gates of the university, where the men shot and killed her. They were dressed in the manner of police but there is no confirmation yet that they were police."

"What do you mean 'in the manner of police'?"

"Black fatigues, black balaclava."

"Then they could be police *or* military?"

"Do you have any reason to believe they might be military?"

"No. Just a professional observation to keep my mind from processing…" His voice drifted off.

Andreas could hear the Brigadier drawing deep breaths.

"How is my wife?"

"I think you better come home. And bring a doctor with you. She looks as if she's in shock."

"Will do. How is Lena?"

"The housekeeper?"

"Yes. She's like Penelope's other mother. Been with us since our baby...was born..."

Andreas heard the sobbing start on the other end of the line. "Please hurry home, sir. We'll stay until you get here."

"Thank you." The phone went dead.

Andreas' eyes jumped between the nearly comatose mother sitting on the couch, and the now silent housekeeper standing frozen in the doorway. He motioned for Yianni to bring the housekeeper over to the sofa. Yianni half walked, half carried her there, and gently nudged her down onto the sofa next to the mother.

For several minutes neither woman moved, only sat in place, staring blankly into the room. Almost imperceptibly at first, the mother's fingers crept toward the housekeeper's hand, and the instant they touched each woman grasped hold of the other as if she were a lifeline, beginning amid tears and embraces the eternal process of mourning the death of their child.

Andreas and Yianni stood in the foyer close by the front door.

"I hope the Brigadier gets here soon."

Andreas looked at his watch. "It's only been ten minutes."

"Seems a lot longer."

Andreas nodded. "I wonder why the Brigadier suggested it could have been military who killed his daughter."

Yianni shrugged. "It has a paramilitary feel to it."

"Are you speaking as an ex-Navy commando?"

"Yes, but every branch of the service has personnel capable of doing what they did." Another shrug. "They train for different purposes than police."

"Sure hope it stays that way."

Yianni nodded toward the women. "They've stopped crying."

"Why don't you get them some water."

Yianni went into the kitchen. The women had gone back to staring off into the middle distance, but now their faces showed the sadness. The mother bit at her lower lip and rubbed at her temples with her fingers, the housekeeper's lips trembled as she fought back tears and clutched a handkerchief in her fist.

Yianni came out of the kitchen carrying two small plastic water bottles and headed toward the couch. He twisted off the caps and handed each woman a bottle.

The mother nodded at Yianni and the housekeeper said, "Thank you."

Yianni returned to Andreas in the foyer. "The Brigadier should have been here by now. The Pentagon's only five minutes away."

"He's probably picking up the doctor," said Andreas.

"He's a general. They have colonels to do that sort of thing for them."

Andreas shook his head. "I pray the day never comes where someone's trying to figure out how I'd react to this kind of news."

"Amen to that."

Andreas' phone rang. He looked at the number before answering. "What's up, Petro?"

"Ballistics has a preliminary report on the shell casings, Chief. They're police-issue calibers, but with a twist."

"A twist?"

"They're handloads, not out-of-the-box ammunition."

"You mean someone made their own cartridges?"

"Yes. The casings were standard issue but the lab found markings on them consistent with handloading equipment. Standard powder loads were replaced with something more powerful. No doubt the bullets were replaced, too, but we'll have to see what the coroner recovers to confirm that."

"His first reaction was that each shooter used different bullets—one to shatter bone, the other to mushroom in the heart."

"Damn."

Andreas stared at the mother as he exhaled heavily. "For sure. See you back at the office, but make sure you don't talk about any of this with anyone."

"Understood, Chief. Bye."

"That didn't sound very encouraging," said Yianni.

"Wait until the Brigadier gets here if you want to see just how very *not* encouraging things can get."

"What's he got to do with this?"

"That's what I aim to find out. It's sounding more and more like we've got a well-planned execution on our hands."

Two minutes later the front door swung open and a vintage version of John Wayne, Greek-style, strode into the room. Military beret and all.

The Brigadier gave Andreas and Yianni a cursory nod as he passed them on the way from the front door to his wife. She burst into tears the moment he walked into the room. He gently pulled her up from the sofa and held her tightly in his arms. At a head taller and half a person broader than she, he looked like a bear embracing a ballerina. He closed his eyes and stood dry-eyed as she poured tears out onto his chest.

When her crying subsided to sobs, the Brigadier eased off on his grip and opened his eyes. He kissed her on the forehead, hugged her, and eased her down next to the housekeeper. Then he reached down and took the housekeeper's hands in his. She looked up at him, her lips trembling. He nodded, she nodded back, and he let go of her hands. She put an arm around the mother. The Brigadier turned and walked to where Andreas and Yianni stood silently watching. He stood a half-head taller than Andreas and looked ten years older, with a barely noticeable potbelly.

"Thank you, both. I appreciate the consideration you showed my wife. Especially after how rude we were to you."

Andreas nodded. "I'm sorry about your daughter."

"I am, too," said Yianni.

"It still hasn't hit me." The Brigadier bit at his lip. "It's just too unimaginable."

Andreas nodded.

"The doctor should be here any minute now. I sent a member of my staff to pick him up."

Andreas felt the I-told-you-so glance from Yianni. "I know this is a lousy time to be asking you questions, but I hope you understand why I must."

"Of course. Besides it might help to keep my mind off…" He coughed in a less-than-successful attempt to contain a sudden sob. "Ask me whatever you want. Let's just do it here in the foyer where I can keep an eye on my wife."

"Let me start with the most obvious question. Who do you think might have done this?"

The Brigadier didn't blink. "How would I know?"

"Not even a wild guess?"

He gestured no.

"When we spoke earlier you said the killers might be military."

"No, I simply said from the way you described their manner of dress they could have been military *or* police."

"Fair point, but what you said got me to thinking. The killers chased your daughter for several blocks. They could have shot her anytime they wanted but held off until surrounded by witnesses and surveillance cameras. And when they did, they managed to tightly group their shots precisely where they wanted on a moving target. That's exceptional marksmanship. Especially for cops."

"I'd call it extraordinary," said the Brigadier. "But how do you know they hit where they were aiming?"

Andreas locked eyes with the Brigadier. "They used special, hand-loaded ammunition with slugs designed to be particularly effective on her spine and heart."

The Brigadier blinked and looked away. "My God…are you saying Penelope was assassinated?"

"That's why I asked who you thought might have done this."

The Brigadier pressed the fingers of his right hand against his brow and rubbed. "She'd been running with a leftist crowd since entering university. But I figured a lot of kids did that in college. Sort of a guilty rite of passage for having parents who could still afford to send them to private schools and spend summers on the islands while the rest of the country was in economic meltdown."

"But why would the left want to kill her if she was one of them?"

"No idea. And I'm not saying they did. I'm just saying that she ran with a crowd known for doing violent things."

"What sorts of violent things?"

The Brigadier closed his eyes, drew in a deep breath, let it out, and opened his eyes. "I have nothing specific in mind. But the media's always showing them burning cars and throwing rocks and Molotov cocktails at police. I'm just doing what you asked, speculating wildly. Sorry if I'm not helpful. I'm not exactly thinking particularly clearly at the moment."

Andreas raised his hands in apology. "Oh, no, Brigadier, I understand completely. We're just trying to come up with a possible motive, something to justify viewing this as more than a random, wrong-time wrong-place tragedy."

The Brigadier closed his eyes. "She was so young. Hard to imagine her making such a hardened enemy who'd go to such lengths to have her killed."

"That's sort of my thinking too. What about you and your wife?"

He opened his eyes. "What do you mean?"

"Do either you or your wife have any 'hardened' enemies?"

"Someone willing to murder our daughter to get back at one of us? That's preposterous."

"It may be preposterous, but I just want to know if it's possible."

The Brigadier paused. "I've done a lot in my career that's harmed a lot of people, but I can't imagine a scenario where someone would go after my daughter to get back at me."

"Terrorists?"

"That's always a possibility, and I work with special-operations forces, but I'm not directly involved in anything that would draw their attention. Besides, terrorists like to claim responsibility for their killings. I haven't heard anything like that in connection with this. Have you?"

"No."

"I wish I could help you, I really do. I want to get these bastards more than anyone on earth."

"I know. We're right with you on that."

"So, what happens next?"

Andreas looked at the mother. "We wait for the doctor and if he says it's okay, we ask your wife and the housekeeper the same questions we asked you."

The Brigadier turned and looked at his wife. "I wish there were some way to avoid that."

"I do too," said Andreas.

The doorbell rang.

"It must be the doctor," said the Brigadier as he went to open the door.

Yianni leaned over and whispered to Andreas. "He's not telling us everything."

Andreas nodded. "I know."

Twenty minutes later Andreas and Yianni left the house. The doctor had allowed them to ask their questions of the mother and housekeeper, but both only said how much the daughter was loved; they couldn't conceive that anyone would want to harm her.

Neither cop pressed the women or the Brigadier further. It was too soon to confront them with more reality than they already had to deal with.

◇◇◇

"What do you think he's hiding?" said Yianni as he steered the marked blue-and-white police car onto Mesogeion Avenue, heading toward GADA.

Andreas gazed out the passenger side window. "No idea. But if it's something that could help us catch his daughter's killers and he still won't tell us, it's got to be damn serious."

"Maybe he already knows who did it?"

"The thought had crossed my mind." Andreas drummed his fingers on the dashboard. "That's about all we'd need right now in Greece, senior military types running personal vendetta operations."

"Or it could just be the natural reluctance of the military to trust civilians. Cops think the same way."

"But we're cops, not civilians."

"To hardcore military types we're not much different from civilians. Just bureaucrats with guns."

Andreas looked at the side of Yianni's face. "So, you think he's going to try running his own investigation? How long do you think he'll get away with that before we start stumbling over each other chasing the same leads? And once we do, all hell will break loose. This country's not keen on the military inserting itself into civilian matters."

"The Brigadier may not see it that way. Or more likely not care. Many in the military think the police are far too lax in tolerating demonstrators—that we let them get away with too much."

"It's not just military types who think that way. But now we have the media about to announce to the world that two Greek cops killed an unarmed twenty-year-old female demonstrator. That's going to raise an outcry against us. So until we identify who actually did the shooting, I'm not eliminating anyone, including demonstrators."

"Do you really think demonstrators masqueraded as government types to cover the killing of one of their own?"

"Not likely," said Andreas, "but as I said, for now I'm not dismissing any possibility."

"Spoken like a true Greek. We thrive on Byzantine conspiracy theories."

Andreas waved his left hand at Yianni. "All we know for sure is that the girl was known by her parents to take part in anti-government demonstrations, and she was hunted down and killed by skilled assassins. If her father knows something that might lead to his daughter's killers, my guess is he'll follow up on it ASAP."

"Do you want to tap his phones? Follow him?"

"I'd like to do all that, but getting a wiretap on a Greek general's phones based on what we have is a non-starter. And putting a tail on him without first getting permission from his defense minister could generate some serious inter-ministry fireworks."

"Which I assume you want to avoid."

"Any minute now we'll be hit head-on with a behemoth media shit storm portraying cops as bloodthirsty killers of a Greek general's daughter. The very last thing we need on top of that is a headline that says 'Cops Investigating Victim's Mourning Father.'"

"So, what *do* we do?"

Andreas smiled again. "I thought I'd leave that to you and Maggie to take care of."

"Maggie?"

Andreas nodded. "You told me generals get others to do things for them. Well, Maggie is our police headquarters' mother superior, with a network of friends and contacts playing similar roles in every Greek government ministry office. Who better to get a line on the Brigadier's likely choice to run such a delicate search-and-destroy operation for him? And whoever that is, that's who we watch."

"She's your secretary. If you think we can get her to ask her friends to betray their bosses' confidences, be my guest."

Andreas nodded. "Yes, it's going to require some convincing to get her to agree."

"And just what part do you have in mind for me to play in your cloak and dagger assignment for Maggie?"

Andreas smiled. "A simple one. You get to do the convincing."

Chapter Four

Andreas and Yianni walked into Andreas' office on GADA's fourth floor to find Maggie and Petro sitting on the couch in front of the windows, staring at the flat-screen television mounted on the opposite wall.

Andreas walked behind his desk and sat down without looking at the screen. "All I want to know is whether they're pronouncing my name correctly."

"Yes, if 'killer' Kaldis sounds right to you,'" said Maggie.

"Cute."

"Would you prefer, 'mad-dog killer cops' or 'government assassins' or 'fascist death squads?' asked Petro.

"That seems to cover the political spectrum nicely."

"It all depends on what channel you watch," said Maggie. "I'd say fascist death squads is the left's favorite. Government assassins is more popular with the right."

"So who's calling us mad dogs?"

"The moderates," said Petro.

Maggie nodded. "Yep, it's not looking good for the good guys."

"Any calls?" asked Andreas.

"It would be easier telling you who didn't call."

"Lila?"

"The wife and family's fine. She said to tell you she's not picking up the house phone, so call her on her mobile."

"That bad?"

Maggie nodded. "The press smells blood in the water, and the video of what you staged in front of the university's gates is running on an endless loop on virtually every station in Greece. They're gunning for you because you're the only cop they recognize and they all have your home phone number and address."

Andreas shut his eyes and shook his head. "Okay, get me our new minister of public order, please."

Maggie stood and walked to Andreas' desk. She dialed the number from memory. "Hello, it's Chief Inspector Kaldis for the minister." Maggie handed Andreas the phone and went back to the couch.

Yianni dropped into a chair next to the desk and gestured for Petro to lower the volume on the television.

"Hi, Babis, I hear you're looking for me."

"Andreas. What's happening and why haven't you returned my calls?"

"Sorry about that, I've sort of been busy, what with having to prevent a riot and inform a family that their daughter's been murdered."

"Yes, I heard it was a woman. A young student at the university. Do you know which of our guys did it?"

Andreas squeezed the phone. "I don't know if any of *our* guys did it."

"Of course they did. Everybody saw it. Video from the university's cameras is playing nonstop on every TV station in the country. They're calling for the killers' heads."

"Well, the short answer is we only know that two men dressed as cops *or military* killed her."

"Military? You think they could be military."

"I said *dressed* as military."

"It would be catastrophic for our people to think the military might be involved in this."

"It's sort of out of our hands. The media will say what it likes, and once it gets out that the victim was the daughter of a Greek general, who knows where they'll go with the story?"

"*A Greek general.*"

"Yes. And an only child."

Babis paused, as if catching his breath. "Despite the militaristic attitudes of the distinguished leader of our government's right wing coalition partner who serves as minister of defense, this government does not countenance violence against lawful demonstrators. And certainly not by the military."

"That's the downside of a free press. People get to think and say what they want."

"You're not funny."

"I'm not trying to be," said Andreas. "But what we should be worrying about is violence against cops."

"That's not an issue here."

"It soon will be, because from the way the media's playing this, every cop in Greece will be a target. Demonstrations and riots will come out of this for sure. So we better be prepared."

"Just find the killers and leave the bigger picture to me. There will be no riots. We know how to handle demonstrations."

Andreas squeezed the phone so hard his knuckles turned white, but his voice remained calm. "Babis, I know how proud you are of your distinguished history at uniting members of your party in demonstrations against government policies with which your party disagreed, but we're talking about passions here, not politics. Should the people start to believe that *our* government is employing the very practices it once so vigorously denounced in opposition—"

"No reason for you to say any more. I know how the people think. They know we'd never betray our promises to them. They will listen to our prime minister and remain calm. All you need to do is find the fascist cops who did this. We must rid their kind from our ranks. That is our promise to the people."

Andreas closed his eyes. "That's all nice to say, but I think you still better plan for civil unrest. Make that *massive* civil unrest."

"There is no reason to. Just do what I said and leave the people to me. And unless you have proof, no more talk of the military being involved in this tragedy. Goodbye, I must speak to the Prime Minister."

The phone went dead and Andreas stared at it for a moment before putting it back in its cradle. "He said not to worry about protecting cops, because he can handle the people, and that I should focus on finding 'the fascist cops' who did this. 'Rid their kind from our ranks.'" He emphasized the quotes with his fingers.

"The leftists' phrase of choice, I see," said Yianni.

"That's what happens when a lawyer who never liked cops gets appointed head of police," said Petro.

"God have mercy," said Maggie.

Andreas opened his eyes and looked down at his desk. "The people elected the government of their choice, and that government has the right to its priorities." He looked up at Yianni. "But, Yianni, I think it's time you told Maggie what sort of help we need from her."

◇◇◇

Andreas, his pregnant wife, and five-year-old son lived at the very heart of Athens' privileged society in a penthouse apartment on the city's chicest street, next door to the Presidential Palace and across from the National Gardens. Andreas' lifestyle came with his marriage to Lila. At first he'd felt he didn't belong, that he was betraying his working class roots. He'd grown up the son of a decorated cop and housewife mother in a shabby but stable neighborhood surrounded by people quick to judge themselves morally superior to any who did not labor as they did to survive. In time, Andreas came to realize that what truly mattered was not what you did or how much you earned, but rather the ethical principles you practiced in living your life.

He'd also be the first to admit it was a hell of a lot easier making the proper life choices when money wasn't an issue.

"Welcome home, handsome," said Lila from a cream-and-blue linen-covered sofa facing a bank of windows looking off toward the Acropolis.

Andreas dropped down beside her and took her hand, his eyes fixed on the Acropolis.

"Not even a kiss? Something serious must be on your mind."

He turned and kissed her on the cheek. "Sorry. Just the state of our world." He patted Lila's belly. "And what it will be like when our little one arrives."

Lila laughed. "Hopefully not that different. My due date's less than a month away."

Andreas leaned over and kissed her again. "You're right. No reason to talk about anything other than happy things."

"I'm not saying that. I'm just tired, a bit anxious, and a lot excited about getting this heavy little ball of love out here into the world." Lila patted her belly.

"Yeah, Tassaki could use a playmate."

Lila stared at him. "Yes, that too." She shook her head. "Men."

"Hey, did I say something wrong?"

Lila patted Andreas' hand. "Don't worry about it. I know what's bothering you."

Andreas bit at his lower lip.

"It was tragic what happened to that poor girl at the demonstration today."

Andreas nodded. "At every level, and now every bastard *malaka* in Greece is looking for some way to spin it to further private agendas."

"Welcome to the twenty-first century, my husband. No one is direct, everyone has hidden motives and aspirations."

"I know, but it still bothers me. "

"Isn't that why we have cops, to keep the really bad ones in line?"

"That's just my point, I'm not sure we are keeping the *really* bad ones in line."

"Where, might I ask, is this conversation headed?" She rested her head on Andreas' shoulder.

He kissed her forehead. "Something isn't right about the girl's death. Her mother's catatonic, the father's in denial. Both are expected reactions, but my instincts are screaming that the father's holding something back, that he knows more than he's told us."

"So how do you find out if you're right?"

"From the way things are going, maybe only when two bodies turn up who happen to be his daughter's killers. I was hoping

Maggie might be able to learn something through her old-girl network, but so far she's come up empty."

"If the father knows, do you think he'd tell his wife?"

"Hard to say. It depends on how he thinks she'll react. He might just want to keep it to himself."

"Wise choice."

"Why do you say that?" said Andreas.

Lila lifted her head off Andreas' shoulder. "Because I know the mother. She's one of the biggest gossips in Athens. Hard to imagine her keeping something like that secret. She'd want the whole world to know if she thought it might help catch her daughter's killers."

Andreas watched Lila rub her belly. "What mother wouldn't?"

She sighed. "I guess you're right. But if you thought she might know something, I could take a run at her for information."

"Uh, uh," said Andreas firmly. "Our prime directive is that you *never again* get involved in any of my cases."

"I know, but I just thought—"

Andreas cut her off. "Last time it nearly cost you your life. And if I'm right, there are far more serious players involved in whatever's going on now. Don't even think about having anything to do with it. If you're bored you can take up something less dangerous, like sky diving, while you're waiting for D-Day." Andreas smiled.

"D-Day? As in 'delivery day'?" Lila shook her head and stared at Andreas' eyes. "Okay, charmer, what do you suggest we do to divert me from my boredom?"

Andreas waggled his eyebrows. "Is Tassaki asleep?"

"I hate it when you do that thing with your eyebrows."

"You didn't answer my question."

"Yes, he's asleep."

"Terrific." Andreas stood, gently pulled Lila up from the couch, and steered her toward their bedroom. "It's diversion time."

She shook her head. "As I said…'men.'"

Tassos had long ago grown used to Maggie's body. He knew

precisely where she liked to be touched. The light was dim and the room a bit warm, but it didn't matter. He had the urge and she always let him. They'd long ago worked around the belly issue; it was passion that drove them. He pulled her closer, firmly gripping her breasts and pressing his thighs hard against her buttocks. They rocked slowly together, she moaning softly as he thrust at a pace in keeping with her breathing. He held her tightly as she came, and moaned into her ear as he soon followed. They knew how to enjoy each other.

They lay quietly together in the darkness.

"At least some things in our country are still worth doing right."

She smacked him on his bare butt. "Is that the most romantic thing you could come up with at a moment like this?"

"Who needs romance? We just had sex."

She laughed. "I'll remember that the next time you start nibbling at my ear."

"It's not your ear I'm interested in." He brushed his finger tips along her breasts.

She smiled in the dark and pressed back against him. A moment passed and she sighed.

"What's wrong?"

"Nothing, my mind was wandering. I was thinking about something Yianni and Andreas asked me to do."

"What on earth could that be to come to you at a moment like this?"

Maggie giggled. "It has to do with that poor girl murdered over by the university."

"The Sigounas girl?" said Tassos.

"Yes." She shifted on the bed. "Andreas wanted me to find out what I could about her father. See if there's anything he's hiding."

"Generals have a lot of things to hide."

Maggie stiffened. "You know him?"

"Some. But I knew his father very well."

"How's that?"

"He was my boss when I worked at that prison on Yaros."

Maggie sat up and turned on the light. She pulled the sheet up to her neck. "But you were working for the Junta then."

"I was a rookie cop, doing a job. I made friends with prisoners and guards alike. It's my nature. And a good thing too," he gently flicked her nose, "because that's how I made friends with Andreas when he was chief of police on Mykonos, and if I hadn't, where would you and I be today?"

Andreas' chance mention to Maggie of widower Tassos, not knowing of their long ago romantic past, had helped put them back together.

"Fine, so what do you know about the Brigadier's father?"

"He was a biggie, had the ear and trust of the Colonels ruling the country."

"What's his name?"

"He's dead now. Passed away a few years back."

"But what's his name?"

Tassos told her.

"That's not the Brigadier's last name."

Tassos nodded. "After the Junta fell, his parents changed his name to his mother's."

"Out of shame over his father's past?"

Tassos gestured no. "Not at all. It was a practical decision. No reason to saddle their son with such a notorious name."

"You mean the military doesn't know about his father?"

Tassos patted her belly. "Darling, of course they know, and that name's not a problem there. His father was a much admired military man—still is, to some—and that makes the Brigadier part of a special clique of multi-generational military types who regard themselves as the true protectors of the nation, no matter who their ancestors may have served along the way."

"Andreas thinks he may be hiding something about who killed his daughter."

Tassos nodded. "If he is, my bet would be he plans on taking vengeance himself."

"That's what Andreas thinks."

"Then what's the problem? Let the Brigadier take care of this mess. I'm sure he'll find a way to restore capital punishment in Greece for the occasion."

"At times it's hard for me to remember you're a cop. You sound more like a thug."

"That's why you work for my squeaky clean buddy Andreas, and sleep with me." He smiled as he tugged at the sheet in Maggie's grip. "You like us bad boys."

Maggie held firm to the sheet. "Well, I'm glad you'll be helping us, at any rate."

"*Us?*" said Tassos.

"Yes. Welcome to the investigation, Cyclades Chief Homicide Investigator Stamatos."

Tassos tickled Maggie's belly through the sheet. "And by what authority are you assigning me a case?"

"The same authority that's going to keep this sheet up around my neck until you say *yes.*"

"That's not very romantic."

"As a wise man recently told me, 'Who needs romance?'"

Tassos frowned a smile. "Hoist by my own petard."

Maggie said, "But look what you've gained," and dropped her hands from the sheet.

Chapter Five

When Maggie arrived at work the next morning, Andreas was sitting behind his desk. She stuck her head in the open doorway to his office. "You're here before nine? What happened? Did Lila throw you out of the house?"

Andreas pointed toward the flickering television on the wall. "Obviously you haven't been watching this morning's news."

"As a matter of fact you're right. What's up?"

"Demonstrations. Everywhere."

"Before noon?" Maggie stepped inside the doorway.

Andreas waved his hand in the air. "Tell me about it, all across the country. Athens, Thessaloniki, Patras, Ioannina, Crete. If it has a university, it has a demonstration."

"Over the murdered girl?"

Andreas nodded. "I'm just waiting for the rock and Molotov cocktail-tossing crowd to move in. International news channels are all over this, so it's hard for me to imagine them staying away."

"I take that to mean you're not a believer in our minister's claimed ability to keep the violent ones in line."

"Why, because his party once tossed the rocks he thinks his government gets a lifetime pass on incoming? The only distinction between his crew and the just-as-bad ones they replaced is in the different promises they made that they won't keep. This government is busy stuffing family, friends, and supporters into every position they can come up with, and pouncing on the same capitalist perks they once denounced. Their arrogance has them thinking the voters they care about don't care, but the people notice. Any day now it'll be his government dodging rocks and bottles." Andreas pointed at the TV. "I just hope today's not that day."

Tassos walked into the office, carrying a small cardboard carton.

"And to what do I owe the honor of this surprise visit?" said Andreas.

"You don't. My love does." He kissed Maggie on the cheek.

"He dropped me off and went across the street for croissants and coffee."

"What's the matter? You're too good for our GADA cafeteria?" said Andreas.

"I'm too old to suffer its indignities."

"Indignities?"

Tassos put the carton down on Andreas' desk and picked out a cup of coffee. "Yes, think indigestion, but working differently on the system."

Andreas waved his hand at Tassos. "Okay, I get it. Spare me the details."

"Shh," said Maggie, pointing at the television. The screen showed police in full riot gear standing outside Parliament, holding shields raised up against a crowd of hooded men wielding clubs.

"Damn it," said Tassos. "There should be a fixed perimeter of barricades out there to protect our boys from being encircled and overrun."

"The new government ordered them all taken down as a sign of 'trust in the people,'" said Andreas. "Let's just hope the damn fools had the good sense to have backup on site, because if the crowd breaks through and our boys sense they're cut off and their lives are in danger…" Andreas waved a hand off into the air.

Tassos picked up a croissant and sat down on the couch beneath the windows. "I never understood the reasoning behind kids with sticks and stones running up against guys with badges and guns."

"I told our *malaka* of a minister to be ready with a plan. Once word gets out that Athens is rioting, it's going to spread."

Maggie nodded toward the television. "It's already happened. There's rock-throwing in Heraklion."

"Great. Athens and Crete. And it's still breakfast time," said Tassos.

Andreas' desk phone rang. Maggie picked it up, listened, covered up the mouthpiece, and said, "It's the *malaka* minister." She handed Andreas the phone.

"Kaldis here."

"*You're* responsible for all of this. If you hadn't moved that girl's body the protestors would have vented their anger by now. Instead, she's become a martyr for every student demonstrator in Greece."

"Not sure I get the logic of how allowing rioters to tear up one part of Greece discourages them from tearing up the rest."

"Kaldis, you're incompetent. I'm bringing you up on charges."

Andreas counted to five. "So nice to hear you're in control of the situation, Babis. Have a nice day." He hung up the phone.

Tassos stared at him. "Did you just hang up on the minster of public order?"

"Yes. He said I was responsible for the riots and he was bringing me up on charges, so I figured what was left for me to say?"

Tassos took a bite of the croissant. "You always seem to draw winners for bosses."

The phone rang and Maggie reached for it.

Andreas put his hand on the receiver. "No need to." He let it ring three times before picking up. "Kaldis here."

"How dare you hang up on me!"

"Did you have something else to say to me? I thought you were finished."

"You're finished, Kaldis. *Finished!*"

"Good, enjoy your day."

As Andreas dropped the handset toward the receiver he heard Babis' tinny voice cry, "*Wait!*"

Andreas brought the receiver back to his ear. "Yes?"

"You owe it to your government to go on television and apologize to the people for what you've done to bring on these demonstrations."

Andreas blinked. "You know, Minister, if I thought that actually had a snowball's chance in hell of working, I'd go for it. But all that's going to do is encourage bad guys to go after more cops."

"I don't care what you think. We're in crisis. Our country is in danger and you must do as I say."

"Minister, out of respect for your office, I will simply say I think you're out of your mind."

"How dare you speak that way to me?"

"Well, my first choice was to tell you to go fuck yourself, but I don't want to carry that visual in my mind."

"Kaldis—"

Andreas raised his voice. "Now you listen. Our country is on the verge of incinerating itself, whether the girl's death or something else triggers it. If you think hanging cops out to dry will change that, think again. We're more polarized as a country than at any time I can remember in my lifetime, and if all you can come up with to deal with this crisis are bullshit political maneuverings intended to protect your party's ass...well, I've already told you what you can do.

"Once you start sacrificing cops, who the hell do you think is going to stand up to the mobs the next time? Your volunteer neighborhood watch groups? Perhaps you'd like to form a protective alliance with Golden Dawn's neo-Nazi party members? And if they're not enough for you, how about calling out the military?

"That should all play very nicely in the international news. Just imagine the headlines, 'Military junta tanks return to Athens' streets.' Should do wonders for tourism."

"We've taken all that into account. Everything is controllable if you do as we say and apologize."

"*We?* Whoever's in your brain trust ought to watch more television news and play less Nintendo. We're way beyond the apology stage. It's head-busting time out there on the streets, and you damn well better do something before someone else gets killed."

Pause.

"Hello, anybody there?" said Andreas.

"What do you suggest?"

"What's worked before, a massive show of restrained police presence. Let the demonstrators know there's steel beneath the velvet glove that allows them to peacefully protest. And damn it, start arresting the violent wolves out there who are stirring up the sheep to fight. Unless, of course, you don't mind risking seeing the country in flames by tonight."

"That's not the way this government does things."

"And how's that been working out for you so far, Babis?"

"I don't need sarcasm."

"Then let me put it differently. Ask your brain trust to consider how it plans on handling those same protestors once they start targeting your cars and homes with Molotov cocktails."

"That will never happen."

"Really? And here I thought you erected those police guard kiosks outside your homes for a reason. Is it just to make your neighbors think you're important?"

"Kaldis—"

"Yeah, yeah, watch the sarcasm." Andreas shut his eyes, drew in and let out a deep breath. "If you let demonstrators think they can burn and loot as they please, just how long do you think it's going to be before some politically ambitious organizer gets the bright idea of delivering an up close and personal message to the big bad government bosses? Sure sounds like great TV to me."

Andreas glared at the phone. "And if you wait until they're about to burn down your own house or car before ordering a police crackdown, imagine the message that's going to send to a country that's watched its government not lift a finger before then to stop the gangs?"

Pause.

"Just a thought."

"I want you at the ministry right away."

"Not for a news conference."

"Understood. Bye."

Andreas put down the phone. "He wants me at the ministry."

"Why?" said Maggie.

Andreas spread his arms wide. "Maybe to fire me. He never wanted me back heading Special Crimes after the Prime Minister replaced me with him."

"No surprise there," said Tassos. "He knows nothing about police work and you do."

"He's not a big fan of yours either," said Andreas.

Tassos smiled. "Is it my fault that being nice to all those political prisoners of the Junta back in the day made me more buddy-buddy with the old lions of his party than he is? It didn't take much for me to convince them that your ministry appointment wasn't political but a temporary placeholder for your ailing predecessor forced to resign for health reasons. It took even less convincing to get them to see that if the new minister got to appoint his choice to run Special Crimes, with its mandate to investigate and root out political corruption, he'd turn it into his private Gestapo for going after his political rivals. Since they already knew him to be an unprincipled, bare-knuckle political opportunist, you were plainly a better alternative and so they insisted on your being reappointed chief of the unit as a condition of his becoming and remaining minister of public order."

"Remind me again," said Andreas. "Am I supposed to thank you for that or take you off my Christmas card list?"

"If he's so distrusted, why's Babis a minister at all?" said Maggie.

"Because he had a strong political following in the election," said Tassos. "Enough to justify a ministry appointment in the new government."

"Thank God he's not as influential as your friends," she said with a smile.

"At least not so far, my love. But he'll keep trying to screw Andreas every chance he gets."

"And on that note, it's time for me to head on over to the ministry and see what he has in mind for me this time."

"Do you need backup?" said Tassos.

Andreas smiled. "That's not a bad idea. Maggie, is Yianni in?"
She nodded.

"Tell him to put on a tie. We're headed to the ministry."

"A tie?" said Tassos.

Andreas smiled. "Yes, I want to make an impression."

Andreas turned off Kanellopoulou Street into the parking area of the currently named Ministry of Public Order and Citizens Protection. He shut the engine and sat staring at the ministry building. He hadn't been here in quite a while. Babis didn't want him around and that was fine with Andreas. Andreas wondered why he even bothered to stay on the force. He didn't need the grief. And his wife had made it clear to him many times that they didn't need the money.

They lived way above his means as a cop, and his natural instincts regarding the subject of a husband living off his wife's money had made that reality a struggle for him to accept. "Stop being a such a *macho* Greek sexist," she'd said. "As long as we're happy, who cares whose money it is? Besides, it saves you from all those temptations thrown at cops struggling to support their families."

Andreas smiled. His domestic situation did spare him all the paperwork associated with reporting attempted bribes, because no one in the know ever bothered trying to corrupt him. *Don't even try, he doesn't need it*, was the word on the street about him.

"Are we just going to sit here?" came a voice from the passenger seat.

Andreas opened his door. "Sorry, Yianni, I was day dreaming."

"Did it bring you any visions of what we might expect to run into upstairs?"

"All I know is what I told you back in the office. My guess is it has to do with implementing crowd-control measures for the demonstrations. Don't worry, you're just along for moral support."

"I thought I was backup."

"Nah, that's only if we'd have to kick down doors. Here we're invited."

"Thanks for explaining the difference."

"You're wel—"

"Hey, is that who I think it is heading into the building?"

Andreas jerked his head around to look at the entrance. "Son of a bitch. It's the Brigadier."

"I doubt it's a coincidence."

"Yeah, sort of makes you wonder what the minister has in mind."

Yianni nodded. "So, what do we do now?"

Andreas stared at the entrance. "Same as before, play it by ear."

"If you say so."

"With one slight modification."

"Being?"

"As of now, consider yourself backup."

Chapter Six

Andreas did not recognize the stern-faced secretary of indeterminate age sitting at the desk outside the minister's office. She, too, was new to the ministry, having joined her boss when he left his position as his party's Assistant General Secretary in charge of Event Coordination, a position the pundits often characterized as "Riot Coordinator."

To give the devil his due, if anyone ought to know how best to deter—if not actually control—demonstrations, it would be the rebels' former organizer-in-chief. But that assumed Babis-the-minister was willing to risk revealing his longtime secrets to his erstwhile enemies. After all, Greek politics being what they were, today's minister could well be tomorrow's anti-establishment rock-tosser.

The thought brought one of Lila's favorite quips from a classic American cartoon character into Andreas' mind: "We have met the enemy and he is us." He smiled at the line.

"Chief Inspector Andreas Kaldis and Detective Kouros to see the minister," he told the woman.

She fixed a frown and her tiny bird-like eyes on Andreas' face. "I'm not sure what has you smiling, Chief Inspector, but the minister said to send you right in." She did not get up from behind her desk.

"A swamp-living cuddly possum named Pogo. No need to show us in, I know the way."

She looked at him as if he were a visitor from another planet.

Perhaps I am, he thought as he and Yianni headed toward a dark, heavy wooden door leading into what until a few months before had been his own office.

Andreas pulled open the door and stepped inside with Yianni right behind him. Babis sat off to the left behind an ornately carved antique mahogany desk far different from the standard-issue desk of Andreas' tenure. The Brigadier sat in one of two bottle-green leather armchairs across from the minister, and a man in a dark brown sport coat with an upturned collar sat in the other.

"Close the door, Kaldis," barked Babis.

Yianni turned to shut the door.

"No, Yianni, let me do it." Andreas stepped toward the door and pulled it gently shut. "It just might be the last thing he tells me to do that I can agree with."

The Brigadier gave a strained chuckle.

"Stop being a wiseass and sit down," said Babis.

Andreas walked away from where Babis sat toward two pairs of straight back wooden chairs facing each other across an expensive oriental rug. He passed by the chairs and chose a chocolate leather Chesterfield sofa at the far end of the office. Yianni stood by the door.

"I like what you've done with the place, Babis. A trifle costly, but as long as it makes you feel more in touch with your roots—"

"Why are you sitting at the opposite end of the room?" said Babis.

"I'm hoping distance might make my heart grow fonder."

The man next to the Brigadier pointed his thumb back over his shoulder at Andreas and said to Babis. "Why do you tolerate a subordinate speaking to you like that?"

Babis shrugged. "I told you he was difficult. But you wanted him here."

"And who, pray tell, are you?" asked Andreas.

"None of your business," said the man without looking his way.

Andreas waved for Yianni to join him on the couch. "*Kali mera*, Brigadier."

The Brigadier turned his head and nodded at Andreas. "Good morning, Chief Inspector."

As Yianni sat down next to him Andreas said, "It might be easier for us to have this conversation, gentlemen, if you turned your chairs around slightly so we're not looking at the backs of your heads."

The Brigadier stood and rearranged his chair. The other man didn't budge.

"By the way, nice dye job," said Andreas to the back of the man's head.

The man flashed Andreas an open palm—the Greek equivalent of the American middle finger—but still did not turn around.

"Who's he?" whispered Yianni to Andreas.

Andreas whispered back. "No idea, but someone who thinks he's important."

"And if he is, you're not exactly charming him."

"I'm not worried. I have you for backup."

"Are you two finished chatting among yourselves?" said Babis.

Andreas nodded. "We're just trying to figure out if the red line on the back of mystery man's jacket collar means it's Prada or a blood pressure indicator."

This time the man in Prada flipped Andreas the middle finger.

"Ah, so you're multilingual," said Andreas. "I take that to mean you're from some intelligence branch. Bet you speak Russian too."

"Enough!" shouted Babis. "We have serious things to discuss."

"On that point," said the Brigadier, "Why don't we begin with someone telling me why I'm here. More importantly, why is he here?" He pointed at the man next to him.

"Patience, Brigadier. We'll get to it in due time," said the man.

The Brigadier leaned toward the man. "In case you've forgotten, I'm a Brigadier in the Hellenic Military and I'm not in the habit of being spoken to that way."

The man in Prada leaned in toward the Brigadier. "You exist only because the people say you exist. You serve the people and you shall act as the people decide."

"I think you should do as he says," said Babis.

"With all due respect, Minister, you are not my minister, and you have no authority to order me to do squat."

"Tsk, tsk," uttered the man. "I would think you'd want to know who murdered your only child."

Color rose in the Brigadier's face and his clenched fist pressed hard on the arm of the chair.

"It's getting interesting," whispered Andreas to Yianni.

"Bet the Brigadier decks Prada."

"Sir," said the Brigadier staring daggers at Prada. "If in the next thirty seconds I don't get a full explanation of what this is about, I'm calling my commander, the minister of defense, for instructions on how to handle what's beginning to smell like a very inappropriate meeting."

"I wouldn't do that if I were you," said Prada, shaking his head.

"You've twenty seconds left," growled the Brigadier.

Prada slapped his hands on the sides of the chair. "Very well, have it your way." He nodded at Babis. "Tell him."

Babis leaned back in his chair. "You are here at the request of our Prime Minister's State Security Police."

"I never heard of any such branch," said the Brigadier.

"Nor have I," whispered Andreas.

"We function under the direction of the Prime Minister," said Prada. "To secure the state from subversive elements seeking to undo the will of the people."

"What the hell?" Andreas jumped up from the couch. "Last I checked, our Constitution doesn't permit secret police."

Not looking at Andreas, Prada said, "I suggest you hold your tongue, Chief Inspector."

Andreas bolted across the room to the man's chair and swung it around with Prada still in it. "Permit me to rephrase it. 'Our Constitution doesn't permit secret police, *asshole.*'"

"I'll have you arrested," snarled Prada, revealing badly mis-aligned teeth.

"Then let me give you something to remember me by." Andreas cocked his fist.

"No!" shouted the minister.

The Brigadier reached up and grabbed Andreas' arm. "Please, Chief Inspector, if any one gets to hit the bastard, let it be me."

Andreas threw up his hands and pointed a finger at Babis. "This has something to do with you. *Explain.*"

"How dare you—"

"No way this asshole could have police powers without your involvement. No way."

Babis cleared his throat. "Yes, that's true. And the State Security Police is a duly formed body under the powers of this ministry. Its chief," he nodded toward Prada, "reports directly to the Prime Minister. Through me, of course."

"Of course," said Prada.

"Wait until the press gets ahold of this," said Andreas.

"The media," scoffed Prada, "they are more concerned with their licenses and staying in the good graces of our government than in the nuts and bolts of police structure. And if you're talking about those few reactionary lackeys intent on terrorizing our people with false reports of our government's aims and aspirations, they are being appropriately dealt with."

Andreas stared at Prada for a moment then looked at the Babis. "I get it, this is some sort of a practical joke. But I think it's in bad taste to involve the Brigadier. So why don't you tell us what's really going on?"

Prada spoke through a clenched jaw. "You, Kaldis, are about to be arrested for interfering with the people's right of free assembly. It was your decision to remove the girl's body from the scene of her murder that brought such horrid turmoil to our beloved country. And you trespassed on university property in direct violation of our Constitution."

Andreas looked at Babis. "Is this guy serious?"

"I gave you the chance to apologize, but you refused."

Prada nodded. "Plus, you assaulted me."

The Brigadier cleared his throat. "And why am I here?"

"Simply to demonstrate to the people your sincere and genuine appreciation to the government for not allowing the fascist cop who defiled your daughter's sacrifice to the people to go unpunished."

Andreas clenched his fists.

"In other words, you want me to give my blessing to what you have in mind for Kaldis?"

"And your wife's blessing, too, of course."

The Brigadier nodded. "And if I don't?"

"It will be a shame to see such an illustrious military career ruined." Prada rocked his head from side to side. "Especially after all you've overcome, what with your father's past."

"I see," said the Brigadier. He rose to his feet and bowed to the minister. "I thank you for inviting me but I'm afraid I won't be able to help you out with this."

"Then you're through," said Prada from his chair.

The Brigadier turned to Prada. "Remember what you said before about Kaldis assaulting you? I don't think I'll be a very good witness for the prosecution."

"Why not? You saw what he did to me, and you have a duty to testify honestly."

"Yes, but all he did was swing your chair around with you in it. That's nothing compared to…"

The Brigadier reached down, yanked Prada out of his chair by his jacket, and threw him across the desk onto Babis' lap. "And if I ever see your hyena face again I'll rearrange your teeth."

"Don't bother," said Andreas putting a calming hand on the Brigadier's shoulder. "It would only improve his appearance."

"You're all under arrest," spit out Prada as he struggled to get to his feet.

Andreas turned to Yianni, who'd come off the couch and stood by the door. "Detective, do your duty. Take us away."

No alarms went off and no one attempted to stop the three men moving briskly away from the minister's office.

"We need to talk," said Andreas.

"Not here," said the Brigadier, looking over his shoulder at two security guards chatting up a secretary. "Who knows what that prick might decide to do."

"Which one?" said Yianni.

"Take your pick."

Andreas smiled. "How about Dal Segno? Is that public enough for you?"

"Sure. I'll see you there in fifteen minutes." They stepped outside the building and the Brigadier waved to his driver. "You're welcome to ride with me. I'll bring you back for your car when we're done."

"Thanks, but it might not still be here when we got back."

The Brigadier nodded, got into the backseat, and was gone.

"I like that waving to his driver bit," said Andreas as he and Yianni walked toward their marked blue-and-white cruiser.

"That only works if you're willing to let someone else drive," said Yianni holding out his hand for the car keys.

Andreas waved him off. "Sort of like our minister."

"Huh?"

"From what I saw upstairs, Babis is definitely not driving the ministry."

"I wonder who that Prada guy is?" said Yianni.

"No idea. I never saw him before."

"Me either. Maybe we can get an ID on him from the photos."

"What photos?" said Andreas.

"The ones I took on my phone while you and the Brigadier were playing beat up on the troll."

◇◇◇

With its fancy shops, restaurants, residences, and reputation as Athens' ritziest downtown area, the Kolonaki neighborhood was a discouraged destination for public appearances by leaders of the current government. The area's affluent lifestyle didn't fit the party's working class image, and at the top of the list of places to avoid stood Dal Segno Caffe with its reputation as the inner sanctum for Greece's old-line political lions.

Which made it the perfect place to meet.

Andreas drove up onto a pedestrian walkway next to the cafenion and parked.

Yianni shook his head. "First assault, now illegal parking. You're a damn closet recidivist."

"Just order the coffees. I'll find us a table."

They headed toward a storefront made of broad glass, polished natural wood, green marble, and Parisian green trim, and walked through a break in a line of sidewalk café tables into the cafenion.

"Pick out some of those too," said Andreas pointing at an array of Italian cookies and assorted sandwiches inside a glass display case.

"I'll have to report you to Lila."

Andreas waved an open palm in Yianni's direction as he stepped out onto an awning-covered patio. He headed toward an empty table tucked away in a corner behind the patio's lone tree.

He wondered how real his risk of arrest was. It made no sense, but if this government truly represented the left wing coup so many accused it of being, anything could happen. Tassos had told him many stories of how the Colonels ran their right wing junta. No reason to think these guys on the left would be any different. After all, Stalin wasn't a pussycat. But he couldn't worry about that. Prada might be hoping to make him a symbol of police aggression, but that would be hard to pull off if the parents of the murdered girl didn't go along with it, and impossible if the Brigadier spoke out in Andreas' defense.

"Screw 'em all," Andreas muttered under his breath as he sat down. If they wouldn't take his advice on how to deal with the demonstrations, that was their loss. He had enough other things to worry about. From here on out, the demonstrators were their problem, not his.

The Brigadier arrived just as Yianni showed up carrying coffees and a plate of cookies and brioches.

"Sorry I'm late, I had to take a phone call."

"I figured you like your coffee black," said Yianni.

"That's fine, detective. Thank you."

"Here's your fat-free cappuccino, Chief."

Andreas looked at the Brigadier. "My wife has everyone around me trying to keep me on a diet."

The Brigadier patted his slight belly. "It's a Greek curse once we pass a certain age."

"See," said Andreas, picking up a biscotti and waving it at Yianni before taking a bite, "the Brigadier's on my side of the pastry issue."

Yianni smiled. "From the way you tossed that Prada guy into the minister's lap, I'd say you stay in pretty good shape."

"Adrenaline helps," said the Brigadier. "Why did you call him Prada?"

"I named him after his sports jacket. It seemed more respectful than asshole."

The Brigadier shrugged. "One of you called him that too."

"Guilty as charged," said Andreas putting the biscotti down on the edge of his coffee saucer. "What's your take on our little get-together with Babis?"

"I was hoping you could tell me," said the Brigadier.

"If Prada actually wanted to pin what he said on me, and needed your help to pull it off, I'd have thought he'd be smart enough to run it by you first."

"If that's your way of asking whether I knew anything about what went on back there before it happened, the answer is no."

"Not at all," said Andreas. "In fact, I apologize for not thanking you sooner for standing up for me in there. I'm just trying to figure out why they thought you would lie for them."

The Brigadier shrugged. "No idea."

"Any idea who Prada is?" asked Yianni.

"You heard what I heard."

"How'd you end up in the meeting?" said Andreas.

"The minister called me to say there'd been a crucial development in the case and that he wanted to talk to me about it in person."

"Did you ask him what it was?"

"No."

Andreas blinked. "Why not?"

"I had no reason to."

"No reason?" Andreas leaned back in his chair and fixed his eyes on the Brigadier's. "With all due respect, sir, from out of the blue the head of the Greek police personally called to tell you there was a crucial development in your daughter's murder case, and you simply let the conversation drop there?"

The Brigadier nodded.

"It doesn't fit with you being a general. Generals are by nature suspicious and used to getting answers to their questions."

The Brigadier smiled. "So are chief inspectors."

"I know," said Andreas, "which leads me to think the reason you didn't ask was because you thought you already had the answer to what he planned on telling you."

The Brigadier stiffened in his chair. "And what are you suggesting that was?"

"The identity of your daughter's killers."

The Brigadier's expression turned grim. "That's preposterous."

Andreas shook his head. "I think you have a very definite idea of who killed your daughter, and thought the minster did too. The part I haven't figured out yet is why you didn't want to hear him say the names?"

"You're way off."

"Am I?" Andreas leaned in toward the Brigadier. "You know as well as I do this wasn't a case of your daughter being in the wrong place at the wrong time. She was a designated target, and your mind's been racing over a list of her possible killers since the moment I told you she'd been assassinated."

The Brigadier bit his lip. "I'm not going to deny any of that. Of course, it's consuming me…" he closed his eyes and let out a breath, "when I'm not worrying about how my wife will bear up at the funeral tomorrow. But I have no one in mind."

"I wish we didn't have to put you through this now," said Andreas, "but we have no choice."

The Brigadier nodded and opened his eyes. "And, yes, when the minister called acting so coy, I thought he wanted me with him as window dressing for some dramatic announcement he planned on making to the press to quell the demonstrations. I had no idea that he and…" his expression twisted into anger, "your Prada guy planned on using me to set you up as the political fall-guy for their PR disaster with the rioting."

"Fair. I'll accept all of that except for the 'no one in mind' part. Even I could have people in mind."

"Fine, then. Chase after them, and leave my thoughts to me."

Andreas leaned in closer. "I wish it were that easy, Brigadier, but I've got the distinct impression something's going on here that's a lot bigger than you're letting on. In fact, I'm pretty well convinced that the only reason your daughter was a target was because she was your daughter."

The Brigadier sprang to his feet. "How dare you suggest she was murdered because of me?"

Andreas waved for the general to sit. "Please. You're disturbing their coffee break." Andreas nodded at two nearby tables filled with customers all staring at the Brigadier.

He drew in and let out a deep breath as he clenched and unclenched his fists. He sat down and leaned in toward Andreas. "We both know there are a hell of a lot of people out there willing and capable of doing seriously bad things. That's why you and I have jobs."

"And all I want to know is whether any of those people spring to mind as a likely candidate for going after your daughter?"

He gestured no.

"Come on, work with me on this. There's got to be somebody out there you can finger as a possibility."

"You mean like terrorists?"

"I mean like anyone."

The Brigadier closed his eyes for a moment. The grim look took over his face again as he opened them. "There are some I know who are quite accomplished at violence and have no love for the path our current government is following. I do not share their views, but I still can't see them going after my daughter because of me."

"Who are they?" said Andreas.

The Brigadier gestured no. "I can't identify them."

"Can't or won't?"

The Brigadier closed his eyes again.

Now Andreas sat grim-faced and waited for the Brigadier to open his eyes. "If you knew terrorists were about to attack Greece, would you warn the country?"

"Of course."

"Then why aren't you speaking out now? Is it because the ones you're reluctant to name are Greeks? Does it matter one iota whether a Greek or a Martian killed your daughter? She's just as dead."

The Brigadier stared into his cup.

"There is a war looming here, Brigadier, and you've got to pick a side."

"Which side is the right side?"

Andreas shook his head. "If you have to ask that question, we're already doomed."

The Brigadier rubbed his eyes with the fingers of his massive right hand. "They're military colleagues."

"Planning a coup?" said Andreas.

"The military tried that with tanks in the streets fifty years ago, and it didn't work out so well. I don't think you can harness the long term support of the Greek people with promises of better living through *coups d'état*."

"Then what are you saying?" said Andreas.

"To my way of thinking, a traditional military coup is out of the question."

"Are you suggesting there's something 'non-traditional' percolating?" said Andreas.

The Brigadier shrugged. "I don't know. But any military man giving serious thought to coup possibilities would know that a coup could not possibly succeed without powerful outside benefactors."

"'Outside benefactors'?"

"Our history is full of them. After all, only with Russian and Western European help did we succeed in our 1821 War of Independence."

Andreas stared up at the tree. "The more things change, the more they remain the same."

"Bet you wish you hadn't asked," said the Brigadier.

Andreas brought his eyes back onto the Brigadier. "It's certainly not the sort of answer I expected."

"Excuse me, Brigadier," said Yianni. "I'm as up as the next Greek for a good conspiracy theory, but if what you said is true, I still don't see why whoever *they* are went after your daughter."

"Like I said, I can't either. I never presented a threat to them."

"That you know of," said Andreas.

The Brigadier chewed at his lower lip.

"So, I'm back to my initial question," said Andreas. "Who are *they*?"

The Brigadier looked away. "We call them the Caesars. They're career military who believe they can run Greece better than its civilian leadership. History is full of that sort. Every military has them. It's why our Constitution places such clear limitations on the powers of the military."

"Do you have any names for these Caesars?" asked Andreas.

"Some are seasoned and frustrated, some young and idealistic, but all are pissed off at how dysfunctional our country's become."

Andreas leaned forward. "What about it, Brigadier, are you prepared to talk about them?"

The Brigadier rubbed his cheek. "They characterize themselves as a military think tank organized to hammer out ideas on how civilian leadership can better help the country. Their members take great pains not to take public positions on any controversial subjects and they offer their suggestions in private to those politicians who wish their assistance."

"Then what makes you think they're dangerous enough to have possibly played a part in your daughter's murder?" asked Andreas.

"I'm not saying they did, just that they're capable of doing it. Remember, their careers are dedicated to preparing to kill for their country. All it would take is one fanatic among them."

Andreas nodded. "Do you have names?"

"I'll give you names, but I think it's better if you decide for yourself what sort of threat they actually present."

"How are we supposed to do that?" said Yianni.

"They've put together a retreat this weekend for senior and general staff level officers to discuss the future of Greece."

"Seniors?" said Andreas.

"Seniors are the equivalent of majors through colonels, and general staff are admirals, generals, and air marshals."

"With all due respect, Brigadier, you can't be serious," said Yianni. "Top level military brass calling an open meeting to plan a coup?"

The Brigadier smiled. "They're not insane, Detective. The stated purpose is to discuss new ways in which the military can help Greece's government negotiate its way through the continuing crisis."

"Sounds rather transparent and non-confrontational to me," said Yianni.

"Yes, precisely like the bullshit Greeks are used to hearing every day from their civilian leadership," said the Brigadier.

"Are you suggesting it's meant to be something more?" asked Andreas.

"Like a means for determining who among them might be sympathetic to using aggressive methods for restoring Greece to glory?" added Yianni.

"Perhaps it's just their way of getting away for a weekend with their buddies," said the Brigadier with a shrug.

"Where's the meeting?" said Yianni.

"Santorini."

"A bit out of season, isn't it?" said Andreas.

"Probably why they chose it. Beauty, calm, and invisibility."

"Do you know where on Santorini?" said Andreas.

"I can get the information for you, but there's no way they'll let you in."

"Just get us the info," said Andreas.

"Don't kid yourselves. These are tough guys, all very security-conscious, and a lot smoother than their Golden Dawn ex-military brethren-turned-members of parliament."

Andreas leaned back in his chair. "And if they're behind your daughter's murder, deadly too."

Andreas tossed Yianni the keys as they reached the rear of the police car. "You drive."

Yianni opened the driver side door as Andreas slid in on the passenger side. "I see you like the Brigadier's idea of having a chauffeur."

"I must respect the workings of an ingenious tactical mind."

"I won't even try to guess what's running through your head." Yianni crept the police car along the walkway through a crush of noontime pedestrians and onto the street.

"I was wrong about the person the Brigadier would be using to track down his daughter's killers."

"Are you saying we should call off surveillance on his aide?"

Andreas nodded. "He knows that if his daughter's murder was meant as a message to him, he'd be risking the lives of others in his family to use someone obviously connected to him." Andreas slapped his right hand on the dashboard. "He's using us to do it for him. No one can say he's behind it because it's only natural for cops to be looking for the killers."

"If that's his plan, then why did we have such a hard time getting him to tell us who's organizing that meeting on Santorini?"

"He could be playing the reluctant virgin," said Andreas.

"There aren't too many of them around these days. Reluctant or otherwise."

"I'll take your word on that."

Yianni patted the steering wheel. "But what you say makes sense for another reason too. If the Caesars aren't the bad guys, and word got out he'd been accusing them, he'd have made some serious enemies and undermined his reputation among his fellow military brass. Cops and soldiers share the same attitude when it comes to distrusting anyone who washes the family's dirty laundry outside the house."

"The Brigadier's style has me wondering how much he actually knew in advance of what the minister had in mind for our little get-together this morning."

"Do you think his standing up for you and tossing Prada across the desk was an act?"

"Can't say, but what he did in there made me feel I owed him big-time. So much so that, one cup of coffee later, here I am committed to going after his Caesars. If they're truly as right wing and fanatic an organization as the Brigadier suggests, they're obviously also a serious threat to the current government. And Prada likely knows that too. Prada also undoubtedly knows that for his leftist government to take the Caesars on openly would only more deeply divide our seriously polarized population along left-right lines."

Andreas shook his head. "Wouldn't it be nice for the government if it could get me, a one-time minister in the former conservative government, to spearhead an investigation that brings down the Caesars, or at least fatally brands the group as terrorist?"

"Sounds rather devious, don't you think?"

"On all levels, by everyone involved. Prada and the Brigadier could be playing together or have separate games all aimed at getting us to focus on the Caesars. I know it sounds crazy, but from his performance back in Babis' office, Prada might have been betting that the Brigadier wouldn't bury me and that he could push him into doing something that made me feel indebted to him. After all, no one tried to stop us from leaving the ministry, and Prada and Babis had to know going into the meeting there wasn't the slightest possibility of my standing up before the press and taking the blame for their screw-up."

Yianni glanced at Andreas. "And you say I'm the one who's hooked on conspiracy theories."

Andreas smiled. "With what we've been through over the last couple of years, is there anyone left in Greece who doesn't think that way?"

"Sure," said Yianni. "But I wouldn't trust them. They've sold out."

Andreas stared at the side of Yianni's face. "Just drive."

Chapter Seven

For centuries after its hellfire volcanic eruption in the mid-sixteenth century BCE, Santorini remained deserted, but its critical location, fertile soil, and awe-inspiring beauty ultimately drew new settlers and conquerors. Phoenicians, Franks, rulers from other parts of Greece, Persians, Romans, Venetians, and Turks laid claim, virtually all enduring earthquakes or volcanic eruptions of varying degrees during their occupation.

Today, the main island of Santorini constitutes the eastern crescent—and by far largest—of five volcanic islands comprising a small circular archipelago. Three of those islands, Santorini (or Thera), Thirasia, and Aspronisi, are all that remain of the original island of Atlantis legend, with Palea Kameni and Nea Kameni born as new islands out of that and other eruptions, including more than two dozen in the Common Era alone.

It seemed only fitting that an archipelago born out of ancient cataclysmic events, would be transformed by a modern catastrophe into the tourist paradise it is today, rivaled in reputation only by its Cycladic cousin Mykonos. On July 9, 1956, a 7.8-magnitude earthquake struck Santorini in what was recorded as the largest to hit Greece in the twentieth century, severely damaging if not collapsing practically every building on the island. But much as with the mythical Phoenix, out of its destruction Santorini rose to what today is a place of fifteen thousand year-round residents drawing 1.7 million tourists annually—nine hundred thousand to its hotels and rooms, eight hundred thousand more from cruise ships.

With forty-three miles of coastline, an east-to-west breadth of between one and four miles, and an overall north-to-south length of eleven miles, Santorini resembles a seahorse standing on its head and staring west—in the same direction as do most tourists.

As reflected in its hotel prices, the island's primary attraction is its view looking west from atop the rim of the volcano's caldera. Away from the caldera Santorini seems much like many other parts of Greece, and its beaches alone are not a draw. But standing on the caldera's nine-hundred-foot red-black-brown cliffs, looking across the seemingly bottomless quarter-mile depths of the crater's sapphire blue lagoon, one faces a true wonder of the natural world.

Few braved that view in winter, though—a time of rain, chill, and fierce winds, a far different experience from what tourists came to expect from glorious springtime through late-autumn weather.

It was a little after eleven in the morning when the rented white Nissan Micra turned left out of the airport and hurried west toward Santorini's central crossroads at Mesaria, a mile away. The roads were dry, but heavily overcast skies threatened to change that at any moment. The car passed shops offering goods and services suited more to locals than tourists, but that was to be expected in Santorini's inland regions.

Locals lived in areas like this, many growing wine grapes cultivated in the unique, tightly coiled, ground-hugging fashion that in winter resembled rows of dull baskets, but in growing season sheltered the enclosed clusters from the wind. Tiny cherry tomatoes, capers, fava beans, barley, and a unique white eggplant were other island growing favorites, with plantings filling practically every arable spot of land.

Although everyone on the island paid homage to some extent to the tourist, most Santorinian hearts still beat as farmers and muleteers. But not so much as fishermen. From ancient times, the island had great merchant trading fleets, and its ships performed heroically in Greece's 1821 War of Independence, but

Santorinians generally preferred to live far away from the sea in places where they could raise their crops and mules. It was tourists who changed all that, starting, it's said, with teaching many a Santorinian how to swim.

At Mesaria, the car turned right onto a road dotted with small tourist hotels, bars, and restaurants, and continued north for another mile or so onto a eucalyptus-lined road into Santorini's capital of Fira. Here the island became a different sort of place. Stretching north six miles along the caldera's western rim—from Fira through Firostefani and Imerovigli into Oia at the island's northern tip—tourists paid hefty premiums for the breathtaking views and promise of romance symbolized by Oia's emblematic blue-domed, bright-white, cliffside churches at sunset.

The road north of Fira yielded no views of the caldera. That property was far too valuable for roadways. Instead, the road ran below and to the east of the towns' perches on the rim, but as if in compensation for that shortcoming, the two-lane road offered unobstructed views of broad green plains running down to deep blue Aegean waters and a panoramic array of neighboring Cycladic islands. But not today. The clouds had darkened, and the horizon faded to where only a shadow of the island of Anafi lingered in the haze.

North of Imerovigli the volcanic rim narrowed to a sliver of privately owned land straddling the caldera's cliffside drop into Mouzaki Bay on the west and a steep, mountainside falloff to the east where a ledge barely accommodated the road. Even the caldera rim's celebrated gray lava and taupe dirt footpath linking Fira to Oia—edged much of the way in smoke-colored volcanic rock and abloom with wildflowers in season—had to merge with the asphalt road for a quarter-mile to get around this pinch point.

A hundred meters past the merge with the footpath, a tiny sign on the left read: SEA AND SKY SUITES. The car sliced across the road and up onto a steep concrete hillside driveway running almost parallel to the road. At a switchback turn leading further up the hill, the driveway opened onto a small parking area close by a two-story white stucco and gray fieldstone building. The car stopped there, next to a door marked RECEPTION.

Two middle-aged men, a younger man, and a woman not older than thirty got out of the car. The youngest man, slim, with flowing light-brown hair, walked up the hill to a bar and infinity pool area just beyond the end of the building. He stood by the edge of the pool for a moment and waved for his companions to join him.

The woman was the first to reach him. "Wow, Christos. I've never seen a view like this anywhere on Santorini."

Less than a mile across the lagoon loomed the neighboring island of Thirasia, a geological chubby mirror image of Santorini but just one-sixth its size, and with only two hundred fifty residents, fourteen churches, and four inhabited settlements, it remained undiscovered by tourism. Directly below the hotel, ultramarine seas touched upon billiard table-green waters lapping against deep brown and black volcanic rocks appearing more as dark shadows than substance.

Christos spread his arms wide and spun around in a circle on one foot. "The caldera lagoon before us, the Aegean laid out behind, how else could you describe this scene but magical?"

"Even in this lousy weather," nodded the woman.

A door slammed shut in the bar area.

"Excuse me. May I help you?" shouted a lanky, dark haired man of about Christos' age. He stepped briskly across the bar area toward the group.

"Why, yes, I think you can." Christos dangled his right hand in the air until the lanky man reached for it and shook it.

"I'm Christos Vlachos, and this is Anna Katsanis." He did not introduce his older two companions. "I'm with GNTO."

"The Greek National Tourist Organization?"

"Yes. And you are?"

"Vladimir Kostikyan. I manage this property."

"I thought I detected a bit of a Russian accent. It's becoming rather commonplace to hear Russian on Santorini."

Vladimir smiled. "I've lived here eleven years. I like to think of myself as one of the pioneers. So, what can I do for you?"

"We're here on an inspection."

"I don't recognize you," said Vladimir. "Where is Mihali from the Syros office?"

"Syros is our regional office for the Cyclades. We're from Athens. I'm sure you're aware of our government's determined efforts at assuring that our precious tourism industry is safeguarded."

"What's that have to do with your being here?"

"We're part of a joint task force with the finance ministry charged with conducting random checks on high-end tourism properties for purposes of confirming compliance with GNTO and revenue-reporting requirements."

"Sounds like a highly profitable line of work."

Christo glanced over at the two men standing by the edge of the pool. "Vladimir, I strongly suggest you don't pursue that line. My two colleagues back there have authority to arrest you on the spot for that sort of talk."

Vladimir pointed at his chest. "Me? I wasn't suggesting anything. I'm just wondering why you picked our dozen villas, with so many larger and far better known hotels to choose from."

"Well, one reason is that you're open."

"Yes, but only for a few days for a private gathering. We've been closed for over a month and didn't plan on reopening until Easter."

"Must be important people if you reopened just for them."

Vladimir shrugged. "I wouldn't know. They're friends of the owner."

"Friends or no friends, they must be paying a lot to get you to reopen."

"Look," said Vladimir. "Let's drop the act. I know why you're here."

Christos stared at Vladimir.

"It's that B & B up the hill," shouted Vladimir waving his finger to the south.

"There's no bed and breakfast around here," said Christos.

"I meant the 'bitch and bastard' couple who own that shit hole of a hotel south of here. They're jealous of what we've done to turn this into a luxury property, but rather than fixing up their hell hole operation, they prefer thinking up ways of getting authorities like you to bust our balls. They must have noticed we're reopening and called you in to screw us up."

"That's a pretty fair description of the Greek definition for 'neighborly,'" said Christos. "But not this time. I'm afraid, my friend, you were just plain lucky. Your name was simply one of several selected at random by our computer for a surprise inspection, and while we were on our way to Oia we noticed that your gate was open, and *voila*, here we are."

"I don't believe you."

Christos waved one hand in the air. "That doesn't matter. What matters is whether we believe your books and records."

Vladimir ran his fingers through his hair. "Look. I've got a very important group of people arriving early tomorrow afternoon, and a lot of work to do between now and then. Can't you come back in a few days, after they're gone? I'll give you all the time you need then."

Christos patted Vladimir's arm. "I understand completely. The only problem is that our unit is charged with making random *surprise* audits. If we wait 'til later it won't be a surprise. Worse still, we've already notified our office we're at your place, so if we leave without doing the audit…well, like you said before… some may start to think we've found 'a highly profitable line of work.' Don't worry, we'll work as quickly as we can. Assuming your records are organized and you cooperate, we should be able to finish up by…" he looked at Anna.

"Early evening," she said.

"What? That means we'll have to work through the night to be ready for our guests. My boss will kill me."

Christos shook his head. "At least you're working for only one boss. Think of us poor public servants who must justify ourselves to an entire nation of bosses."

Vladimir's back stiffened. "I want to see identification."

"I thought you'd never ask."

Christos displayed a card identifying himself as Deputy Inspector General of GNTO, and Anna's ID showed her to be the Finance Ministry's Field Audit Compliance Chief for the Southern Aegean.

Vladimir bit at his lower lip. "What about them?" pointing at the two other men.

"They're the ones with guns and badges who make sure we stay safe."

Vladimir threw up his hands. "All right, okay. Just tell me what you want to see and let's get started."

"A good attitude, Vladimir. Why don't you, Anna, and I go back to your office and begin with your books. If you'd like to save a lot of time, give me the keys to the villas and I'll have my colleagues get their equipment out of the car and confirm that the villas' measurements and appointments are as represented in the hotel's GNTO filings."

"All the villas are unlocked, open, and airing out."

"Great."

Vladimir stared at Christos. "But I want you to know I don't believe you. I still think the bitch and bastard up the hill are behind this."

Christos smiled. "Some bitch or bastard perhaps, but I can assure you, not them. At least not this time."

Each villa was of new construction with essentially the same two-story layout. The front door opened into a large L-shape living-dining-kitchen area decorated in traditional Santorini blues and white, and a similarly toned separate master bedroom and bath took up the remaining floor space. A narrow spiral staircase at the rear of the living area led to a second-floor bedroom, bathroom, and outside roof deck, complete with a Jacuzzi overlooking the caldera.

The two men worked quickly, burying listening devices in wall plates in every room and a repeater transmitter on each roof tied into the Jacuzzi's electrical system. They passed on installing video, considering it too tricky to pull off in the time available if they wanted to cover all twelve villas for sound.

They did manage to hide one camera and mike behind the bar adjacent to the main building, piggybacking on a camera already in place to keep the bartender honest.

At twenty minutes per villa, plus another thirty at the bar, nearly five hours had passed when they walked into Vladimir's office.

"Where the hell have you been?" said Christos, his sleeves rolled up and his elbows planted on a desk covered in open accounting books and binders filled with invoices and receipts.

Vladimir sat next to him, looking as if he'd been dragged behind a bus for eternity.

"You told us to be thorough," said the shorter of the two men. "Those are big rooms, with a lot of things to verify. We had to measure the rooms and the closets, check to make sure that everything worked. Every light switch, every outlet, every faucet, every—"

Christos raised one hand. "Okay, Francesco, I get it."

Francesco nodded. "Unless you have something else for us to do, Dimos and I will wait outside."

"How about reading some invoices?"

"Not our job."

Christos looked at Vladimir. "This is the sort that the old administration left for us to work with. No willingness to help out their comrades."

Francesco shrugged and looked at Vladimir. "Do you mind if we wait at the bar?"

Vladamir sighed. "No. Feel free to help yourself to a beer."

"That's *one* beer," said Christos. "We don't want any misunderstandings here."

The two men left.

"How much longer will we be at this?" said Vladimir.

Christos looked at Anna, "What would you say, another thirty minutes or so?"

She nodded. "That sounds about right."

Vladimir looked relieved. "Terrific."

Christos smiled. "Assuming, of course, that our colleagues at the bar did everything I wanted."

"They better have after I just bought them a beer."

"Stay here. I'll go check."

Christos caught up with them standing by the bar talking about soccer. As soon as Christos joined them, Francesco pushed a speed-dial button on his mobile.

A loud "Hello" came through the phone.

Francesco held the phone up to his ear. "Could you hear us?"

"You mean all your wishful thinking about the chances of your football team doing well this year?"

Francesco smiled and nodded to Dimos.

"Perfect," said the voice on the phone. "Just as clear as you came through from the villas. Good work, guys."

"Great. So, when do we get out of here and back to Athens?"

"What's your hurry? You're in tourist paradise."

"Funny, my wife said sort of the same thing. It's why she wants me back home tonight or tomorrow morning at the latest. She was pissed when I told her I had to catch the afternoon ferry here. She wanted to know why I couldn't fly in the morning, and when I told her Dimos and I had to take the van, she didn't believe me. I used to spend a lot of time on Santorini and she's worried I might run into some old friends."

"Sounds like you're going to have a lot of sweet-talking left to do to convince her you're suffering during your stay."

"*Stay?* Whoa, whoa, whoa, Petro. What the hell are you talking about?"

"Sorry to be the one to give you the news, but since you guys set up all the equipment here and in the hotel, we now have orders from the chief for you to stay with me and babysit everything in case something goes wrong."

"For how long?"

"Until the targets leave."

"Damn."

"I hear you, Brother."

Francesco walked to the end of the bar area at the edge of the caldera, looked north at a white church sitting atop and west of a path running along the caldera, and flipped a finger at the hidden camera.

"Crystal-clear image, thank you."

"Can't believe that church is going to be our home for the next few days."

"You'll love what I've done with the place since you and Dimos went off to pick up the Athens folk at the airport."

"God help us."

"Hey, the views are great."

"How do we get there from here?" said Francesco.

"Come in from the Oia side where we parked the van and lugged the equipment up to the church. We wouldn't want Vladimir getting a glimpse of you and Dimos traipsing across the hills like fugitives from *The Sound of Music.*"

"You're not funny."

"I'm saving my best stuff for our weekend together in church."

Francesco shut off his phone and walked back to the bar.

"Everything okay?" said Christos.

"Aside from the fact that Dimos and I are staying here, yes."

"What do you mean?" said Dimos.

"I'll tell you later."

"Do you need me to stay?" said Christos.

Francesco gestured no. "You've done more than enough. We couldn't have done it without you distracting Vladimir."

"Anything for Uncle Tassos."

"How's Anna with all this?"

"She's cool. Treating it as a real audit. In fact, as far as she knows, it is. I'm the only one who knows there's something else going on." He raised his hands. "And I don't know what it is or want to know. Uncle Tassos said to buy you time and that's all I needed to know. Period."

Francesco patted Christos on the shoulder. "I like your style. Somewhat more subtle than your uncle's knock-down-the-door approach, but it works for me."

"That's the first time anyone's ever called me subtle. Flamboyant maybe."

"Uh, guys," said Dimos. "Don't you think we should get back inside before that Vladimir guy starts wondering what we're doing out here?"

"Don't worry about him," said Christos as he went behind the bar. He took three beers out of the cooler and put them on the bar. "From what I've seen of his books, he's got nothing to worry about and Anna will give the place a clean report. He'll be so happy, he'll probably put us on his mailing list."

Christos opened the beers and handed one to each man.

"*Yamas*," said the men as they clinked bottles.

All but Francesco took a sip.

"What's the matter?" said Christos. "You don't drink"?

"Not until after I call my wife to tell her I won't be home this weekend."

"That's crazy," said Christos. "A sip isn't going to fog your mind, and she can't smell beer on your breath over the phone."

Dimos shook his head. "You don't know his wife."

Christos laughed.

Francesco didn't.

Chapter Eight

After dropping Christos and Anna off at the airport for their late flight to Athens, Francesco and Dimos drove west along a winding mountainside road toward the picturesque mid-island village of Pyrgos, with its labyrinth of medieval stone houses and passageways winding up toward fifteenth-century Venetian castle ruins atop the highest village on the island. Until the early nineteenth century, Pyrgos had served as the capital of the island, but today its five hundred residents depended upon tourism, as did most of the island, indeed most of Greece.

Petro stood waiting at the edge of the road, near the base of wide, well-worn pebble and stone steps leading up into the village.

"You got here quickly," said Francesco through the open driver side window.

"Your suggestion that we who are condemned to spend a weekend together in church should have a final meal together on the outside, inspired me." Petro nodded toward a red and yellow Suzuki Ninja motorcycle parked by the steps. "And that little rented wizard did the rest."

"Get in," said Francesco.

"I thought we were going to dinner," said Petro, cramming himself into the backseat.

"We are, but in the next town. I just thought it was easier for you to meet us here. We got a recommendation from Christos. Just look for signs to the village of Exo Gonia."

A few minutes later Dimos pointed. "That must be the place up ahead. Christos said it looked like a concrete bunker with trash bins out front and TAVERNA scrawled on the wall in whitewash."

Petros leaned over the front seat and stared at Francesco. "Just how well do you know this guy Christos? You didn't by chance insult his mother or something?"

Francesco flicked Petro's chin. "He's Tassos' nephew, and a big gun with the Tourist Office. He wouldn't steer us wrong. And I don't even know his mother."

"What about his sister?" said Dimos.

Francesco parked alongside the trash containers. "Hey, you're going to give Petro the wrong impression about me."

Dimos smiled as he opened the door. "You mean the same one your wife has of you?"

Francesco waved off his friend as he got out of the car, and the three cops made their way down the hillside toward the taverna. They stopped by a broad open terrace overlooking a distant blanket of sparkling lights running off toward the sea.

"It must be beautiful in season," said Petro.

"Bit nippy tonight," said Francesco.

Dimos pointed to a door. "That must be for inside seating." He pulled the big iron door handle and held the door open for Petro and Francesco.

They stepped into a room with no view, no sense of the outdoors, and no promise of romance. Two long rows of tables covered in white linen ran the length of the room from the door to the back wall, with banquettes anchored along each wall. A tiny bar area, kitchen entrance, and hostess station stood at the far end. Every piece of wood in the place was dark-gray fieldstone trimmed in white stucco adorned each sidewall, and a vaulted white stucco ceiling spanned it all.

They'd stumbled into what could have been a cave, filled with smiling faces packed together in shared harmony and conversation rumbling along at a pleasant hum.

A man standing in the middle of the room holding an order pad waved for them to come to him. "Gentlemen, how can I help you?"

"We're here for dinner on the recommendation of a good friend," said Francesco.

"I love good friends like that," said the man. "Please give me a few minutes and I'll set something up for you. Okay?"

Francesco nodded. "Okay. Thanks."

The man nodded and went back to taking his customers' orders.

Petro and Dimos followed Francesco as he wandered over to a corner where a female cashier sat on a bar stool behind a well-distressed, podium-style hostess desk. She was young, unsmiling, and overworked.

"Are you always this busy?" said Francesco.

"Usually it's worse. I just sit here listening to people complain about how long they have to wait for a table, as I try to figure out ways to make their lives more miserable than mine."

Francesco cocked his head and nodded toward the man with the order pad. "Is he your father?"

"What makes you say that?"

"You have the same smile."

She stared at Francesco. "I get it. You're the charming one in this crew."

Dimos laughed.

"What's so funny?" she said. "He's here trying to hustle me while you're waiting for the owner to get you a table and I've got to endure it. Can't you two keep him busy or something? The guy's a piece of work. Telling me I have the same smile as *him*," pointing at the owner. "Lord, have you no mercy?"

Petro burst out laughing.

"And what's with you, giant man? Is the air so thin up there you can't understand what I'm telling you? Read my lips. 'Keep the great romancer busy and away from me.'" She pointed at Francesco. "Puh-lease."

Now all three cops were laughing.

She waved to the owner, "Smiley, would you get over here and seat these three? They're killing me."

"Why do I feel we're part of a show?" said Francesco.

The owner waved for the men to come to him. "Let me spare you any more of Sappho."

"Don't laugh," she said. "That's my real name. Now you know why I'm like I am. With a name like Sappho you've got to have a sense of humor."

Petro stood staring at Sappho, a grin from ear to ear.

"What's with you? Chow's ready, move on."

Petro didn't move.

She pointed him toward the owner. "Go."

Petro didn't move.

With a dramatic sigh, Sappho stood and came around the desk. She was almost as tall as Petro.

"Surprised you didn't I?" She spun him around and led him by the arm over to the table where Francesco and Dimos sat.

"Hey, guys, you forgot one." As she pushed him toward an open chair, she stood on her toes and whispered in his ear, "I think you're cute," pinched his butt, and sashayed back to her desk.

Petro stood there, watching her walk.

Without turning around Sappho yelled back over her shoulder. "So, tell me folks, is he watching my butt?"

A roar of "*YES*" came up from the crowd. She spun around, sat on her stool, and smiled at Petro.

Francesco grabbed Petro by his coat and pulled him down onto the chair. "It's embarrassing watching you fall smitten in front of an entire restaurant full of strangers."

Petro looked at Francesco. "I'm just interested."

"Interested is in a menu. Smitten is in a woman."

"So, let's look at a menu already," said Dimos.

"Do you think she's married?" asked Petro.

Dimos and Francesco looked at each other.

"Don't look at me," said Dimos. "You're the one with the bright idea of us all going out for dinner. He's your problem."

"Are you ready to order?" said the owner.

"Why don't you just start bringing out the food and we'll tell you when to stop," said Dimos.

"And same thing with the wine," said Francesco, "especially the wine," pointing to Petro.

The owner picked up the menus. "No problem." He patted Petro on the back as Petro stared at Sappho. "You're a good sport. I like you." He paused. "My wife likes you, too."

The blood drained from Petro's face and he turned to face the man.

"I'm sorry, sir, I didn't know she was your wife."

He patted Petro on the shoulder again. "Not Sappho, the one over there watching you from the kitchen." He pointed to a plump, dark-haired woman standing in the doorway behind Sappho.

The woman smiled and Sappho laughed.

But not as much as Francesco and Dimos.

The food came in tranches, overrunning the available space on the table and pressing into service adjacent empty chairs. First, Santorini *fava* with onions and capers; baked white eggplant in tomato sauce with feta and fresh basil; grilled Haloumi cheese with grilled tomatoes and olive oil; and grilled Santorini spicy sausages alongside fried potatoes and parmesan cheese. Next, a salad of spinach, red and green leaf lettuce, spring onions, dill, orange, walnuts, parmesan, pomegranate, and balsamic vinaigrette with honey; a second salad of cucumber, tomato, onion, green pepper, boiled potato, Cretan cottage cheese, olives, croutons, fresh olive oil, capers, and Cretan salt; and grilled octopus with fresh oregano and balsamic vinaigrette. Following came spicy fried pork with peppers, onions, leeks, Santorini cherry tomatoes and feta; lamb in yogurt sauce with mint, coriander, and cracked wheat; and beef filet in *vinsanto* sauce accompanied by wild mushrooms and basmati rice.

By the time they finished eating, the place had virtually emptied out, and Sappho was sitting next to Petro, engaged in a running monologue for the benefit of all three men on the nature of their species. She took time out only to encourage them to eat more and pour more wine for them and herself. "Eat, eat. The fatter you get the less likely you are to be a threat to the virtue of Greek women."

Petro couldn't remember ever laughing harder or longer in his life. "So, you've worked here all your life?"

"Yep." She took a sip of wine. "Except for my university days in Patras."

"What did you study?"

"Chemical engineering." She leaned toward Francesco. "My turn to interview. So what are you three musketeers doing on Santorini in the off season?"

Petro said, "We're here to—"

"Stop hogging the lady's attention. Give some other guy a chance," said Francesco. "We're here to check out some hotel properties with an eye to investing in them."

She nodded. "A lot of people come here in the winter looking to do that. Never understood why. My friends tell me the only time you make money in the small hotel business in Greece is when you sell it."

"It's all a matter of how you market it."

"And getting it at the right price," said Dimos.

She poked Petro on the arm. "What do you have to say about the hotel business?"

Francesco spoke quickly. "He's our money guy. He's not part of the business."

She leaned back and ran her eyes up and down Petro. "You're rich? Wow you're a great catch for some girl." She pulled her chair closer to his and rested her head on his shoulder. "Please take me away from all this. I want to bear your children."

Petro laughed.

She sat up straight in her chair. "What! You dare to laugh at my proposal?" She jumped out of her chair and headed toward the kitchen, yelling to her father as she passed him. "And you just sit there as my honor is besmirched by these rude strangers."

Her father kept talking to his remaining customers, ignoring his daughter.

Francesco glanced toward the kitchen before leaning in toward Petro. "My boy, be careful. A woman wound as tightly as this one comes with problems. Guaranteed."

"But she's funny. "

"Yeah, a regular life of the party," said Dimos.

"Great fun, but when they're alone, and not the center of attention…" Francesco shook his head.

"The word you're looking for," said Dimos, "is depression."

"Just be careful, is all I'm saying."

"Look guys, I'm just having a good time. Thanks for the fatherly concern but I'm not getting married."

Francesco looked at Dimos. "Did he just say 'married'?"

"Again."

"Screw you both."

"Hey," said Dimos, "your girlfriend's heading straight for us and she's waving a chef's knife."

The cops all spun around in their chairs.

Right behind Sappho marched her mother bearing a melon, a plate of pastries, and silverware. She put everything down in front of Petro, pinched his cheeks, and smacked her hands together. All with a big smile and not saying a word.

Sappho walked to where she'd been sitting and leaned over the table to cut the melon.

Petro studied her face, not more than a lean-in away from his own. Long dark hair framed a slightly coffee-colored face set with sparkling dark eyes, a broad nose, and a prominent, dimpled square chin. A traditional Greek-looking woman.

"I hope you're dying to kiss me," she said without looking at him.

"Absolutely, but why do you ask?"

"So I can entice you into telling me why you're really on Santorini."

"We told you why," said Francesco.

She caught his eye. "I've spent my life surrounded by military types and hotel types. They're very different breeds. And you're definitely not hotel types."

"You think we're military?" said Dimos.

She shook her head from side to side and went back to cutting the melon. "The Air Force base is just down the hill from here at the airport, we have a lot of regulars from there. In fact some of the guys talking to my father are from the base. There's some big gathering this weekend and they want to take over the restaurant to hold a dinner." She shifted her eyes to Petro's. "If you're here because of that, maybe I'll get to see you again."

Petro smiled. "I certainly hope so, but it won't be because we're military. I'm just a working stiff trying to get by in a worse-than-lousy economy."

She smiled. "I thought you're supposed to be the rich kid."

"My friends slightly exaggerated. I'm the one with the contacts. That makes me the moneyman in their parlance. But it's OPM."

"OPM?"

"Other people's money."

She nodded. "Fair enough. So what are you doing the rest of the night? It's still early."

Petro laughed, reached around Sappho's waist, pulled her toward him, and gave her a big kiss on the cheek. "I promise you I'll be back. My schedule, though, is not my own this weekend. But if there is any way, I'll let you know."

"You liar. You haven't even asked for my number."

Petro smiled again. "Don't need it." He held up a matchbook imprinted with the name and number of the restaurant.

"Quick recovery." She pulled out a pen and scribbled on a paper napkin. "Here's my mobile number and e-mail address."

Sappho stood straight up and nodded to Dimos and Francesco. "Night guys, a pleasure meeting you." She crouched down, gave Petro a quick kiss on the lips, and scurried off into the kitchen.

Petros took out his phone and fiddled with it.

"My God," said Francesco, "can't you at least wait until after we're out of here before putting your new girlfriend's number in your phone? Look at those guys at the other table. They're laughing at you."

"Yep, they sure are," said Petro still fidgeting with his phone. "It saves me from having to ask them to smile for the camera."

"Camera?" said Francesco.

Dimos laughed. "Good move, kid."

Petro smiled at Dimos. "I thought you might like that." He put down his phone and placed his hand on Francesco's shoulder. "And I hope you realize, my friend, that with those photos I just took of all the military types gathered around that table, this meal is now officially a business expense."

Francesco's face lit up. He swung around in his chair and waved to the owner. "Check, please. This is my treat. Don't even think of giving the bill to my buddies."

Chapter Nine

The hike to the church from where they parked the motorcycle and car took a lot longer than Petro remembered from their middle-of-the-night treks up the hill the night before. Far steeper too. But that was in adrenalin-driven preparation for an operation, not an alcohol-impaired stagger off to bed under the glow of an almost full moon playing hide and seek among the clouds. Francesco and Dimos said hardly a word the whole way, concentrating instead on keeping their footing.

At least it wasn't raining.

Petro was the first to reach the church nestled at the crest of the hill. He lifted a rope blocking the few steps up to the church. A sign dangled from the rope: CLOSED FOR REPAIRS AND PAINTING.

"Nice touch," said Dimos.

"We'll see if it works. The word 'NO' seems to attract our countrymen."

The steps led to a low-walled stone terrace abutting a blue-domed white church aligned with its front door facing west, and a complementing small all-white structure snug up against the church's north wall. Petro reached above the lintel, pulled down a key, and opened the church door. Inside, a soft flicker of light from an oil lamp reflected off a row of well-lacquered, hand-painted icons hung along a simple dark-wood iconostasis separating the main part of the freshly whitewashed church from the altar area behind it.

"I sort of feel funny about doing all this in a church," said Dimos.

Petro nodded. "I said the same thing to the chief. He said the Church has always been there for our country in crisis, so he was volunteering its services for this one."

Dimos rolled his eyes. "Yeah, sure. But does that mean no one from this church knows we're in here?"

"Somebody does, because someone left the key above the door."

Dimos shook his head. "Whatever."

"What's with Francesco? Why's he so quiet?"

"My guess is he's still recovering from the shock of paying the dinner check. It probably just hit him it's not as easy getting reimbursed as it used to be in the good old days of the EU picking up practically every tab."

"Screw you. I'm just exhausted." Francesco pulled a sleeping bag out from among three piled in a corner and unrolled it close by the door. "Is there a toilet around here or are we supposed to aim for the caldera as I did most of the morning?"

"There's one in that building next to us," said Petro. "It was built for tourists hiking the trail."

Francesco opened the door and went outside.

"I'm going to check the equipment," said Dimos stepping behind the iconostasis.

"Using the altar area to set up our equipment is really testing the Church's dedication to the cause," said Petro.

"It gives us the best angle on the hotel. The window aims right at it."

Petro walked to the edge of the iconostasis. "That's a big sucker of a parabolic dish and mike you've got set up there."

"It's our best shot at picking up conversations on the terrace overlooking the caldera."

Petro nodded. "Seems a natural place for having a serious talk. Like planning coups."

"Is that what you think this is all about? A *coup d'etat*?"

Petro scratched his ear. "Whatever it is, I doubt it's related to furthering the democratic process."

Dimos smiled. "Are you one of those idealists who still believes we have a democratic process?"

"I'd like to think so."

"And I'd honestly hoped the new guys in power would back away from corruption and favoritism and actually care about what happens to us. But nothing's changed. Just different faces on the same sort of crooked politicians saying whatever they need to say to stay in power and screw the country blind."

"You sound like you'd rather be hanging out with the guys we're supposed to be watching."

Dimos gestured no. "Not a chance. At least the bastards we elected to run the country have to follow the rules if they want to put their opposition into prison. From the track record of our military, I don't see dissenters getting much of a break." He smiled. "Except, of course, their legs. Oh, screw it all. I just wish there were some way of getting better people to run the government and not just the same old family names, generation after generation."

"You sound like an American," smiled Petro.

"Or an Englishman, Frenchman, Italian, Spaniard, you name it."

"Seems about the only ones these days not complaining about their leader are the Russians."

"Which only proves my point about militants in power. Everyone knows how the Russians really feel about ex-KGB chief Putin, but they're too afraid to say anything, worried if they do that the next thing they'll likely hear is, 'Welcome to Siberia.'"

The front door swung open and Francesco stepped inside. "There was a couple sleeping inside the bathroom."

"What?" said Dimos.

"You heard me. Young Australians looking to spend a night on the caldera but they couldn't find an open place to stay they could afford."

"What did you tell them?" said Petro.

"To wait outside until I was done."

"That's it?"

"What was I supposed to do, chase them away because we're on a secret mission for God? They'll be gone by tomorrow. Just knock before you enter if you need to use the facilities. The romance of the setting might just bring on an overwhelming rush of passion in them."

"Remind me not to sleep next to you," said Dimos.

"Don't worry, honey," said Francesco climbing into his sleeping bag. "I'm too tired. Which reminds me to ask, what time do we start tomorrow?"

"You mean today," said Petro. "It's nearly four. By ten we need to be up and running, just in case our guests show up earlier than expected. Military types can be like that. They like to surprise."

"Great," said Francesco, curled up in the sleeping bag. "You two can set up and take the first watch."

"Why us?" said Dimos.

Francesco extended a hand from his sleeping bag and flipped Dimos off. "Because I paid for dinner."

◇◇◇

Petro wondered why church bells were ringing so early. In fact, why were they ringing at all? He lifted his head out from inside the sleeping bag and squinted at the light. *What time is it?*

Nothing moved in the other sleeping bags. The bells had stopped. He looked at his watch. Seven forty-five. Damn. *Who goes to church that early?* The bells started up again. They were ringing in his pants on the floor next to the sleeping bag. He grabbed for the pants and pulled out his phone. He looked at the caller ID and sat up.

"Yes, Chief."

The other bags moved.

"Did I wake you?" said Andreas.

"Not really. There's not much happening yet so we're just hanging out."

"Are you sure?"

"Hold on." Petro jumped out of his sleeping bag, kicked the shapes still buried in the other two bags, and ran behind the iconostasis to the window looking down at the hotel.

He lifted a pair of binoculars off a small table and, standing back from the window, held them up to his eyes. Uniformed military were all over the hotel.

"Francesco, Dimos, *get the hell in here, now.*" Petro put the phone back to his ear and swallowed. "When did they get here?"

"My guess is just before daybreak."

"They're early."

"They obviously believe in the old adage about the early bird getting the worm. Let's hope that doesn't apply to Francesco's and Dimos' handiwork."

"How did you know they were here?"

"Someone else apparently is watching that hotel and is an early riser. She and her husband called Santorini's police chief at home to complain about a military invasion of their neighbor's property. Luckily, it just so happens the chief's an old friend of mine. Even luckier, he's the same old friend who arranged for you to get that key to the church and is making sure you're left alone. He figured this was just too much of a coincidence not to have something to do with me."

Francesco and Dimos poked their heads in the doorway.

"Sorry, Chief." Petro pointed at the window and silently mouthed the words, *They're here.*

"It's not about sorry. We didn't expect them this early. I assume they're out there for security reasons, and searching for listening devices, for sure."

"Francesco and Dimos should hear this. I'll put you on speakerphone."

"Good morning, Bright-Eyes."

"Morning, Chief."

"So tell me, guys, are they going to find what you left for them?"

"Not a chance," said Francesco.

Dimos nodded. "They'd have to get lucky. We expected them to run a sweep. That's why we're not turning on any equipment until after they're done with their games. And when we do, what we installed won't read as anything out of the ordinary."

"But won't they check in the same places where you hid your equipment?"

"Not likely, but if they do the mikes are designed to look like part of the wiring, and the repeaters are buried where they look like they belong, unless you happen to know what runs a Jacuzzi."

"So, you're saying it would take some really skilled guys to find your work?"

"Magicians," said Francesco.

"Sort of like military-intelligence experts?" said Andreas.

"An oxymoron," said Francesco. "They don't do that sort of work. It's our civilian counterintelligence boys we'd have to worry about, and even they would have to physically look for our stuff to find it. They won't pick it up on instruments."

"Chief, it's Dimos, and if this is a routine sweep of the sort the military does, they'll miss it. I can say that because we helped train them."

"It's comforting," said Andreas, "to know you're holding back secrets from those you're supposed to be helping keep our country secure."

"We're like master chefs. We hold back some ingredients from our published recipes," said Francesco.

"It makes us seem indispensable."

"Okay guys, just consider this a multi-purpose wakeup call. Those people you're watching obviously aren't afraid to let folks know they're out and about. Which means they'll probably have security stationed in places to keep an eyeball on the hotel. There may be competition for your church. Be prepared. And don't get spotted peeking out the window."

"Will do, Chief."

"Now stay alert. More importantly, stay safe. If these are the bad guys, they're very bad guys. And don't forget to check in every half hour. Sooner, if something goes down. Got it?"

"Got it," said Petro.

"Great. Bye."

Petro closed his eyes as he shut off his phone. He pinched

his fingers nearly together and opened his eyes. "We came this close to seriously screwing up."

"Eh, close only counts in horseshoes," said Francesco.

"Bzzzzzz. Wrong answer," said Dimos. "Close is also highly effective with hand grenades."

"Francesco, you and Dimos are not going to leave that window until we know the equipment is secure and operational."

"But, we just told the chief—"

"I heard what you told the chief, Francesco, but shit happens, and *no more shit* is going to happen on an operation that has my head on the line. Understand?"

Francesco chuckled and slapped Dimos on the arm. "See, I told you someday we'd end up working for the kid. I just didn't expect it to be so soon."

Dimos smiled at Petro. "He's trying to say we like you. Especially the way you didn't try to push what happened last night off on us."

"Last night? What last night?" said Petro.

"I like that sort of thinking, kid," said Francesco.

"Good," Petro walked past them, picked up his pants, and started putting them on. "I hope you'll remember that when the time comes for you to put in for reimbursement for a dinner that never took place."

Dimos laughed.

Francesco didn't.

Andreas hung up his mobile phone, and lay on the bed staring up at the ceiling.

"Is everything okay?" said Lila peeking out from under the duvet cover.

"As okay as anyone on watch aboard the good ship *Titanic* could be."

"Sounding a bit dramatic, are we?"

"We're using shoestring budget equipment, improvising as we go, to eavesdrop on some of our nation's top military brass planning God knows what. Of course, we have absolutely no authorization for any of it, so dare I need explain what's likely to happen should we get caught?"

"I see an iceberg analogy on the horizon."

"Hitting an iceberg head-on would be a great kindness compared to what the minister and his boys will put us through should this achieve its full cluster-fuck potential."

"How elegantly put."

"Just think of a swan dive off the rim of Santorini's caldera as far less painful."

"Yes, I far prefer that image. So romantic. We should go there."

"Assuming I'm not locked up, we'll go in the spring, after the baby's born."

"If worse comes to worst, I'll send you a postcard from there." Lila rubbed her belly.

"I can't believe that in less than a month Tassaki will have a little sister."

"He's so excited."

"I know, he insisted on helping me paint her room."

"Tell me about it. Remember who supervised the cleanup?"

"Hey, artistic expression isn't always neat."

"It's why the good Lord invented housepainters."

"I'll always remember that room as a father and son engaged in a labor of love."

"Great, and this soon to be mother in labor will remember it as a latex paint-remover nightmare."

Andreas smiled. "Okay, next time you get to be in charge of the painting."

She poked him in the side. "Don't give up so easily, I actually liked your color choice. Pepto-Bismol has always been a favorite of mine."

"You just can't stop." Andreas reached under the covers and tickled Lila's belly, his eyes still fixed on the ceiling.

She pushed his hand away. "I'm not the one whose phone went off in the middle of the night and got this routine up and running."

"It was daybreak, and I offered to talk in another room."

"Once I was up, why would I want to miss out on the action? Just one question, did Petro screw up?"

"No, we had no idea they'd show up this early. If it was anyone's fault it was mine for not telling him to expect it."

"Good. He's a nice kid. Better you screw up than he."

"Thanks for the support."

"You're welcome. Any word from the Brigadier?"

"Not a peep. He told us where the meeting was taking place and said we're on our own from there on out. His precise words were that he 'couldn't risk doing anything more.'"

"Considering all that's happened, I'm not surprised."

"Funny," said Andreas. "Considering all that's happened, I *am* surprised. If someone murdered my daughter," he crossed himself three times, "I'd be moving heaven and earth to chase down every possible lead."

"But you're a cop. He's a soldier. Maybe he doesn't want to risk anyone else in his family getting hurt until he has a better fix on the enemy?"

Andreas turned his gaze from the ceiling to his wife's eyes. "As I always say, Mrs. Kaldis, you're not just a pretty face."

"You used to always say, 'and hot body.'"

He put a hand on her breast. That, too, but don't get me started."

"Don't worry, I still know how to finish." She slid her hand down his belly to where he was showing a growing appreciation of her attention.

"Just one thing," said Lila, sliding down toward his waist.

"What's that?"

"Turn off your damn phone."

Andreas sat at his desk drinking cafeteria coffee out of a paper cup. Maggie wasn't in yet to make her special brew. He looked at his watch. Not yet nine. Petro had called him every half hour since their daybreak conversation. All appeared calm. The military guys seemed more interested in the view from the caldera than the villas.

Our nation's conscripted forces at work, thought Andreas.

Depending upon the branch of service, all able-bodied Greek men were required to serve up to a year of military duty. The Air Force recently undertook to make their branch more career-oriented, but still, those with connections generally drew the best duty. Like serving their time on Santorini. Savvy career military types saw opportunities in befriending those in their charge who might be useful to them once civilians again, which made busting their balls on routine assignments a low priority.

Andreas hoped whatever rigorous searching might be going on inside the hotel villas was confined to soldiers seeking to retrieve messages and picking out caldera photos to post on their smartphones. He'd take any break he could get, lucky or otherwise.

He'd meant what he'd said to Lila that morning, though he'd made it sound like a joke. If this blew up, the minister and his Prada buddy would go after him in the media with charges of treason, or whatever else they could trump up, whether provable or not. Hard core leftists saw things in black and white. Their values were white, everyone else's black. Unless, of course, green was involved. Then the color of money trumped all others.

"Why am I doing this?" said Andreas aloud. *If the dead girl's father doesn't care enough to push the envelope, why the hell am I?*

The door to his office swung open and Maggie walked in carrying a pot of coffee, followed by Yianni carrying two cups.

"I see you're in early. That's not a good sign." Maggie put the coffeepot on a pad of paper on Andreas' desk.

Yianni poured a cup of coffee and held it out for Andreas.

Andreas waved him off. "You keep it. I prefer to suffer along with what I'm drinking. I'll switch to Maggie's when I'm done hearing bad news."

Yianni took a sip and looked at Maggie. "Well then, it looks like we're not going to need this cup for him, after all."

"What's that supposed to mean?"

"I just told Yianni that your Prada friend is asking about you."

"That doesn't surprise me. It's what guys like him do."

"But he's asking GADA senior administrative staff, secretaries and the like, what they know or have heard about your political opinions."

"He's doing that personally?"

"Yes. Just this morning I've heard from a half-dozen different people he's spoken to."

"But you just got in."

"That's why I'm late. They called me at home. Apparently he's been calling since seven."

Andreas leaned forward. "Why would he be in such a hurry to call so many so early in the morning? And why people who hardly know me?"

"I can't answer the first question," said Maggie, "but maybe he knew it would get back to you that he was checking up on you, and did it just to let you know he hadn't forgotten about your get-together in Babis' office."

"Could be," nodded Andreas.

"Your second question's easy to answer. We're invisible. You just think we don't know you. No one notices us, but we're always there, always listening to whoever has dealings with our bosses, and the bitching by our bosses about those they deal with. It gives us a unique view of people and how they're thought of by their peers."

"I'll have to remember that," said Andreas. "But why are they talking to him?"

"Because they've been ordered to by Babis."

Andreas shook his head. "They're gunning for me even before Santorini blows up. Christ, I'll be crucified."

"Nicely put," said Yianni.

"Damn."

"I like that better," said Maggie.

"I don't know what he's looking for, but the bottom line to my politics is simple. I believe all politicians should be required to earn a living, and not live off the earnings of those who elected them."

"In other words, you're against them all," said Yianni.

Andreas smiled. "You could say that."

"Not sure where that puts you on the political spectrum," said Maggie, "but it sure makes you loved by me and my friends."

"Meaning?"

"I don't think he's going to find any ammunition for going after you. He's an arrogant narcissist. No one missed that. He thinks he's smarter than everyone and can masquerade as a friend of the people. No one bit at his efforts to say something bad about you."

"That we know of," said Andreas.

Maggie nodded. "But I wouldn't worry about any of this now."

"Why not?"

"You've got the Santorini operation to worry about."

"Thanks for making me feel better." Andreas looked at his watch. "Petro's been calling in like clockwork. Now he's nearly ten minutes late."

"Why don't you call him?" said Maggie.

"Uh, uh," said Andreas. "I have to assume there's a reason why he didn't call. The last thing a man in the field needs when something's going wrong is for his boss in the office to be nagging for updates. I'll find out why he's late when he calls in."

"I wish I had your patience," said Yianni.

"It's not patience, it's anxiety. And you're more than welcome to it." Andreas' eyes jumped between his watch and the phone.

"Come on, damn it." Andreas smacked his hand on the desktop. "Call already."

Chapter Ten

Petro sensed he'd been holding his breath forever, beginning with the first knock on the church's front door.

"Who the hell is that?" he'd whispered to Francesco.

"No idea," shrugged Francesco.

"What's happening?" said Dimos peeking around the iconostasis from the altar area.

Petro waved at Dimos, "Get back to the window. And let us know if you see anyone else coming up the hill."

"No one's come up the hill. Whoever it is must have come the other way."

"Hello, I know you're in there. Open up. Please."

Francesco scrunched his eyebrows together. "He's speaking English." He walked to the door and opened it slightly.

"Yes, my son. What can I do for you?"

"My girlfriend and I wanted to know if it would be okay to stay here another day. We won't be any trouble."

"I'm sure," said Francesco, "but to be honest, if the bishop ever finds out that I've let people stay here without his permission, I will have eternal hell to pay."

"You mean the Greek Church would deny someone shelter?"

Francesco smiled. "Nice try, but allowing two Aussies on their trek around the globe to shack up on church property doesn't exactly fit the image you're trying to conjure up here."

"Are you a priest?" said the boy.

"Don't be misled by how I'm dressed. I'm working here. That sign on the rope you stepped over to get up here mentioned that."

"Oh." The boy bit at his lower lip.

"I wish I could do more for you, son, but I can't. But take your time gathering up your things."

The boy looked down at his feet and rubbed one beat-up sneaker against the other. "Would it change your mind, father, if I told you my girlfriend and I plan on getting married?"

"Congratulations, but you're not married yet, so there's really nothing I can do for you." Francesco shook his head. "Sorry."

The boy sighed. "Thanks, anyway," and walked away.

Francesco closed the door, turned around, and leaned back against it. "Whew."

"Well done," said Petro looking at his watch. "Damn, I'm late calling the chief." He reached into his pocket for his phone.

"You better hold off on that," yelled out Dimos. "We've got more company coming up the hill. And from their weapons I'd say they're not tourists looking for a priest."

Petro ran to the window. Two men in military fatigues, H&K 7.62 assault rifles strapped over their right shoulders, trudged up the hill, about seventy-five meters away.

"Maybe they'll keep on going," said Dimos

Petro gestured no. "Their weapons look to be standard issue and from the way they're moving, not likely well trained, but unless they're brain dead, they're going to check out this church."

"What if we just keep the door locked and windows covered until they leave?" asked Dimos.

"That assumes they won't break down the door," said Petro stepping back from the window and heading into the front room. "Or find two Aussies in the bathroom who'll promptly tell the soldier boys all about the priest inside the church."

"Damn," said Francesco. He moved quickly to a cabinet in the altar area and rummaged inside before pulling out a neatly folded black garment. "Guys, hide everything behind the iconostasis and, Dimos, once they're inside, act as if you're a local churchgoer watching out for the place."

"Inside? You're going to let them in?" said Petro.

"Only as a last resort. But we have to be ready for that," said Francesco.

"What am I supposed to do?" said Petro.

"You'll never pass as a churchgoer. Stay hidden behind the iconostasis and don't make a sound."

"That's it?"

"Feel free to pray."

"And precisely what will you be doing?" said Petro.

"Trying my best to get us out of the mess I created. Lock the door behind me."

With that Francesco was gone.

"Is he serious?" said Petro.

"I sure hope so. Otherwise the odds are looking pretty good that we'll end up spending the rest of our chummy weekend together as guests of military hospitality."

Petro picked up three sleeping bags in one hand and three backpacks in the other, and lugged them into the altar area. Dimos rearranged the benches and candle stands to make the space look more like a church than a dormitory.

Petro had just gathered up water bottles and food containers from the front when a hard knock sounded on the door.

"Open up," barked a husky voice.

Dimos grabbed anything else that didn't look to belong in a church and stashed it in the altar area.

Seconds later came three harder knocks, "*I SAID OPEN UP.*"

"Now what?" said Petro.

"It's Francesco's play. We'll have to let him make the first move."

Six hard poundings on the door followed by, "OPEN UP OR WE'LL BREAK DOWN THE DOOR."

"Screw this," said Petro. "If they break down that door I'm breaking their heads." He started toward the front door.

Dimos put a hand on Petro's chest and whispered, "Wait."

Over the sound of more pounding they heard another voice. "Gentlemen, gentlemen, is this any way to respect a house of God?"

Dimos whispered to Petro, "It's Francesco."

The husky voice said, "We have orders to search this church."

"And I have orders from a higher power to resist all those who seek to defile this place of sanctuary."

"Father, we aren't trying to defile your church, just search it," said a different, softer voice.

"For what reason?"

"I can't say," said the soft voice.

"Ah, precisely the sort of reason that has haunted the innocent through the ages. I cannot allow it."

"You have no choice in this matter," said husky voice.

"Oh, my son, you are very misguided. I have a lot of choice in this matter. We are not a church lost in the hills of the Peloponnese where no one will know or possibly even care what you've done. We are a venerated church on the caldera of Santorini, known around the world, and I can assure you that your defilement of our hallowed place will by the end of this day resound across every television screen and newspaper in Greece, including those favored by your superiors."

Silence.

Dimos gave Petro the thumbs-up sign.

"But I appreciate your predicament, gentlemen. You are sheep in the military's flock who must follow the orders of your shepherd or be punished. I do not want that on my hands. And so I will allow you into my church."

"Is he nuts?" muttered Petro.

The soft voice said, "I heard someone inside."

Petro blanched.

"Of course you did, it is my attendant, Dimos, readying the sanctuary."

"Readying it for what?" said the husky voice.

"I'll show you," said Francesco. "In fact, you are welcome to participate. Dimos, open up."

"He's definitely insane," whispered Petro retreating to behind the iconostasis.

Dimos opened the door slightly.

"Are we ready?" said Francesco dressed in a black priest's cassock.

Dimos eyes jumped between the faces of the soldiers. "Yes, Father."

Francesco turned to his left and waved in the direction of the bathroom. "Come, my children, these soldiers mean you no harm," he said in English. "They have come to share in your great joy."

The soldiers exchanged befuddled glances.

Around the corner came the Australian boy and his girlfriend, holding hands and smiling.

"This is so very nice of you, Father," said the boy in English.

"Yes, we'll remember this moment for the rest of our lives," said the girl in English.

"As will I, my children, as will I."

The soldiers started to step into the church but Francesco grabbed them by the back of their flak jackets. "No, the bride and groom enter first."

The soldiers turned to allow the Aussies to pass. "You mean this is a wedding?"

Francesco nodded as he passed between them. "Of course it is. What else did you think would be happening up here so early in the morning?"

The soldiers followed Francesco into the church and looked around at what appeared to be a neat, traditional church, with everything in all the proper places. The soft speaking one headed toward the altar area.

"Uh, uh," said Francesco. "I see you are not aware of our ways. You are not allowed back there."

"Why?"

"Only the soon-to-be wed and I are allowed back there to commune with the spirit blessing this occasion. We cannot allow it to be corrupted by another presence."

The husky-voiced soldier shook his head. "You Santorini locals sure have some weird superstitions."

"Weird is in the mind of its beholder, my son. Dimos, have you made preparations for the service?"

"Uh, yes, Father. Everything you need is back by the altar."

Francesco nodded. "Good, I will now go and prepare."

"How long is this going to take?" said the soft voice.

"Not more than a couple of hours."

"A couple of hours!" said the husky voice.

Francesco shook his head. "Would you deny these young people the full measure of the blessing of the church?"

"It's another reason why I'll never get married," said the husky voice.

"That and the unlikely chance of finding someone who'll marry you," said the soft voice.

Husky looked about to punch his partner, but didn't. "Let's get out of here."

Soft Voice turned to the bride and groom and said in English, "I'm sure you don't understand Greek but we wish you a life full of flowers, *vion anthosparton*."

Both soldiers nodded at Francesco and Dimos, then left.

Francesco stared at the front door, not saying a word.

"Father, is everything okay?" said the girl.

"What? Oh, yes. I was just contemplating the moment."

"We all were," said Dimos in Greek.

"Are they gone?" said Francesco.

Dimos stepped out onto the terrace and came back in. "They're headed north, but they might come back."

"I doubt it. Not unless they've reconsidered attending the wedding service."

"Yeah," said Dimos, "what was all that bullshit about a two-hour service, and the altar area being off-limits?"

"Improvisation my friend, improvisation. Which reminds me. Hey, Petro, don't say anything until the newlyweds are out of here."

"You're not actually going to perform a wedding service, are you?" said Dimos.

"It's up to them." Francesco switched to English. "My children, before we begin may I see your marriage license?"

"Marriage license?" said the boy.

"Yes, it's required that you have one from our town hall."

"I didn't know that."

"Well, if you want the marriage to be legal, you must have a marriage license."

"Can we get one now?"

"I'm afraid it takes a couple of days. So sorry."

Tears welled up in the girl's eyes. "I was so looking forward to this moment, taking our vows together on Santorini."

Francesco rubbed at his collar. "But there's nothing I can do. Without the license you will not be legally married."

The boy looked at the girl, then back at Francesco. "Just say the words. We'll consider this our wedding day, but do it officially next week."

The girl squeezed her boyfriend's hand and smiled. "Yes, Father, please. It would mean so much to us."

Francesco looked at Dimos.

"Hey, don't look at me," Dimos said in Greek. "You're the one who came up with this brilliant idea. But don't worry, I'm sure you know enough about weddings to fake it, and these two won't know the difference anyway. But if you do decide to go through with it, please do everyone a favor and stick to an abbreviated version. Now, if you'll excuse me, I'll be stepping behind the iconostasis to keep an eye on the folks at the hotel, and leave you to your wizardly performance for the visitors from Oz."

Dimos smiled and disappeared into the altar area.

Francesco cleared his throat and began speaking slowly in English.

The young couple held hands.

Petro made a phone call.

Andreas grabbed the phone out of its cradle before the first ring had finished.

"Yes."

"Sorry, Chief, but we had visitors."

"Petro, I can hardly hear you." Andreas put the phone on speaker.

Yianni and Maggie leaned in to hear.

"I have to whisper. I said we had visitors. Two soldiers."

"Are they still there?"

"No."

"Then why are you whispering?"

"It's a long story, but Francesco is performing a wedding."

Andreas stared at the phone. "Sounds interesting indeed.... Are things cool?"

"Looks like it. The military left without searching the altar area where our equipment is set up."

"How'd you manage to get away with that?"

"It's part of the long story."

Andreas shook his head. "How long until the wedding is over—you did say a wedding?"

"Yes, I did. Dimos told him to move it along, but he seems to enjoy being a priest."

Maggie laughed. "Sounds like Francesco."

Andreas didn't smile. "Tell him to end it *now*."

"Will do."

"What's the news on the hotel? Any of our anticipated guests show up yet?"

"No one except security, as far as I can tell. But let me check with Dimos. His ears are glued to his headphones listening to the mikes."

Petro's voice paused. "It's the chief. He wants to know if anyone's shown up yet."

A few seconds later Dimos said, "I overheard a maid making up a room say that two men are in the office waiting for more to arrive."

"Do we have audio in the office?"

"Negative. We didn't have time to get in there and set anything up."

Andreas picked up a pencil and began tapping the eraser end on his desktop. "Sounds like the party's about to begin."

"And as soon as they make it over to the bar area we'll have video on them," said Dimos.

"What if they don't go to the bar?" said Andreas.

"No problem, once they're on the terrace staring down at the caldera, we'll be in paparazzi heaven up here. No way they'll be able to resist that view."

"Let's hope so. I want you sending me photos as soon as you take them."

"Will do."

"Good."

Petro came back on the line. "Anything else, Chief?"

"Yeah, as soon as Francesco sends his newlyweds on their way, call me."

"Ten-four on that."

"Bye." Andreas turned off the phone.

"Francesco is performing a wedding in the middle of a top secret surveillance operation?" Yianni laughed. "I can't wait to hear the story behind that one."

Maggie smiled. "In his younger days he was an entertainer. Once he joined the force, his acting talent landed him playing undercover roles. He took a bullet that nearly killed him in an assassination attempt by a homegrown terrorist group he'd infiltrated."

"How'd they find out he was a cop?" said Yianni.

"How do you think?" said Maggie. "Some asshole in the department tipped them off."

"Bastard."

"But once Francesco recovered, rather than walk away, he asked to be transferred to special crimes. That was before the chief's time. He gave up doing undercover work—his wife threatened to kill him before anyone else had the chance if he didn't—and teamed up with Dimos, our resident techno-geek, in finding ways to plant whatever we needed wherever we wanted it."

"Did he ever find the bastard who turned him in?" said Yianni.

"If he did, he never said a word of it to anyone, as far as I know," said Maggie.

"Smart move," said Andreas. "That makes it so there's no way to suspect him if the bastard simply disappeared someday."

"Is that how you'd handle it, Chief?" said Yianni with a smile.

Andreas grinned. "You'll just have to wait and see, though, with so many high-ranking folks out there gunning for me, it may not be that long a wait."

Andreas' desk phone rang. He looked at the caller ID. "It's Petro. Everybody get a box of popcorn, I think we're about to hear a story of epic legend potential."

"If Francesco's telling it," said Maggie, "make that two boxes."

It turned out to be a rather pleasant day for December, and just overcast enough to be perfect for taking photographs. Virtually every arriving guest went straight to the edge of the caldera, cell phone camera at the ready. Within an hour of Francesco's telling his much-exaggerated tale of how he'd single-handedly saved the three of them from being marched down the hill in irons, Dimos had sent Andreas near portrait-quality photographs of two dozen men.

As the photos came in, Maggie and Yianni matched them up against military personnel records, and within another hour every face had an associated name, rank, and bio. It was a gathering of majors through generals, squadron leaders through air marshals, and lieutenant commanders through admirals from the Army, Air Force, and Navy. Each branch had four general officers and four seniors, with one general officer and one senior officer from each branch sharing the same villa.

The planted video and audio worked perfectly, capturing every private conversation, and when all twenty-four men met together for several hours in the late afternoon in the largest villa, not a word was missed.

Despite all that good fortune, Andreas wasn't smiling. For hours he'd been listening over the speakerphone to the live feed coming into the church from the late afternoon meeting in the villa, and his mood had progressively darkened in pace with the evening sky.

Maggie had made herself scarce, and Yianni sat on Andreas' couch snoozing through barely feigned interest in the eavesdropped conversations.

"This is going nowhere," barked Andreas, slamming his hand on the desk.

Yianni jerked up on the couch. "Not what you expected?"

"It's like listening to a bunch of cops on a retreat planning for the next generation."

"But they're criticizing the government."

Andreas waved his hand at Yianni. "Stop trying to sound as if you were awake and paying attention. They're gossiping and guessing—the same as every other Greek on the planet. No one has any idea where this government is taking the country." Andreas pointed at the phone. "These aren't guys planning to take over the country. They're looking to come up with a plan for keeping up with the current government's intentions, as incomprehensible as they may be."

"But why involve so many low-ranking officers in such a high-level operation?"

"Think of it as mentors and their protégés. From the bios I read, those twelve seniors are among the military's most talented, promising officers. Bringing them in early as participants in the planning stage ties them in at the grassroots. Don't forget, down the road those same senior officers will likely be the general officers called upon to implement decisions made this weekend."

"Are you saying that what we're doing is a waste of time?" said Petro over the phone.

Andreas leaned in toward the speakerphone. "No, not a waste of time. Just that we're getting nothing out of this."

"At least not yet," said Petro.

"I admire your persistence," said Andreas.

"You know, Chief," said Yianni, "this is a hard crowd to be openly pitching revolution to. As you said, these are the military's best and brightest young minds. Most likely also its most loyal and patriotic. Only a fool would preach coup to these types right from the start."

Andreas picked up a pencil and began tapping it on his desktop.

"You make it sound like a seduction," said Petros.

"I like the analogy," said Yianni.

"Yianni could be right, Chief. If a senior officer could be made to think it was his idea that a coup would be best for the country, and found the courage to raise the idea with a general officer he regarded as his mentor, the general officer would have hooked him for life."

"A simple but diabolical variation on your mentor and protégé theme for the weekend," said Yianni.

Andreas ran his fingers through his hair. "So you think all this unfocused, frustrated bullshit we've been listening to on how to plan for the country's future is actually intended to steer the seniors into suggesting a more aggressive strategy?"

"Could be," said Petro. "Most of the talk we've heard has been from the general officers. The seniors have kept relatively quiet."

"That's probably a big reason they've been so successful in their careers," said Andreas.

"I'll try to keep that in mind," said Yianni.

"But among themselves, Chief, the seniors are likely to talk more openly of tougher tactics. After all, it was colonels, not generals, who pulled off the coup in 1967," said Petro.

Andreas stared at the phone. "Do you really believe that every general officer in that hotel room is somehow involved in orchestrating a conspiracy to have their seniors suggest a coup?"

"You don't need them all," said Petro. "Just the ones steering the conversation. Those who have that view are looking for traveling companions. And those who don't probably won't pick up on what's happening. It's all buzzwords, innuendo, and gestures."

"I think you've been watching too many spy movies," said Yianni. "Besides, if it's all code words, how are we going to know when someone bites, let alone nibbles, at the bait?"

Andreas spoke up. "By continuing to listen to every word they utter."

"Uh, Chief…"

"Yes, Dimos."

"The meeting's about to break up."

"Good. If Petro's theory has legs, the more aggressive talk will come in private."

"But they're going off-property," said Dimos.

"Where?"

"To a taverna they've taken over for the evening."

Andreas slammed his hand on the desk. "Damn, damn, damn."

"Chief?"

"Yes, Petro?"

"I know the place, and there might be a chance for me to be inside while they're having dinner."

Francesco could be heard laughing in the background.

"What's so funny?" said Andreas.

"He's an asshole at times," said Petro. "He took us all to dinner the other night and by coincidence it's the same place they're headed to."

"How's that going to get you inside?" said Andreas. "There'll be security for sure to keep the party private."

"He's got a free pass," yelled Francesco. "The owner's daughter is sweet on him."

A muffled "Fuck you," came across the phone from Petro.

"Enough," said Andreas. "Is that true? Can you get inside?"

"I think so."

"Then do it. I don't care what it takes, just do it. Dimos, can you wire the place for sound?"

"It'll be tough," said Dimos.

"What about wiring Petro?"

"That will be really tough," said Francesco. "To pull this off the kid's likely to be extensively searched from head to toe. Many times." He laughed.

Another muffled, "Fuck you."

"We'll try, Chief," said Dimos. "But we'll have to go portable and set up our van close by the taverna."

"Just do your best."

"We could do better if we had satellites like the Americans."

"Christmas is coming, Dimos. Put it on your wish list."

"What time's dinner?" said Yianni.

"Ten," said Dimos.

Andreas looked at is watch. "You better get moving, it's almost eight."

"Uh, Chief…"

Andreas put his head in his hands. "Yes, Francesco. What is it now?"

"Speaking on behalf of those of us tightly gathered together in shared, close quarters, may I suggest that we get Petro to a hotel for a shower before his big date?"

Yianni burst out laughing.

"Laugh all you want, Yianni," said Francesco, "but remember for the want of a nail a kingdom was lost. Do we want to risk all that for the want of a bar of soap?"

Andreas dropped his hands from his face, shook his head, and smiled. "As I said, whatever it takes. Even soap."

"And don't forget to shave," said Yianni.

Over the phone came a clear as a bell and very loud, "Fuck you."

Chapter Eleven

"Hi, Sappho, it's—"

"It took you long enough. My phone's grown cobwebs waiting for you to call."

Petro laughed. "I just got off work. It's the first chance I had."

"I'm not even close to believing that line. Try another."

"My dog ate my phone."

"Better. But keep going."

"I didn't want to call until I had the perfect words to say to you to convince you to see me again."

Silence.

"Sappho, are you there?"

"I didn't want to interrupt you. You're on a roll, man."

Petro laughed again. "Does that mean we're on for tonight?"

"Tonight? No can do. We're booked solid for a big party."

"I'm not looking for a reservation. I just want to see you."

"Sadly, my life is here. If you want to see me between six at night and whenever, it can only be here."

"That's fine. I'm willing to just sit with you while you work."

More silence. "Are you for real? Or did you run out today and buy one of those books with a title like *Ten Perfect Things to Say to a Woman?*"

"It was actually twelve. I've ten more to tell you." Petro paused. "So, can I see you tonight?"

"You're too much. But I don't know how I can pull this off. I'll have to ask my father."

"But I thought your father liked me?"

"He does, and my mother *loves* you. But this is a sort of special dinner and no strangers are allowed."

"No strangers, huh?"

"Before you say it, okay, you're not a stranger. At least not a total stranger. How about tomorrow night?"

"I may have to go back to Athens."

"Oh."

"Or I may not. Just not sure. And I want to see you."

"I think there's only nine lines left from your book."

"That wasn't a line."

"Make that eight. Give me a minute so I can speak to my father."

Petro stood in front of the iconostasis staring at the icons of the saints. He felt badly about lying to the woman. *But the fate of my country could be on the line. I must do my duty.* Thinking those thoughts didn't make him feel any better about lying to her. But he did want to see her. So it wasn't a total lie. She was different from all the other women he knew. Not sure if that was good or bad.

"Hey, hotshot, do you have your working papers with you?" Sappho was back on the phone.

"Sure, why?"

"My father didn't think it was a good idea, but mother made him see the light."

"What light?"

"We have twenty-five hungry men coming for dinner all at the same time at the same table. There's no way we pull that off effectively with just my mother cooking, my father taking orders, and me serving. We need another hand. Congratulations, you're our busboy for tonight."

"Will it give me time to hang out with the cashier?"

"Don't worry, honey, we'll be bumping into each other all night. Twenty-five guests all wanting to be treated like royalty will turn the place into a madhouse."

"I'm sure it will be a wonderful evening. How could it not now that I get to spend it with you?"

"Please do bring that book with you. I can't wait to see what you're holding back for later."

"Quite a bit."

"*Enough.* I've got to concentrate on the place cards."

"Place cards?"

"There's assigned seating, with a chart we have to follow. As I said, twenty-five men wanting to be treated as royalty."

"What time should I be there?"

"Can you make it in an hour?"

"I'll try, but it will be tight. I need to take a shower."

"We have a shower here. You're free to use it. Hurry. Bye."

Petro stared at the phone.

"So what did she say?"

"I'll be bussing tables this evening for twenty-five guests."

"Twenty-five?" said Dimos.

"Yeah, I wondered about that too. We've only got twenty-four in the hotel."

"Maybe she was just speaking in rough numbers?" said Francesco.

Petro shook his head. "I don't think so. She said she was given a list of assigned seats. Restaurateurs count seats."

"That's good news," said Dimos. "With that list and you working the table, we can plant our equipment close to the most likely coup-planning candidates."

"And who would they be?" said Petro.

Dimos shrugged. "That's why we have a chief. We'll let him make the call."

"Good idea, but make it fast because we've got to get lover boy to a hotel for a shower," said Francesco.

Petro shook his head. "That won't be necessary."

"I thought we resolved all that in our talk with the chief?"

"We did, but Sappho told me I could take a shower at the taverna."

Francesco's face lit up.

"Don't even think of saying what I know is on your mind," said Petro.

Francesco, put up his hands. "Hey, I admire what you're doing for our country. I'm just worried you might be martyred in action."

"How's that going to happen taking a shower?"

"Showers are known to be dangerous places. Just be careful who hands you the soap."

Dimos nodded and forced a serious expression. "Especially if there happens to be a father with a shotgun nearby."

"That's not martyrdom," said Francesco. "That's marriage."

There were a lot more vehicles on the roads than Petro expected for the off-season, but then again it was an unusually warm Friday night and unlike most places in Greece, locals on Santorini had money to spend. Drivers didn't seem as unpredictable here as in wild party places like Mykonos during tourist season or in Athens at any time of year, so he drove without fear of triggering a macho reaction in those he flew up behind, then passed. His only concern was an unlikely run-in with a cop for ignoring just about every speeding and no-passing law on the books.

Getting stopped wasn't what concerned Petro. He worried he'd need to identify himself to avoid arrest, and that risked word getting out that a special-crimes unit cop was on the island. If the military brass he was supposed to be serving tonight should happen to get wind of that, and bother to pull his photo, for sure he'd be recognized from the taverna. Still, Petro saw getting to the taverna ASAP as his primary concern. Dimos and Francesco left in the van at the same time he did, but they didn't have to hurry. They had plenty of time to find a spot close by the taverna and set up the equipment. But Petro had a lot to do beyond taking a shower.

He hadn't worked in a restaurant for years but, like riding a bike, it wasn't something he'd forgotten. He just had to come up with a believable background story for himself in case one of the customers, or more likely, their security folks quizzed him. Plus he'd have to coordinate his answers with what Sappho, her father, and mother might say.

◇◇◇

"Right on time," said Sappho looking at her phone as Petro came through the front door carrying a small gym bag and heading straight for her. "I like employees like that."

"As a matter of fact, I'm early." He stopped a foot in front of her.

She nodded. "So you are." She leaned forward and kissed him on both cheeks.

"That's it?"

"We've work to do."

"What about my shower?"

"Later. You've got more sweating to do to earn it."

Petro shrugged. "You're the boss."

"More words to quicken a lady's heart." She smacked Petro lightly on his belly with the back of her hand. "What's in the bag?"

"A change of clothes and a razor."

She nodded. "If you know how to set up a table, the plates, glasses, and silverware are in the big cabinet behind me next to the kitchen door. Salt, pepper, olive oil, vinegar, and napkins are on trays just inside the kitchen. If you have no idea what I'm talking about, I think I'll cry."

"Don't worry, I can handle it."

"Finally, my knight has arrived."

"Which table?"

She pointed. "The long one set up in the middle of the room. The linen is already on it. They want only chairs, no banquettes. Twelve on the side facing into the room, thirteen on the side facing the banquettes."

"No settings at the heads of the table?"

Sappho gestured no. "That's how they wanted it, that's how they'll get it."

"Okay, let me get to it." Petro walked to the banquette closest to the table and laid his gym bag on it. He walked back to the cabinet behind Sappho and began quietly shuttling piles of dinner and bread plates to the table.

Sappho watched him with a smile on her face. "I see you like to concentrate on your work."

"I figure the sooner I get done with this the faster I can start flirting with the cashier."

"So, you *have* worked in restaurants before."

Petro smiled but didn't reply and started arranging plates on the table.

Sappho walked behind her desk, picked up an envelope and a sheet of paper, and held them out to Petro. "Here, now that I see you're an experienced table setter, I'm promoting you to card placer. There are place cards inside the envelope. Put them on the table in precisely the order set out on this seating chart." She waved the paper.

Petro walked over and took them from her. He bowed. "Thank you for your confidence in me."

She nodded. "Don't mention it. I'll be in the kitchen helping my mother. Just yell if you need me."

"Maybe I should say hello to her."

Sappho held up her hand. "Later. I know she's sweet on you, but she's really busy. Even has my father cooking. I'll give them your regards."

Petro watched her walk into the kitchen. She sashayed through the doorway the same as she had the night he met her, but this time she threw no wisecrack over her shoulder. Maybe she needed an audience. Or maybe something else.

As soon as Sappho was gone, Petro's eyes raced over the chart. His eyes fixed on one entry. *That would be my pick.* He walked over to the table and with his back to the kitchen took a picture of the chart with his phone and sent it off to the chief and Dimos. He went back to setting the table as he waited for a response.

He'd just about finished when he felt the buzz of his phone in his pocket.

It was a message from Andreas. BE SURE TO COVER THE ONE NAMED "GUEST," AND EVERYONE BESIDE AND ACROSS FROM GUEST.

It was his pick too. Petro smiled at the message.

"Is your wife wondering where you are?"

Petro didn't even look up. "Nah, she wants to know what I've done with our dozen children."

Sappho didn't move from the kitchen doorway. "Are you married?"

He looked up. "No. Are you?"

"Not anymore."

"Kids?"

She gestured no. "He was an asshole. He'd drive me to work, hang around here long enough to pick up tourist girls he could take down to the beach by the airport to fuck, and be back in time to take me home."

"Ouch. How long have you been divorced?"

"Six months."

"I hear it takes about two years to get back to where you were before."

"Why would I want to get back there? I want nothing more to do with the life that got me into that mess in the first place."

"I hear ya."

"You seem like a nice guy."

Petro held up his right hand. "Cross my heart, I am." He dropped his hand back to his side. "But that doesn't mean I'm perfect. Far from it."

"If both of us were perfect that would be a problem."

"Well, I hear opposites attract."

Sappho nodded. "Yeah, the trouble with that is, when they separate it's an explosion."

Petro laughed.

She waved her hand off into the air. "Just keep setting the table and don't try to figure out what's going on in this screwed-up bitch's mind."

Petro smiled. "Whatever you say, Boss."

She feigned a slap, followed by a wink, and turned back to the kitchen.

Petro stared at the empty doorway for a couple of seconds before looking at the chart. The word GUEST appeared in the seventh position on the thirteen-seat side of the table. No name, just a seat in the very center of the action.

He took his bag from the banquette and set it on a chair shielded from the kitchen by the table. He unzipped it and took out seven thin, shiny metal clamps, each looking vaguely like a square-shaped question mark. They were the classic form of clamp used in virtually every taverna in Greece to hold table-cloths in place.

But these clamps were special. Dimos had developed them as his go-to mikes for on-the-run surveillance. You could quickly switch them for the real clamps, and only someone looking very closely at one might notice a mottled rather than smooth pattern on the side facing up.

Petro had to hand it Dimos. The guy probably could actually hide an elephant under a tablecloth. With microphones hidden in the tablecloth for good measure.

Petro staggered the new clamps in among the old in a zig-zag pattern, starting on the twelve-seat side with new clamps placed between seats two and three, six and seven, and ten and eleven, and on the thirteen-seat side between seats four and five, eight and nine, and twelve and thirteen. The final clamp he tucked to the immediate left of "Guest," between seats six and seven.

Dimos had come up with that pattern for giving them maximum coverage for their equipment in that table arrangement. He'd given Petro several patterns, each for a different table configuration. Dimos said it was like designing football plays to counter anticipated defenses. He liked doing that sort of thing.

Petro had just slipped the clamps taken off the table into his bag when he heard, "Are you finished yet?"

"Almost. I just have to bring out what's on the trays from the kitchen and put them on the table."

"Plus the bread."

"Will do."

"Hurry up. I'll get the hot water started for your shower."

Petro cocked his head at her.

Sappho turned and walked three meters to the left of the kitchen entrance to a door marked PRIVATE.

She smiled at him. "It's down here in the basement. But don't worry, handsome, the soap's all yours. I don't need a *hot* shower."

She opened the door. "But fair warning. Mother's angling to bring you the towel."

It took Petro fifteen minutes to shower, shave, dress in dark pants and a white shirt, and be back in the dining room. Sappho stood by her desk wearing a tight fitting, knee-length black skirt and snug white cotton blouse in the deeply plunging décolletage style so favored by Greek women. Perfectly centered between her breasts hung a heavy gold and emerald cross on a black lanyard.

"You clean up nicely," she said.

He tried not to stare at Sappho's breasts. "You don't look so bad yourself."

She adjusted her neckline. "I figured if I dressed like this, they'd pay less attention to you."

He watched as she finished. "That's very considerate of you."

"It's to protect us. We don't want our guests discovering there's a stranger among us since we promised it would be only family."

"So, who should I say I am?"

"Where are you from?"

"Athens."

"I mean before that. Where's your family from?"

"Argolis."

"In the Peloponnese?"

"Yes."

"Great. You're my father's godson and the son of my father's best friend. What's your father's name?"

"Ilias. But that still doesn't make us family."

"Are you kidding? You're a godson, which makes you more than family. He had no choice with me, but with you he did."

Petro smiled. "You sure do have a strange way of looking at things."

"And you've been working with us for the past three summers."

"What if they check your records?"

She smiled. "Off the books, of course."

"But what if they don't believe my story?"

She touched the buttons on her blouse. "I'll undo another one. Or two. Don't worry. Just don't talk. Let my father and me be the life of the party."

Before he could answer, the taverna's front door swung open and a line of straight-backed men in casual dress began parading through it.

Petro swallowed hard.

Showtime.

Chapter Twelve

Nearly an hour passed and not one of the men had sat down. They stood in small groups, drinking, talking, and grabbing *meze* off the table almost as quickly as Petro brought more appetizers out from the kitchen. Sappho spent the time circulating among the men, plying them with drinks and flirting up a storm in a theater-in-the-round troubadour performance worthy of an Academy Award—and making it highly unlikely that anyone would sit anytime soon near a microphone.

The operation had jumped off the tracks headed straight for the realm of FUBAR. The only good thing Petro could think of to say about the way the evening had gone so far was that Sappho's performance had made him invisible. Everyone acted as if he weren't in the room.

He'd been able to match every face to photographs taken of the men staying at the hotel. That meant twenty-four men. He counted heads to confirm. No number twenty-five yet, no unrecognized face, no mysterious guest.

A loud voice rose up from one of the groups. "Gentlemen, it's time to take our seats for dinner. I assume no one as yet has had so much to drink that he won't be able to find his way to his own name at the table. I emphasize *as yet*."

Amid courteous laughter everyone promptly moved to his assigned seat.

"A good beginning," said the same man after everyone had sat. He was a swarthy, buzz-cut fellow in his early fifties who likely hadn't missed a meal in a very long time. "We all made it safely to the table." He looked to his right and paused. "Except for one. But we're not going to wait for the straggler."

He waved at Petro and pointed to the empty chair and place setting next to him. "Take all this away." He leaned over and looked at the place card. "If Mister Guest is not here on time, he doesn't get to eat with us."

Petro nodded and quickly removed the setting and chair to another table. *Who the hell was number twenty-five?* He shook his head. *This now was officially Fucked Up Beyond All Repair,* he thought.

"Hey, Petro. Get it in gear, man. We've got a lot of hungry people to feed." Sappho stood with her hand on the shoulder of the man who'd ordered him to remove the place setting. "And be sure to start with our host, dear friend, and savior of Santorini skies from the Turks, our beloved air marshal." She patted Buzz-Cut on the shoulder.

The air marshal waved dismissively but his face beamed at the praise.

Petro forced a smile and headed into the kitchen. For the next forty minutes he did nothing but shuffle back and forth from the kitchen, holding plates of food in each hand and more plates lined up along his right forearm. Whenever he caught a glimpse of Sappho she'd be reaching over one man or another pouring wine. More than once he heard her laughingly tell someone that she only poured wine, so he'd have to service himself with his other requests.

He watched Sappho's father work his way around the table, smiling and joking with his guests, all the while taking orders for their next course.

Sappho's mother and her three female Bulgarian assistants remained in the kitchen, quietly working away, though all smiled at Petro each time any one of them caught his eye.

He'd done his best to eavesdrop on the conversations at the table, but nothing he heard was much different from what he'd expect to hear in any other group of guys out for the night.

Sports, new clubs, vacation plans, women and—of course—Sappho's tits. What they didn't talk about is what caught Petro's attention. Not one word about politics, an unheard of situation in a gathering of Greek men out for the night. It was as if they'd been ordered not to discuss the subject in public.

Petro stood at the kitchen counter, avoiding eye contact with the women while he waited for more food to carry to the table. He wondered why, despite how badly this evening had gone for his unit's surveillance operation, he was having such a great time. He really enjoyed helping this family do its thing.

Perhaps tonight's undercover disaster was meant as God's way of suggesting to him that police service might not be the best career path. Yes, the Lord surely did work in mysterious ways. Perhaps even in a kitchen.

One of the women smiled at him.

Perhaps as a Bulgarian cook.

On that thought, he allowed himself a wide smile, blew all the women kisses, and laden with plates, walked back out to the table.

He caught a glimpse of someone standing by the front door. "Sappho, you've got company at the door."

She yelled over to the man, "Sir, may I help you?"

Everyone turned to see whom she'd called to.

The man walked toward her. "Sorry to be late, but my plane was delayed in Athens."

The air marshal jumped to his feet. "Ah. So you're our surprise guest. Why didn't your office tell me instead of keeping it a secret?"

The man shrugged. "You know how things are these days. I'd rather keep my agenda to myself." He looked to be in his mid-forties, slim, of less-than-average height, and most likely not military.

The air marshal nodded. He pointed at Petro. "You. Set a place for my friend at my right hand." He patted the man on his back and helped him off with his coat. "Come, sit. We have a lot to talk about."

Petro quickly set a place for him next to the air marshal,

taking great care to position the tablecloth clamp between the two men. He held the chair for the man to sit down, then hurried back to the kitchen, glancing skyward as he did. *Thank you, Lord, thank you.*

Within fifteen minutes after his arrival, every general officer had made a point of getting up from his seat to say a few words of respect to Guest. When one officer asked to have his picture taken with him, Guest turned to Air Marshal and whispered in his ear.

Air Marshal immediately announced to the table, "There will be no photographs this evening." He then called out to Sappho, her father, and Petro. "That applies to you, too. No photos. In fact, turn off your phones."

"Yes, sir," said Petro. *Nice idea but too late.* Someone fidgeting with a smartphone these days was practically invisible. All it required was a bit of technique and a silent shutter setting so as not to tip off your subject. He'd long ago taken and sent along photos of everyone at the table, including more than a dozen of Guest.

For the next twenty minutes Guest and Air Marshal sat locked in hushed, eye to eye conversation. Air Marshal turned away from the conversation first.

He picked up his wineglass, leaned back in his chair, and took a long sip. He held the glass for several seconds before putting it down and clearing his throat. "Gentlemen, I need your attention." His voice was firm and clear, but not loud.

Some voices immediately stopped; others continued as if they'd not heard him.

He repeated in the same tone, "Gentlemen, I need your attention."

More voices stilled, and those that didn't were nudged to silence by those who had.

Petro took Sappho by the arm, put his forefinger to his lips, and steered her into the kitchen. Her father had beaten them there.

"They don't want us in there now," said the father.

Petro nodded. "It's best that we just sit here and listen for when they call us."

Sappho opened her mouth as if to speak, but instead glanced out through the doorway at the table. "Yes, let's just sit here in the kitchen and listen." She nodded at two chairs. "Bring those in here and follow me."

Sappho walked along the wall separating the kitchen from the dining room, and stopped under a vent. Pointing up she whispered, "We'll sit here, right below the vent. But be quiet, because they can hear us the same as we can hear them."

"This is crazy."

She leaned over and whispered in his ear. "There's another vent above their table. It's our unofficial intercom with the dining room. When we're really busy, we stand under it and shout out the orders."

"Your customers must think you're crazy."

"I should hope so, what with all I do to make them think I am. But at least this gets the orders working faster."

Petro put down the chairs. "Are you sure we should be doing this?"

She nodded and sat. "Aren't you curious?"

Of course he was. But he knew the microphones would pick up everything, so there was no reason for him to risk someone from the table walking into the kitchen and catching him eavesdropping. The chief would skin him alive.

Sappho reached out and touched his hand. "Okay, if you're not curious, just think of this as humoring me." She sat focused on the vent, and tugged at Petro's hand without moving her eyes. "Please, sit next to me."

Petro shook his head, dropped onto the chair without letting go of her hand, and listened.

Air Marshal's voice came roaring through the vent. "Gentlemen, it is our great privilege and honor to have with us this evening our Prime Minister's most trusted and respected advisor. He has shown himself on countless occasions to be the man whose counsel our Prime Minister treasures most. We have known each other for many years, and though we have our differences, I respect him as a forceful, determined advocate who once committed to a cause will not rest until it succeeds."

He paused. "Now if only we could convince him that a strong military remains Greece's best hope for a secure future in these restless times."

Over applause he introduced the guest by name to the others at the table.

"Thank you, Air Marshal. I, too, am deeply honored, for you have given me the opportunity of addressing our country's finest, most dedicated military minds. You are Greece's strong right arm, the modern day embodiment of our ancient warrior tradition carrying on with a proud history of valor that serves as inspiration to heroes everywhere."

Applause.

Guest smiled. "Thank you for that. Applause is something we in government receive precious little of these days."

A few men laughed.

"I'm particularly gratefully for your applause now," he continued, "for once I've said what I've come to say, I dread I may hear no more."

Nervous glances bounced around the table.

"I was asked to speak on the topic of domestic terrorism, but I have something far more important to share with you. I do not have to tell you, gentlemen, that every day our democracy is locked in battle with economic catastrophe. Not since the horrors of the World War II German occupation have so many of our countrymen faced suffering of such third-world proportions. Our efforts to reason with our creditors only intensify their demands for deeper carvings into social programs they see as unnecessary, wasteful, or simply too generous for our times. They do not grasp that what they ask saps the very marrow of what makes us Greeks."

A couple of officers applauded but abruptly stopped when no one else joined in.

"Many have given up hope. Our brightest youth flee for studies and careers elsewhere. The poor are getting poorer, the rich have already moved their wealth to foreign shores, and the middle class fears being no more. Tax evaders are more blatant, criminals more forceful, and all feel prey to their neighbors' envy. The very fabric of our nation is at risk.

"We cannot permit that to continue. And I am here tonight to tell you we shall not."

Silence.

"Our Prime Minister has weathered many difficult times. He's been forced to accept concessions he despised, dictated by foreign powers in order to keep our ship of state afloat. He is no stranger to hard choices, and I'm about to inform you of another he's forced to make. I doubt you'll agree with it, but as he's convinced of its wisdom it shall come to pass. I am here merely to tell you to prepare.

"There is no country in Europe with a bigger military for its size than Greece. There is no country in NATO as militarized as Greece, and no country in the EU with a bigger proportion of its Gross Domestic Product dedicated to military spending than Greece. Until the financial crisis struck, we numbered among the world's five biggest arms importers and even today have four times the number of German-made, top-of-the-line Leopard tanks as Germany's own military."

He shook his head. "Our Prime Minister does not see how he can justify spending of that magnitude in the face of the extraordinary amounts owed to our creditors and the crushing economic and social toll that burden takes from our people every day.

"He is convinced we need a new direction, one that rejects outdated thinking and wasteful ways. He asks, what are the concerns that fuel our military budget? Turkey? The Turks may rattle their sabers but would never dare invade our NATO country. FYROM? It may call itself Macedonia, but it too would never dare act upon its desire to run its southern border into the heart of northern Greece."

He waved his hand dismissively. "Our Prime Minister sees all of that as scary tales told to the Greek people by politicians of the old order for but a single purpose. To justify their ongoing corrupt dealings with our nation's armorers. Their greed has cost our nation billions, and made them and their patrons very, very rich.

"I am here to tell you those days are over. We shall embrace our NATO and European allies as our protectors and spend our precious resources on fulfilling our party's promises to the people, not on buying foreign armaments. Gentlemen, embrace the new order. For it is here."

Silence.

The air marshal coughed. "Thank you for sharing the Prime Minister's views. I'm sure you realize many of us have very different opinions on how best to address our nation's predicament."

A chorus of agreement arose from around the table.

"But I see no reason to ask you to defend the Prime Minister's thinking with us here tonight. We came for an evening of camaraderie and fun, not serious discussions. There will be time enough for that later."

He held up his glass. "I propose a toast. Here's to Greek valor. May no war require it, but may it ever be ready for every foe."

In one loud voice the entire table responded, "*Ya mas!*"

Sappho looked at Petro. "That's our cue to get back in there."

"Especially the wine-pourer. My guess is after that little speech they'll be doing a lot of drinking."

She let go of his hand, stood, and headed toward the door. "I sure hope the budget cuts don't kick in until after they pay our bill."

"Spoken like a true Greek. Ask not what I can do for my country, but what can I get out of it."

"What can I say? We're incorrigible."

"And look where that's got us."

She stopped to turn and look at him. "Perhaps I missed something back there, Mister Super Patriot, but it sure as hell sounded to me that a lot of big-time military brass just learned that their cushy lifestyle is now bye-bye. I don't want to be the idiot left holding their empty money bag."

"So, what are you going to do about it?"

"Make them pay before they leave. No more 'send us a bill.'"

"Won't that offend them?"

She turned and headed back toward the door. "Better they're offended than we're stiffed."

Guest left the dinner cold sober within twenty minutes of finishing his speech, but the last of the decidedly-not-sober military did not leave the taverna until after sunrise. Another hour passed after that before Petro felt he'd helped clean up sufficiently to announce he had to leave.

Sappho hugged him. "I wish we could have spent more time together. But I know you're tired. We both are. How about tonight?"

Petro laughed. "Let me get some sleep first."

She looked up at him without loosening her hug. "You know I like you?"

"And I like you too." He kissed her on the forehead and headed toward the front door.

Sappho's father caught up with him at the door and pressed an envelope into his hand.

"What's this?" said Petro.

"Your pay."

"I don't want this." He pushed the envelope back toward the father.

"Absolutely not, you earned it. And I hope you realize that any time you want a job you have one here."

"Thank you, but I didn't come here to work for pay. I came to spend time with your daughter."

"I insist. Besides, it's mostly your share of a very big tip."

Petro smiled. "In that case…" He took the envelope and put it in his pocket. The two men hugged and Petro left. He was outside less than thirty seconds when his phone rang.

He looked at the caller ID. "Yes, Chief."

"Don't take the job. We need you in the unit."

"Glad to hear the clamp mikes work, even in my bag."

"So you were able to switch them back out for the real ones."

"While cleaning up."

"Good. You must be exhausted."

"I am."

"You did some first-class work back there."

"Thanks."

"And as soon as you're back at the church call me. We have a lot to talk about."

Andreas and Yianni had spent the night in Andreas' office, alternating shifts between listening to the live feed from the taverna and napping on the couch. But neither man slept during the gathering's heated debate over the implications of the Prime Minister's message that erupted the moment Guest left the taverna. Naptime only returned after the talk deteriorated into a bitching session about politicians in general, on its way toward the evergreen topics of fishing, sports, holidays, and women.

Now they sat wide-awake, staring at Petro's photographs of Guest.

"What the hell was he doing there?" said Yianni.

"Somehow, I don't think it was simply to deliver a message from the Prime Minister."

"Hell of a message. More like a declaration of war against the military. I couldn't think of more unifying hot-button issues for the military than Turkey, FYROM, and cutbacks."

"Almost as if he were trying to provoke them," said Andreas.

'But why? The Prime Minister's been pretty content up to now with not going after the military's sacred cows."

"Or rattling its very comfortable cages."

"Like the air marshal's in Larissa, a town known for having both the Air Force's main base and more Porsche Cayennes per capita than any other place in Europe."

Andreas shook his head. "Something's not right about this. He just told a room full of military that the Prime Minister is planning a one-eighty reversal on the nation's basic national security strategy without a single word of any of that having leaked into the press."

"That's just the sort of dynamite stuff someone turns over to the media in exchange for getting a big-time favor. Maybe the PM's office has been extraordinarily careful to keep a lid on this?"

"Not likely if what we heard him privately tell the air marshal just before making his speech is true. He made a careful point of telling the air marshal he did not agree with the PM's strategy and had vigorously but unsuccessfully argued against it. That's the kind of high-level discord that fuels leaks."

"And he had to know the air marshal would repeat that kind of juicy gossip," said Yianni.

"Which is precisely what we heard him do with several people over the course of the night. By now everyone who was at that table knows or will know by morning that there's a disagreement between the PM and his most trusted adviser."

"It's as if he wanted them to know of his differences with the Prime Minister."

Andreas nodded. "As I said, something's not right."

"But we knew that about the guy from the first time we met him."

Andreas looked closely at the photos. "I can't tell if he's wearing his jacket with the red striped collar."

"With or without it, he's still that asshole Prada."

The phone rang on Andreas' desk. Andreas hit the speaker button.

"Chief?"

"Yes, Petro, I'm here with Yianni."

"Great work, kid," said Yianni.

"Thanks." A yawn came over the speaker.

"Yianni and I were just talking about your guest who came to dinner."

"Who is he?"

"He's the head of State Security Police, whatever the hell that is. It seems to be where he's parked himself for a paycheck and power base while he serves as an advisor to the Prime Minister. We met him at our meeting with the Brigadier in our minister's office. Yianni calls him Prada. His real name is…" Andreas looked at a note on his desk and said the name.

"Never heard of him."

"That's apparently how he likes things. He and Babis organized most of the major violent demonstrations for the Prime Minister that helped bring their party to power. Prada served as the brains and Babis as the front man. Prada kept a low profile then too. Let others take the credit."

"And shielded the Prime Minister from taking the blame," said Yianni.

"Well, the military top brass certainly knew him," said Petro.

"That surprised me," said Andreas. "I wouldn't have thought he'd be that close to the military."

"Certainly not as a leftist revolutionary," said Yianni.

"Any idea why he delivered a scary message to the military instead of what they expected him to talk about?" said Petro.

"We were just tossing that around," said Andreas. "What's your take on what you saw?"

"He certainly shook everyone up. Especially the young ones. I could tell from their faces. It was as if someone near and dear to them had just died in front of them."

"Did they seem angry?" said Andreas.

"Hard to say. They drank a lot and that muddies your emotions. But for sure they'd come to Santorini expecting to be anointed the military's next generation of leaders only to learn that their dreams had just crashed and burned, courtesy of the Prime Minister."

Andreas picked up a pencil and began tapping it on his desktop. "What did they say about Prada?"

"Not much. They took him as the messenger."

"Did they mention anything about his not agreeing with the Prime Minister's strategy?"

"Not that I overheard. Is that true?"

Andreas filled Petro in on what they'd picked up from the microphones.

"Very interesting, but I never heard them talking about that."

"Okay, try to get some sleep, because as soon as your big tippers wake up, I want you glued to those mikes."

"The tips weren't that big."

"No matter, you earned them. But be alert. I'm sure what Prada said will now be their number-one agenda item. I want to know where this is headed so we can try to be out in front of it for once."

"Any guesses?" said Petro.

"None that I want to make until after I hear what the men have to say when they're sober."

"I'll call you as soon as they're up and talking."

"I've a better idea. Call Yianni."

Yianni did a double take at Andreas. "Let me guess. So you can sleep?"

Andreas stood and headed toward the door. "The benefits of rank, Detective. But don't worry, now the couch is all yours. Sleep tight, guys."

Andreas never saw the pillow coming, but felt it hit just before he made it out the door.

Chapter Thirteen

"So, what do you think of this color for the baby's room?"

Andreas pulled the pillow off his head. "I thought you liked the Pepto-Bismol pink Tassaki and I painted it."

"I changed my mind. Being left alone as much as I've been has given me an opportunity to re-think some choices."

Andreas pulled the pillow back over his head. "It's perfect."

"I'd respect your opinion more if you actually took the time to look at what I'm holding in my hand."

"I'm sleeping."

"And I'm dealing with a color-blind painter. It's almost noon. Aren't you embarrassed to leave your pregnant wife to deal with tradesmen?"

"Nope, they're no match for you. Besides, I didn't get to bed until three hours ago."

Lila walked to the foot of the bed. "Not my problem." She tickled his toes.

Andreas yanked away his legs to protect his feet. "Stop that."

"Not until you tell me what you think of the color."

Andreas twisted his head and looked at the piece of painted board in her hand. "Brown? For a baby's room. Ugh."

"My sentiments exactly. What do you think of light lemon yellow?"

Andreas forced a smile. "Perfect. May I go back to sleep now?" He shut his eyes.

"If you'd like, though Yianni said to tell you to call him as soon as you were up."

"When did he call?"

"Five minutes ago."

Andreas swung his feet around and over the side of the bed.

"So, this wasn't actually about the painter."

Lila smiled. "I just wanted to have some fun. It gets lonely having a husband who stays out all night eavesdropping on other people having a good time."

"Remind me to take you along the next time."

"Oh, sure. You know how to show a girl a good time."

Andreas stood and headed toward the door.

"I suggest, dear husband, that you put on a robe. I don't think the painter will appreciate your Adonis-like nude form as much as I do."

"You mean there really is a painter?"

"And he is color blind."

Andreas put on his robe, walked through the foyer into the study, nodding to the paint-speckled Polish lad standing outside the baby's room as he did. "My wife will be right with you."

He closed the door and called Yianni.

"Didn't mean to wake you," said Yianni.

"Of course you did. So what's happening?"

"The meeting's in full swing, and the only topic of conversation is what will happen if the Prime Minister goes forward with his plans."

"What do you mean if?"

"Their word, not mine. As we thought, everybody now knows Prada doesn't agree with the Prime Minister, and there is a lot of speculation over how that might be exploited."

"Exploited how?"

"You name it, they've suggested it. Some have even gone so far as to suggest financially backing Prada to split from the PM's party and form his own."

"I don't see that ever happening. Once it got out he was the military's candidate, he'd be dead. Possibly literally."

"Yeah, that wouldn't sit too well with his leftist buddies."

"Besides, I don't see him as the charismatic type that appeals to the electorate."

"That's what the air marshal said. His thinking is to get the media involved. Play up how dangerous is Greece's Mediterranean neighborhood, and that the waves of illegal immigrants streaming across our borders calls for an even stronger, better-equipped military presence. That way, instead of battling the Prime Minister over cuts, the Prime Minister has to fight public opinion calling for an increased military budget."

"That approach might have worked in the past," said Andreas, "but I don't think it's going to play well these days. The people are numb to preachings of disaster. All they've heard over the past couple of years in one election after another is sanctimonious politicians preaching milk and honey if you voted for them and utter disaster if you didn't. But no matter which party won, nothing changed, things just got worse. They don't believe a thing they're told by a politician or the political parties' mouthpiece media outlets. Political promises are meaningless, facts are made up, lies are everywhere."

"Have you been listening to the recordings?" said Yianni.

"What are you talking about?"

"You just repeated the essence of what practically every senior officer said in that meeting. 'The times are different,' they say. 'The old ways won't work.'"

"So what are the young ones suggesting?"

"That's what they're debating now."

"How big is the difference of opinion between the general and senior officers?"

"I wouldn't call it a mutiny in the ranks, but considering how carefully politic these senior officers must have been to get this far, I'd say it's a rather dramatic development for them to be openly expressing their differences with the general officers."

"Sounds like they took the message Prada delivered from the Prime Minister to heart," said Andreas.

"For sure. Both levels of officers see Prada as the key. The question is, how to use him to turn the Prime Minister."

"Let me know if they come up with an answer."

"Right now they're trying to come up with the right person to approach Prada."

"Approach him for what?"

"To feel him out, see if he's willing to try again to change the Prime Minister's mind. If not, they have to come up with a different angle."

"Hate to drop the word, but any talk of a coup?"

"Not even a hint. A cynic would say it's as if they know they're being recorded. I'd say it reaffirms the military's loyalty to the nation and its recognition that any talk of that sort is treasonous," said Yianni.

"You sound like you might want to re-enlist."

"As hard as it may be to believe, I think I actually got more sleep as a Greek Navy commando than a cop."

"I get the hint. I'll see you in about an hour. You can catch some sleep then."

"Can hardly wait."

"Good. And while you're at it, make a list of the officers you think are most enthusiastic about using Prada."

"Why?"

"Just a hunch. But if a painter can be color blind, maybe we're missing something too."

"I won't even ask what that means. Bye."

Andreas put the phone back in its cradle. *Not sure I know either.*

◇◇◇

"Francesco, what are you doing?" said Petro.

"Just what it looks like. I'm getting ready to head out for a walk."

"To where?"

"Anywhere. I'm going stir crazy. I spent all last night cooped up in a van listening to military types rattling plates, and for the last five hours to them rattling sabers."

"Don't you have to help Dimos?"

"It's all under control. Right, Dimos?"

"Gotcha covered. Just don't stay away too long, your wife might call."

"Cover for me. Tell her I'm out chasing terrorists."

"On Santorini?"

"Okay, tell her they're price-gougers. She dislikes them even more."

"Did you guys rehearse this routine or what?" asked Petro.

"Don't worry, Dimos will cover for you with Sappho, too."

"Damn, I forgot to call her. What time is it?"

"Nearly four," said Francesco.

Petro reached for his phone.

"Hold on guys," said Dimos. "You're going to want to hear this. I've got it going live to the chief, too."

Petro and Francesco crowded in next to Dimos and listened through a pair of shared earphones.

Dimos nodded at the phones, "It's the air marshal and a rear admiral alone in the admiral's villa," said Dimos. "That's the admiral talking now."

"—you're right, a real tragedy. I knew the girl. Really nice kid. Not at all like her mother."

Laughter.

"Too bad the father wouldn't join us," continued the air marshal. "If there's anyone who might be able to convince our dinner guest to straighten out the Prime Minister's thinking, he's our man."

"The two of them are that tight?"

"They go back to childhood school days. One went into the military, and the other into leftist politics, but they stayed close friends right up until a couple of years ago."

"What happened?" said the admiral.

"Not sure, but I heard it was our dinner guest who steered his buddy's daughter into her passion for leftist causes."

"How'd he do that?"

"No idea."

"And now she's dead. I see why there's not much of a chance

of getting him to ask his old friend to convince the Prime Minister to change his mind."

"You got it…Now, if you'll excuse me, Admiral, I must head back to my quarters for a nap. That is, if I want to have any chance of keeping up with our late-night partying colleagues."

"Are they going out again tonight?"

"No idea, but I want to be ready in case they do. Can't let them see the old man sweat."

Laughter, and the sound of a door opening and closing.

Dimos looked at Petro. "Does that make any sense to you?"

Petro bit at his lip. "I'm sure it will to the chief."

Yianni stared across Andreas' desk at his boss. "Son of a bitch."

"I think what we just overheard calls for something more like, *MISERABLE MOTHER FUCKER*," shouted Andreas pounding his fist twice on his desk. "The asshole's daughter was murdered and he's holding out on us."

"'Holding out' is a colossal understatement. The bastard never bothered to mention a word about his relationship with Prada."

"Sort of makes you wonder about how much of what went down in Babis' office was staged."

"And how much of what he told us in the cafenion was true."

Andreas ran his fingers through his hair. "But why tell us about the meeting on Santorini at all? He had to know it could lead us to discover his history with Prada."

"Maybe he didn't think it would come up?"

Andreas picked up the phone, looked at a number written on a pad on his desk and dialed. "I'm tired of maybes." He began tapping a pencil on the desktop.

"Hello, Brigadier, this is Andreas Kaldis."

Pause.

"I'm fine, but I need to see you right away."

Pause.

"I know you're busy, so am I, but this is urgent."

Pause.

"No, I can't talk about it on the phone and this time I'm afraid you'll have to come to my office."

Pause.

"I must insist. Get here as soon as you can. Goodbye." Andreas thrust the phone back onto its cradle.

"So much for being politic with the military brass," said Yianni.

"I thought I was rather restrained."

"Since he's coming, I'd say you got the message across."

"That we know about his relationship with Prada?"

"That we know something not nice about him. You didn't exactly sound like an investigating cop talking to a grieving father."

Andreas scowled. "If he wants to be treated like a grieving father, then he should start acting like one and cooperate with the investigation."

Yianni got up and headed toward the door.

"Where are you going?"

"To get a quick bite to eat. I don't want to sit through what's coming on an empty stomach."

"Just be here when he arrives."

"Don't worry, I wouldn't miss this for the end of the world. Which in fact it may turn out to be, considering the Brigadier's temper."

"I can handle his temper."

"The question is, can he handle yours?"

Yianni ducked as Andreas launched a pencil across the room at his head.

Andreas sat silently at his desk, nibbling at the *spanakopita* Yianni had brought back for him from the cafeteria. The most difficult thing about preparing for confrontation was determining how best to deal with all the competing scenarios playing out in your head. No matter the outcome, you wasted substantial time and attention on things that would never happen. That's why Andreas decided to stop thinking about the possibilities, and concentrate on how to put what he knew straight to the Brigadier. Whatever happened after that, he'd deal with it. At least that was the plan.

Maggie's voice came crisply through the intercom. "Chief, the Brigadier is here."

"Show him in."

Yianni shifted on the couch.

Andreas stood up as the door opened and the Brigadier walked into the office wearing civilian clothes. Andreas extended his hand, but did not move from behind his desk. "Brigadier, thank you so much for coming."

The two shook hands and Andreas pointed at one of the two chairs in front of his desk. "Please."

The Brigadier sat down and crossed his legs. "I'm not at all happy about your dragging me down here on a weekend."

Andreas forced a smile. "I don't like working weekends either, but sometimes we have to if we want to catch bad guys who do bad things to other people's children."

"What's that supposed to mean?" The Brigadier uncrossed his legs and leaned forward in his chair.

"Precisely what you think it means. We're trying to find out who killed your daughter, and we think it's time you started telling us the truth so we can do our job."

The Brigadier's face turned crimson. "Are you calling me a liar?"

"No, I'm saying you don't seem to give a shit about telling us what we need to know if we're going to find who's responsible for murdering your daughter."

The Brigadier lunged out of his chair, swinging his right fist across the desk at Andreas' face.

Instead of ducking, Andreas deflected the punch across his body with his left forearm, and used the Brigadier's momentum to yank him sailing over the desk and into the wall behind him.

Yianni leaped off the couch and raced around the desk to help.

"No need, Yianni," said Andreas gripping the Brigadier's right hand in a firm wristlock. "I'm sure the general sees the wisdom of learning to control his temper and behaving in a more civilized manner."

The Brigadier tried to wrestle out of the wristlock, but Andreas gripped tighter and pressed hard against his elbow, drawing a noticeable wince from the larger man.

"Have you had enough yet or would you like a bit more pain?" Andreas pressed harder at the elbow.

"*Enough*. Okay. Stop."

Andreas released his grip. "Back to your chair, please."

The Brigadier shuffled to his feet and rubbed at his arm and wrist as he walked toward the chair. "I—I'm sorry. When it comes to my daughter…"

"Apology not accepted."

"What is it you want from me?"

"Here's a hint. Sorry your flight over my desktop didn't end as comfortably for you as the one you sent your buddy on in the Minister's office."

The Brigadier drew a deep breath, shut his eyes, exhaled, and dropped into the chair. He opened his eyes. "If you know our history, then you know throwing that bastard across the desk was the least of what I've been wanting to do to him for a very long time."

"What do you mean *if* we know your history? You sent us off to Santorini to eavesdrop on some hush-hush military powwow that has your childhood friend turning up as its guest of honor and you thought we wouldn't find out about your relationship?"

"He was there?"

"Don't toss me any more bullshit. You knew he'd be there."

"No, I didn't. I swear."

Andreas shook his head. "You had to know that sooner or later we'd find out about your past together. How could you be so stupid as not to tell us? Or did you think we were too stupid to figure it out?"

The Brigadier dropped his head and stared at the floor. "I didn't want to open a can of worms."

"*A can of worms?* We're trying to find out who murdered your daughter and you're worried about a can of worms."

"He had nothing to do with her death."

"How can you be so sure?"

The Brigadier bit at his lip. "He was her godfather."

Now Andreas drew in and let out a breath. Agreeing to be a godparent was a serious undertaking in Greece. By accepting, you gave your word to raise the child as your own should something happen to the parents. If Prada had been involved in the assassination, it would have been like killing his own child.

Andreas waited until the Brigadier raised his head. "What's the can of worms?"

The Brigadier rubbed at his forehead with the fingers of his right hand. "I didn't want my wife traumatized any more than she already is." He looked Andreas in the eyes. "We were lousy parents, and I didn't want that to become public. The media would chew her up."

"What do you mean by 'lousy?'"

"We were so involved in our own lives we left Lena to raise her."

"Your housekeeper?"

The Brigadier nodded. "Lena made her breakfast, took her to the playground, made sure she did her homework, and tucked her in at night."

"If that's your definition of lousy, there are an awful lot of lousy parents out there. I don't see that as generating bad press."

"The lousy part was how Lena was treated." He stared back down at the floor. "My wife yelled at her constantly. Nothing she did was ever right. She would scream for Lena to walk up three flights of stairs just to hand her something sitting on a table right next to her. And she'd do it front of everyone, including our daughter."

"And you let her?" said Yianni.

"I wasn't home much, and when I was, I took the path of least resistance. I didn't want to fight with her."

"Why didn't your wife fire her if she was so unhappy with her?"

"She wasn't unhappy, just threatened by Lena's relationship with Penelope. I took it all as a power play to show who was in charge. If Lena had quit, my wife would have been utterly lost. Lena knew that too."

"Then why did she stay?"

"Because she loved our daughter. She had no children of her own. She just tuned out my wife's screaming and went about her business."

"Frankly, Brigadier, beyond your wife coming across as—if you'll excuse the expression—a bitch, I still don't see any story angle to this that makes it a can of worms."

The Brigadier audibly sighed. "It was my wife's constant hounding of Lena in front of our daughter that fueled Penelope's attraction to radical politics. If my wife hadn't treated Lena as badly as I allowed her to, I'm certain Penelope would never have rallied to the cause of 'the exploited workers tormented by the monied classes.'" He emphasized his final phrase with finger quotes.

"How's that all tie into your not telling us about Prada?" said Yianni.

"Prada? Oh, that's your nickname for him." The Brigadier smiled. "It fits his style these days." He stretched and shook his wrist. "You've got a pretty strong grip there, Chief Inspector."

"Just tell us how it all ties into Prada," repeated Andreas.

The Brigadier shifted in his chair. "He was a regular in our home, dropping by all the time for dinner and to rage on in debates with me over politics. It was a routine we'd followed since childhood. He always took the side of workers uniting against oppressive bosses, leaving me to play the right wing bad guy. I saw our arguments as fun, a link back to our days as kids. Neither of us ever took it seriously or expected to change the other's views."

He shook his head. "I never realized how the combination of our tabletop debates and my wife's treatment of Lena had radicalized our daughter until it was too late. She saw her mother's relentless hounding of Lena as proof positive of the validity of Prada's arguments."

"And when was 'too late'?" said Andreas.

"When Penelope went off to university and joined the far left radical crowd that got her killed. I tried to get him to talk sense into her, to get her to back away from the rock- and bomb-throwers, but he refused. He said it's up to her to make her own decisions, lead her own life. Then he had the balls to tell me, 'Don't be so worried. It's just a phase kids go through in university. When she gets older and wiser, she'll come back around to your right wing way of thinking. They always do.'

"I thought he was joking but he assured me he wasn't. He gave me a speech. He said he'd been around long enough to know ideals didn't matter. All politicians, whether left or right, shared the same stage, bit players directed in their roles by global forces. The costumes might be different, but they shared the same dressing room, took bows before the same audience, wooed the same critics, and dined at the same trough. Speeches were just that—wave the flag, blame the immigrants, promise the masses what they wanted, do whatever it took to keep moving the sheep toward the pen. The far left was in power now, but on a course likely to banish it from power for generations."

The Brigadier clenched his fists. "The callous bastard didn't believe his own rhetoric. He was a fraud who'd radicalized my daughter, his godchild, and then refused to help her get her head back on straight."

"That's when you stopped talking to him?"

The Brigadier nodded, his face coloring. "And never will again. He cost my daughter her life."

"Why do you say he's a fraud?" said Yianni. "It sounds as though he was just making an observation and trying to comfort you as a father."

"It's more than that. He could have talked to her. She'd have listened to him. But he didn't want to risk his leftist credentials by getting her to turn her back on his radical cronies. I watched him grow up. Saw him make whatever alliances it took to get what he wanted. Yes, he's made his mark espousing leftist causes, but I've no doubt he'd move to the right in a heartbeat if he thought it benefited him. He's a practical man. He keeps his options open. I'm sure even his friendship with me was purposeful. I served as his link to the military right."

"Why would he want a link to the right?" said Andreas.

"For the same reason I imagine he went to Santorini. He's always believed that once the far left attained power, if it faltered, the far right would be the next to rule. He sees them as two sides of the same coin, equally appealing to voters so easily seduced by radical promises of better lives once the party's targets of blame are eliminated."

"You're saying he's a hypocrite?" said Andreas.

"No, I'm saying he's a ruthless opportunist utterly devoid of ethics. He'll do whatever it takes to benefit himself."

"Like seeing your daughter dead if it might have benefited him?"

The Brigadier shut his eyes for a moment, opened them, and stared straight at Andreas. "From the bottom of my heart, as much as I'd like to say yes, I have to say no."

Yianni coughed. "Excuse me, but let me run something by you, Brigadier. Prada claimed to be on Santorini at the request of the Prime Minister for the purpose of delivering a very unwelcome message to some high-ranking military. The sort of a message that some might say inspires coups. Does that sound like your buddy's style?"

"If you mean benefiting by fomenting discord, absolutely. But why would he want a coup? His party is already in power."

"But it's moved rather briskly from its classic, far left communist roots toward the center," said Yianni.

"That's consistent with Prada's vision of politics as a process of moving to the right with maturity. Besides, the Prime Minister booted out the party's most extreme leftist members in the last election, and its ruling coalition partner is a party of right-wingers with its head serving as minister of defense. The Prime Minister's party is on an obvious march to the right, so I don't see why he would be trying to provoke a conflict with the military."

"Are you suggesting Prada lied when he said he was delivering a message from the Prime Minister?" said Andreas.

"Hard to see why he'd deliver such a message, because you'd think it's the sort of thing that would get back to the Prime Minister, making Prada look, at best, a fool if what he said wasn't true. And if there's one thing he's not, it's a fool."

"But he did deliver that message," said Andreas. "No doubt about it."

The Brigadier shook his head. "Then I suggest you find out whether what you overheard actually came from the Prime Minister. And if not, who's the powerful son of a bitch that convinced Prada to deliver it. One thing I can tell you for sure is that's not the sort of wild-ass political risk he would take on his own. He likes his power, but only takes chances when he's certain he has political cover from above."

The Brigadier swallowed. "For the same reason that he wouldn't risk his political future by telling my daughter she was in with the wrong crowd, he wouldn't dare cross the Prime Minister unless he thought he was covered by the right crowd."

"So the question is, why did Prada do it?" said Andreas.

"Where the hell do we start to figure that out?" said Yianni.

Andreas sat back in his chair, closed and opened his eyes. "By asking the Prime Minister."

Chapter Fourteen

Andreas did not know the Prime Minister personally, and knew it would be impossible to expect his boss, the minister of public order, to arrange a private meeting between Andreas and the Prime Minister, even if Andreas were prepared to trust him with his reason for the meeting. Nor could Tassos convince one of his contacts to set up such a meeting without confiding its purpose to the intermediary in advance. Heads of state did not like surprises.

Andreas had to find another way. He doubted that becoming Facebook friends with the Prime Minister would work, so he settled on an old-fashioned method: He asked Lila to do it for him—a wise decision that yielded immediate results.

Though the Prime Minister had risen to power as a symbol of the exploited masses, his mentor in all of that was one of the most socially prominent and wealthiest women in Greece. It took Andreas' wife only a brief telephone call peppered with catty gossip and well-placed flattery to get Greece's Lady Rasputin, as some called her, to assure Lila that the Prime Minister would see her darling husband at once.

And so he did, that very afternoon.

The Prime Minister's offices were in the Maximos Mansion at 19 Irodou Attikou, an extraordinarily convenient meeting place for Andreas because it stood just up the block from where Andreas lived. But there was a snag. The Prime Minister scheduled their meeting for his home: a modest apartment in a seven-story building amid a sea of unattractive concrete apartment buildings jammed into the staunchly working class Athens neighborhood of Kypseli. About one mile roughly due north of GADA headquarters, and a world away from the Maximos Mansion, this once elegant neighborhood had seen ill-conceived construction and an ever-expanding immigrant population turn it into what's said to be among the most densely populated neighborhoods on the planet.

Andreas parked his unmarked car directly across from the Prime Minister's building in a spot marked NO PARKING. Two marked police cars sat in the street on either side of the entrance to the apartment building. He'd been surprised by the graffiti-covered walls up the block, rubbish-littered empty lots, and abandoned properties, but not by the black-clad soldier wearing a combat headset and carrying a H&K MP5K submachine gun stepping briskly toward his open window.

Andreas held up his ID and said he had an appointment with the Prime Minister. He sat with his hands on the steering wheel while the soldier relayed the message and waited for instructions.

"Okay, sir, you're cleared to go up."

"Thank you," said Andreas, opening the door and getting out.

The soldier pointed at a burly, bald man in civilian clothes standing by the front door to the building. "He will take you up, sir."

As much as Andreas wanted to joke about the fortune in euros all this security must be costing the nation simply to demonstrate that the Prime Minister remained a commoner, he doubted that would get a smile out of the Prime Minister's security detail. Besides, this long neglected neighborhood could use the additional police attention.

The burly man met him just inside the front door. "May I have your weapon please, Chief Inspector?"

Andreas handed over his nine millimeter.

"Thank you. I'll give it back when you leave."

"Don't you want to search me?"

The man smiled as he pointed toward the elevator. "No need, the doorway you just passed through did a full body scan."

Oh yeah, he's living just like the common folk.

Andreas and the man stepped inside the elevator. The man pressed 4. Andreas wondered whether the building's tenants had come to accept their working elevator as just another perk of their illustrious neighbor's presence in the building.

The elevator door opened and the burly man pointed left at two more men in civilian clothes, one standing on either side of an apartment door no different from any of the floor's other beige metal doors. The burly man nodded and one of the two men leaned over and opened the door.

Andreas went through the doorway not knowing what to expect on the other side. He found a living room reminiscent of the one he'd grown up in, furnished on about the same budget as his father's cop salary. Nothing of great monetary value jumped out at him, and family hand-me-downs seemed everywhere. Conspicuously absent were photos of powerful or celebrated friends. The only photographs were of the Prime Minister and his family. It was the perfect setting for his just-like-us public persona.

There was no way of telling what might lie in the other rooms, but no matter what the actual truth might be about the PM's rumored family wealth, Andreas had to admit he knew how to project an image.

As if on cue, a man about the same age as Andreas burst into the room carrying a tray laden with two large mugs, a carafe of coffee, milk, sugar, two spoons, and a plate of cookies. In rolled-up shirtsleeves and no tie, the Prime Minister smiled. "Welcome, Chief Inspector Kaldis."

"May I help you, Prime Minister?"

"No, I'm fine, thank you." He gestured with his head toward a sturdy, wood-framed sofa done in heavily varnished dark floral carvings and a nondescript, faded-beige chenille upholstery. "Please, sit there."

Andreas sat on the sofa as the Prime Minister placed the tray on a coffee table in front of him.

"Sorry, about the informality of all this, but the kids' mom had to work today and I had to get them started on their homework for Monday. I barely had time to boil water for the coffee. I hope that's okay."

Andreas smiled. "More than okay, sir. Thank you."

This guy really knows how to play the role.

Still standing, the Prime Minister picked up a mug, poured in the coffee, and looked down at Andreas. "Milk? Sugar?"

"Just black, thank you."

The Prime Minister handed him the mug, poured one for himself, and sat across from Andreas on a chair matching the sofa. "That's something else we seem to have in common."

"Pardon?"

"Black coffee." The Prime Minister smiled. "And a deep appreciation of the value of the mothers of our children."

Andreas laughed. "Yes, it's because of the latter that I have this chance to try the former."

The Prime Minister's smile relaxed into something more genuine. "Well put." He leaned forward and picked up the plate of cookies. "Here, try these *koulourakia*. I get them from a bakery around the corner. Best in Athens."

Andreas took a butter cookie. "Thank you."

The Prime Minister leaned back in his chair. "So, what is this urgent matter threatening my government that my good friend told me I must hear from your lips in person?"

"Your friend is very insightful. My wife never said that to her, but it's true."

He nodded. "She is one of the most intuitive people I know. She senses the unsaid."

"A valuable skill."

"And one whose advice I've learned not to follow at my peril." He sipped his coffee.

"Do you have other advisors you value for the same reason?"

The Prime Minister paused in mid-sip. "My turn to say, 'pardon'?"

"To get straight to the point, sir, I'm here because in the course of a homicide investigation we picked up a conversation involving one of your senior advisors."

"Involved in a murder?"

"No. He turned up unexpectedly at a dinner arranged by top military personnel, and it's what he said to those attending the dinner that brings me here."

"What did he say?"

"He described what he characterized as your new defense policy."

The Prime Minister seemed to squeeze his coffee mug before putting it down on the table. "Who said that?"

Andreas told him.

"And what precisely did he say?"

Andreas told him.

The Prime Minister sat quietly for a moment. "Do I understand you to be telling me you have incontrovertible proof of top members of our nation's armed forces being told by one of my most trusted advisors that I plan on Greece no longer employing a strong military to facedown its historic enemies, but rather will rely upon NATO and Europe to defend our homeland?"

Andreas nodded. "That sums it up."

The Prime Minister smiled. "That must have ruined the military folks' evening."

The smile surprised Andreas, but he played along. "It did add to their bar bill."

"What was their reaction to what they heard?"

"Once your advisor left, they openly disagreed with what they understood to be your position, and talked a lot about finding some way of getting you to change your mind."

"What sort of way?"

"Finding someone capable of persuading your advisor to convince you to change your position."

"I'm getting the impression my advisor made it appear he didn't agree with what he'd described as my strategy."

"Yes, sir, that's correct."

"Was there any talk of more aggressive means for getting me to change my mind?"

"There was some talk of convincing your advisor to form his own party to run against you."

The Prime Minister laughed. "Anything a bit more realistic?"

"Nothing."

"You're certain of that?"

Andreas nodded. "I am. They only talked about using their influence to change your mind, not their might to change the government."

The Prime Minister smiled. "I like your way of putting things."

"Thank you."

The Prime Minister nodded. "I understand there's a question you wanted to ask me in person."

"Yes."

What is it?"

Andreas swallowed hard. "Is it true what he said about your strategy?"

"You're asking me whether I plan on instituting a revolutionary shift in Greece's military policy? That strikes me as a subject far above your security clearance."

"With all respect, sir, I have the clearances. Besides, if what he said is true, it's no longer a secret. Someone claiming to be authorized to speak on your behalf broadcast your alleged plan to two dozen hard-drinking military men. The real question is, who doesn't know about it by now? In fact, I'm surprised you haven't had the press at your throat about this already."

The Prime Minister fixed his eyes on Andreas. Andreas stared back, saying nothing.

"If that were my plan, revealing it as he did could be seen as an effort to fire up the military against it before I've had the chance to put it in place, and my instinctive reaction would be to consider his behavior a political betrayal." He picked up his mug. "If that weren't my plan, but he said that it was, a sinister plot comes to mind, one on the order of an effort to turn the military against me and remove me from office. That I'd call treason."

The Prime Minister took a sip. "But in either case, if confronted, he'd likely say it was a trial balloon floated out there by him, not me, to test the chances of such a dramatic policy change actually surviving the military's ire. He'd call that an act of loyalty, attempting to spare me a political disaster."

He put down his mug. "So what is it, Andreas, political betrayal, treason, or loyalty?"

Andreas hesitated for an instant at the use of his first name. "I hardly know the man. I can only pass along the facts. It's up to you to interpret them."

"I want your instinct."

"You already have someone for that sort of advice."

He smiled. "I see why our minister of public order is always screaming for me to get rid of you. You're far better at this political fencing than he is." After a momentary pause, the Prime Minister slapped his hands on his thighs. "Okay, here's what we do. This conversation never happened. You continue with your investigation, following it wherever it takes you. And once you have an 'instinct born of facts,'" he used finger quotes, "I want you to tell me right away. I'll take it from there." He stood and extended his hand. "Okay?"

Andreas stood and shook the Prime Minister's hand. "You still haven't answered my question. Is that your new strategy?"

He put his hand on Andreas' shoulder and led him to the door. "Let's just call our little political fencing match a draw on that subject."

"Whatever you say, sir."

But be ready when the boys with the real swords come after you.

Andreas sat in his car, staring up at the Prime Minister's apartment building. This time the soldier ignored him.

Andreas had never been a fan of the PM, but for that matter he'd not been a fan of any Prime Minister in recent memory. None ever did what he promised. This one most of all. A declared Marxist-Leninist practically since birth, he was elected on promises of standing up to Greece's European creditors and restoring jobs and social programs amid a catastrophic financial meltdown. An impossibility, his right wing rivals said.

Once elected, he staged a dramatic show of resistance to his nation's creditors but ultimately capitulated to all their demands and implemented societal changes far more severe and conservative than any right wing leader ever imagined could pass through Parliament. Yet his left wing supporters still loved him enough to elect him again.

The man was a political magician.

And Andreas could see why. You couldn't help but like the guy on a personal level, even though you knew you couldn't believe a word that he said. Not that he was a liar…no he was the consummate political animal. He existed to be elected and remain in power. For successful politicians, Andreas supposed political philosophies must give way to that principle. Politics was all about being practical, and Andreas would have bet this guy didn't even own a pair of nonsensible shoes.

Though the Prime Minister had carefully avoided giving Andreas an answer for why Prada had said what he did on Santorini, he'd indirectly told him plenty. He'd neither embraced nor rejected Prada, admitted nor denied Prada had spoken the truth to the military, but he'd given Andreas the green light to go forward with his investigation. Something the Prime Minister never would've done had Prada been acting on his behalf in delivering that message to the military.

Andreas nibbled at his lower lip. On the other hand, if the PM had told Andreas to stop the investigation, it would be a direct confirmation of Prada acting on his behalf. With all the subtle ways the Prime Minister had at his disposal to prevent Andreas from ever learning the truth, it made no sense for him to say anything to make Andreas think Prada didn't have the full backing of the Prime Minister's office.

He rubbed at his right temple. The Prime Minister had taken great care to mention that Babis wanted Andreas' head. He'd said it in a way that suggested the Prime Minister had Andreas' back. Still, all it would take was a "Do what you think is best for your ministry," phone call from the Prime Minister to Andreas' boss and Andreas would be history.

I'll know soon enough, thought Andreas, shaking his head as he started the car. *Politics.* Andreas hated the process. He glanced up and down the street, still not believing this was where the Prime Minister of Greece lived. His eye caught a street sign and he smiled. Perhaps that explained it. This had to be the only place in Greece where the Prime Minister could find what the name on that street sign promised. Andreas pulled away and drove off, leaving Harmony Street behind.

Andreas marched into his office carrying a box of pastries and a bottle of *tsipouro.*

Yianni stared at him from a chair in front of a row of empty coffee cups aligned along Andreas' desk.

"Glad to see one of us is in a party mood. For the last four hours I've been sitting here listening to our military's best and brightest engage in a marathon booze and bitching session over their rapidly fading futures, only to have you show up with this." He pointed at the bottle of *tsipouro* in Andreas' hand.

"What can I say? After my meeting with the Prime Minister and your time here, I figured we could both use a drink."

"But this stuff is like gasoline."

"No, gasoline would be its Italian cousin, *grappa.* This one has just enough anise to make it pleasant. Besides, we're civilized… we mix it with water."

"Spoken like a true Greek."

Andreas put the bottle and pastry box on his desk and sat down in the chair next to Yianni.

"Went that badly, huh?"

Andreas shrugged, opened the box, and took out a cookie. "Either the Prime Minister is with us or against us. No telling. But I'm going to act as if we have his full support and plunge ahead on that assumption."

"And if you're wrong?"

"You and I will have a lot more time for *tsipouro.*"

"Great. Did he tell you if what Prada told the military was true?"

Andreas gestured no. "But my instinct is it wasn't."

"Instinct? Maybe I'll have that *tsipouro,* after all."

"Any news from our boys on Santorini?"

"They're just as bored as I am. As for the two-dozen military men on whose every word we're hanging, they've been drinking for hours. The more they drink, the more the younger ones urge the older to pressure Prada."

"And the top brass?"

"They just listen to the younger ones vent. It's as if they don't want to be quoted."

"Sounds like a wonderful time is being had by all." Andreas bit into the cookie.

"Prada's little speech put a real damper on the weekend."

Andreas nodded. "Just like he intended."

"What do you mean?"

"He had to know the effect his words would have on that group. And assuming he knew what he said wasn't true, he also knew that sooner or later the whole episode would get back to the PM. That adds up to Prada having had one hell of a powerful reason for taking such a risk." Andreas drummed the fingers of his right hand on the desktop. "All we have to do now is figure out his motivation, determine who else is involved, and how it all ties into the murder of Penelope Sigounas."

Yianni opened the box and took out a *galaktoboureko* custard pastry roll. "Oh, that's all? I feel so much more relaxed now."

Andreas ignored him. "His purpose in going to Santorini had to be to get a rise out of that group. But why?"

"If that was his goal, as I said, he certainly succeeded in pissing off the younger officers."

"But you're sure none of the general officers jumped in on the bitching or at least encouraged it?"

"Not as far as I heard. The closest any big brass came to what I'd call encouragement was when one said, 'If you feel that strongly, why don't you go talk to him directly?' 'Him' being Prada."

"Who said that?"

"The air marshal."

"Sounds a bit out of the usual chain of command, wouldn't you say? An air marshal telling lower-ranking officers to take their gripes directly to the Prime Minister's right-hand man?"

Yianni yawned. "It came after a long, droning diatribe by one officer in particular. To me it seemed Air Marshal said what he did more out of frustration with the officer's yammering than anything else."

"Who was the complainer?"

"A Colonel Retsos."

"A colonel? Well, that certainly raises warm memories."

Say the word "colonel" and Greece's junta dictatorship years immediately popped into the minds of those who lived though them.

"I told the Prime Minister there's been a lot of bitching but no mention of any use of force. Is that still true?"

Yianni nodded.

"Good."

Yianni took a bite of the pastry, and a sip of coffee. "So, let me get this straight. If you're right about the Prime Minister not authorizing Prada's little speech last night, aren't we back to square one as far as figuring out how any of this makes sense?"

"You could say that, but I have an idea."

"Should I be afraid?"

"Not yet, but don't worry, there's still time. There just might be a party I want Petro to crash later."

"Sounds like you're about to make his day."

Andreas reached for the *tsipouro*. "Let's drink to Petro and good luck."

Yianni slid two empty coffee cups toward Andreas. "How about good luck for us all?"

"Let me see if I understand you correctly," Petro told Andreas. "You want me to find out where Colonel Retsos plans on having dinner tonight, go there, make friends with him, and learn all that I can about what he plans on doing to get our Prime Minister to change his mind on our nation's military policy?"

"Yep, that about sums it up," said Andreas.

Petro pulled the phone away from his ear, stared at it, and shook his head.

"Petro, are you there?"

"Yeah," he said bringing the phone back to his ear. "I'm just wondering how the hell I'm supposed to do any of that, let alone all of it in one night."

"It's not as difficult as it sounds. I doubt the colonel and his buddies will stay cooped up in the hotel, so just listen to where they plan on going."

"That'll be the easy part. How am I supposed to make friends with the guy? For sure he'll recognize me from the restaurant, and I doubt some hotshot colonel will be interested in making friends with his busboy from the night before."

"Don't be so negative. See, you've already hit upon common ground for striking up a conversation. Just let your natural charm carry you from there."

Petro closed his eyes. "Why do I sense Yianni is in the background hooting and hollering while you're telling me all this?"

Andreas laughed. "What can I say, that's Yianni. But we both have faith in you to pull this off."

Petro heard Yianni shout in the background, "All you'll need is a little luck. We're rooting for you."

"Sounds to me like you're drinking for me too."

"Pardon?" said Andreas.

"Not you, Chief, I'm talking about my cheering section in the background."

"He means well," said Andreas.

"So, what precisely are you hoping for me to get from this colonel?"

"I want to know whether he plans on hooking up with Prada and who, if anyone, is encouraging or assisting him to do that."

"Anything else?"

"If the subject comes up, what he plans on doing if he can't get the Prime Minister to change his mind."

"I can't imagine him telling those things to a complete stranger."

"Just go in confident and play it by ear. No telling what you might learn."

"Do you want me to wear a wire?" Petro glanced at Dimos.

"No need to risk them finding out they're under surveillance," said Andreas. "We have days of them talking the subject to death. Just find out what you can about any plans for getting to Prada."

"I'll try. No promises."

"None expected. Just try your best. Bye."

"*Good luck*," shouted Yianni.

Petro shut the phone in one hand and smacked his forehead three times with his other.

"Sounds like you have a busy night ahead of you," said Dimos. 'You heard?"

"Of course I heard, I'm a professional eavesdropper, with the equipment to prove it. Besides, I'm standing right here and your phone volume's too loud."

"How am I ever going to get close to that guy? He'll shoo me away like a cockroach."

"You mean like a cat. A cockroach he'd probably step on."

Petro raised his hands. "Okay, a cat. It's still the same problem."

"You need a distraction, something that will make him want to hang out with you."

"Like what?"

"Sappho."

"What are you talking about? She's not that kind of girl."

"*Malaka*, I'm not saying set him up with her, I'm saying that she's fun and everyone on this island knows her. All you have to do is show up with her, and before you know it she'll be in conversation with them. It's the way she is. You'll just have to take it from there."

"She's a bit of an unguided missile on the conversation front."

"As long as you don't tell her what you're up to, who cares how outrageous she gets? It will only charm the colonel and his buddies more. Guys like hanging out with funny, fast-talking women. She'll be the hit of the night."

Petro shook his head. "I don't know—"

"Let me stop you right there. What you don't know is whether you want to get her involved in this. That I can understand. But don't say it's because it wouldn't work. It will work, or at least has a better chance of working than you showing up solo."

Petro sighed. "Maybe Retsos will decide to stay in tonight and this whole scheme will just fade away."

Dimos held up a piece of paper. "Sorry to break the news to you, but while you were on the phone with the chief, Colonel Retsos made reservations for twelve at twenty-two-hundred hours at a restaurant called Alexi's on the main road to the airport in the town before Mesaria. It ain't romantic, but it makes you feel right at home. The perfect place for making new friends."

Petro glared at the piece of paper before snatching it out of Dimos' hand.

"Enjoy your evening."

Chapter Fifteen

Petro and Sappho sat at a table close by the kitchen. There were only a half-dozen tables in the place and they wouldn't have had a table at all if the owner's son hadn't offered them the one he sat at to serenade customers with his *bouzouki* playing. He said that was the least he could do for his grade school sweetheart and promptly hugged and kissed Sappho hello far more vigorously than one would expect in casually greeting an old friend.

Sappho shrugged off his enthusiasm with a comment about how she hoped he played the *bouzouki* with a more sophisticated touch than the one he'd just applied to her backside. He laughed and walked away, leaving Sappho and Petro to their table.

"Quite a fan you have there."

"He's stoned all the time," said Sappho. "It's the curse of our island. Drugs. They're everywhere."

"At least he gave us the table."

"His mother would have killed him if he hadn't. We're in the same business. You take care of each other."

"Was he really your boyfriend?"

"Ah, you're jealous."

"Just curious."

"I let him feel me up once in eighth grade. The poor guy's never forgotten it. Probably the last female breast he ever touched. Other than on a chicken."

"Too much information."

"You asked. But while we're on the subject of information, why did you pick this place?"

"Why not?"

"It's just not known to many tourists."

"One of my buddies that you met the other night suggested we come here."

"I guess he didn't want to expose you to a romantic setting."

Petro smiled. "Any place with you is candlelight and roses."

"I see you're still reading that what-to-say-to-a-woman book."

"I'm just happy you agreed to come on such short notice."

Sappho reached across the table and squeezed his hand. "Why wouldn't I? Our restaurant isn't busy tonight and I like spending time with you."

Petro sat quietly.

"Did I say something wrong?"

"No, I'm just waiting for the punch line."

"Tonight I decided to be sincere."

"Not sure I can handle it."

"Don't worry, it's like water skiing. Just relax and let the boat pull you up." She squeezed his hand again.

"Hi, Sappho," said the waiter.

"Hi, Giorgio. How are things going?"

"Terrific. I've got a job. That's enough to make any Greek feel terrific these days."

"I hear you."

"What can I get you guys? By the way, if you're in a hurry you might want to put in your order right away. We've got a party coming in any minute that will take over the rest of the tables, and they'll likely be pressing us hard for attention all night. Military types."

"Tell me about it." Sappho looked at Petro. "We had to deal with that sort all last night."

"Yeah," said Petro. "At least they're big tippers."

"So, should I put in your order?"

Petro looked at Sappho. "I'm not in a hurry, are you?"

She smiled at Petro. "Not me. I have all night."

"Okay, guys, I get it. I'll bring you the wine and some *meze* and just let me know when you need me for anything else."

"Thanks, Giorgio," said Sappho.

The waiter patted Sappho on the back, "Any time, darling," and headed off to the kitchen.

"Everybody seems to like you," said Petro.

"Are you surprised?"

"Totally. I thought it was only me who felt that way."

"*Stop* already. You're killing me with all this."

"Don't worry, I'm just booking credits for when you'll want to smack me."

"You mean there are exciting times to come?"

Petro smiled. "For sure."

Sappho nodded toward the door. "Like right now, for instance. You'll never guess who's coming through the front door."

Petro turned his head in the direction of Sappho's stare. "My God, we're reliving last night. It's the same crew."

"I knew this island was getting too small."

"Oh, well, don't worry, we'll just ignore them."

Sappho smiled and leaned forward close enough to almost kiss him. "Yes, it's just the two of us in the room, and no one else."

"*Sappho*! You're here. What a surprise," said one voice.

Come, you've got to join us," said another.

Sappho dropped her head toward the table. "I can't believe this."

"As our guest," said a third.

"And bring your father's godson with you."

The officers pushed four tables together, seated Sappho in the middle directly across from Colonel Retsos, and banished Petro to a far end.

Petro couldn't help but admire her. He knew she didn't want to be dragged into the middle of a stag party, but yet there she was, the centerpiece of an otherwise all-male night on the town. She knew just what to say. Who to encourage, who to discourage. Even though this wasn't her family's place, they were her family's customers, and by showing them the attention they craved, she was respecting her family's business.

Petro's thoughts had drifted toward a feeling of pride at how masterfully she handled herself, until shame crept in for his part in tricking her into playing that role. *But I honestly did want to be with her*, he thought. And what he'd said to her he'd meant, even though the words also served the purpose of his job. He wondered if that made what he'd said any less sincere. He hoped not.

"Hey, godson, get with it, will you? You're the damp rag at this party."

Petro raised his glass to the clearly drunk major calling him out from the other end of the table. "*Stin yia mas.*"

"*Yamas,*" said the rest of the table raising their glasses and toasting to everyone's health.

"Hey, Major, go easy on him," said Sappho. "I'll need him in one piece for later on. He's more than my father's godson—he's my boyfriend."

That brought on a host of shouts and hoots from around the table and what Petro thought for sure had to be a broad blush across his face.

An Air Force wing commander sitting next to Sappho jumped up and said, "Godson, sit here. I don't want to separate you two hard-working kids on your night out."

The drunken major staggered to his feet and said, "I'll take your seat if you don't want it. I'm willing to risk breaking up the two lovebirds." But before he could move, officers on either side of him pulled him back down onto his chair.

The wing commander waved to Petro, "Get over here, son, that's an order."

"Thank you, sir," said Petro.

"Pussy," shouted the drunken major waving his glass of whisky in the general direction of Petro.

"Cool it, Major," said Colonel Retsos.

The drunken major stared in the general direction of the colonel but said nothing, instead taking a swig from his glass.

"Sorry about that," said the colonel as Petro sat across from him. "He's really not a bad guy, just under a lot of pressure at the moment."

"I bet," said Petro with a smile.

The colonel extended his hand across the table. "The name's Retsos."

Petro shook his hand. "A pleasure to meet you, sir."

"Again, I apologize for his behavior."

"No reason to, Colonel. I get it. He's just blowing off steam. The Mediterranean is one big tinderbox filled with crazies running around lighting matches, and Greece sits on the edge of it all looking to you guys to keep us from going up in flames."

"Well said."

Petro smiled. "Feel free to use it. I've a lot of career military buddies, and you guys get nothing but blame while you should be catching only praise. Every significant problem Greece faces, from FYROM, to the masses of immigrants streaming in through Turkey, puts you on the front lines."

The Colonel smiled. "You're starting to sound like a PR flack for the Defense Ministry."

Petro shook his head. "Could be worse, I guess. You could have called me a politician."

The colonel laughed. "Forgive me, please."

Petro lifted his glass and held it up to the colonel. "Forgiven."

They clinked glasses and launched off through many glasses of wine, accompanied by grilled eggplant, tomato *keftedhes*, *fava*, local cheeses, and a host of other Santorini appetizer specialities, into focused conversation over sports, fishing, the world of the military, and how lucky Petro was to have Sappho in his life. Though busy entertaining the rest of the table, at the mention of that final subject, Sappho jumped in on their conversation with a one-liner that let both men know she hadn't missed a word of what they'd been saying.

"I think we'd better pick a less dangerous topic, Colonel," said Petro, reaching over to pat the back of Sappho's hand.

She turned her hand over, took hold of Petro's, gave a quick squeeze, and let go.

"I've been so busy talking about myself, I haven't given you a chance to tell me anything about your life," said the colonel. He waved at Petro and Sappho. "Other than the obvious, of course."

'What would you like to know?"

"Well, I don't know…how about what you do for a living?"

"I'm trying to get into the hotel business. As I see it, it's about the only career in Greece that looks to have a future."

"Good thinking. Just be sure you find the right location. Like here on Santorini, for instance."

Petro nodded. "Yes, but it's tough breaking in on this island without the proper backing."

"For sure. You need the right backing for everything in life."

"Even in the military?"

"*Especially* in the military. If you don't have connections, you're fucked." He glanced at Sappho, who didn't appear to be listening. "Sorry about that," he said to Petro.

"No problem," said Sappho, without looking at either of them.

Petro shook his head and the colonel laughed.

"She's amazing," said the colonel.

"For sure. She doesn't miss a trick."

"I bet she could introduce you to backers."

Petro leaned toward Sappho's ear and said loudly, "Won't ever happen. She wants to keep me working in the restaurant so I'm never out of her sight."

The colonel laughed again. "Well then, maybe I can borrow her for an introduction…."

"To whom?"

The colonel took a sip of wine. "That civilian who came to dinner last night."

Petro hoped his face remained steady. "Which guy was that? You all wore civilian clothes."

"The one who arrived late and left early."

"I don't know him."

"Maybe she does?" nodding toward Sappho.

"Let's ask her," said Petro.

"No, please don't." The colonel reached across the table to grab Petro's forearm. "I don't want to raise the subject at the table. It's sort of a touchy one."

"Touchy?"

"We've been going back and forth all day over whether we should try to meet with him on a policy issue. Some said yes, some said no. The brass has left it up to us to decide because they don't want to hear any more arguing over it. In fact, that's why they passed on joining us for dinner. They didn't believe us when we promised not to talk about it tonight."

"I take it you're on the side that wants to talk to him?"

Colonel Retsos nodded.

"I don't understand why you need an introduction. Couldn't you just call him up and say you want to meet with him? After all, it's not as if you're complete strangers. You did have dinner together a night ago."

"You're probably right. But I still have to convince a few more of my colleagues that the brass meant it when they said we could speak to him if we wanted. Trouble is, none of the brass is willing to introduce us to him. So, despite what we were told, my colleagues are worried the brass will be pissed if we do manage to get in to see him."

"Sounds like some folks are afraid to rock the boat."

"Bingo," said the Colonel pointing at Petro with his wine glass. "At all levels. But what they don't understand is that meeting with this guy is our only chance of keeping the boat afloat."

Petro raised his glass. "To floating your boat."

"And to Greece."

They clinked glasses and drank.

"Amen," said Sappho reaching over and squeezing Petro's thigh. She leaned in and whispered in his ear, "I probably could arrange an introduction for him, if you'd like."

Petro whispered back. "Thanks, but it's better for you to stay out of this." He kissed her on the ear.

She turned her head and looked at him. "Well, that's a start."

"What is?"

"The kiss."

◇◇◇

The colonel and Petro talked straight though the main course of lamb *kleftiko*—lamb and potatoes cooked in waxed paper—and *paidaikia* (lamb chops), but neither said a further word about the disagreement among the troops over approaching Prada.

Petro saw no purpose in pushing the subject. He had his answers for Andreas: Colonel Retsos had no plan for hooking up with Prada and no one was encouraging or assisting him to make it happen. *No one, except perhaps Petro, with his unintentional suggestion that he call Prada directly.*

As for Andreas' desire that he fish for what Retsos might do if he couldn't get Prada to change his mind, Petro saw no non-suspicious way of raising the subject. But he did have a strong instinct on the point. He didn't see the colonel as the *coup d'état* type. He came across as a good soldier committed to the separate roles of civilian and military leadership, and to working within that framework. He also struck Petro as not the sharpest blade in the military's drawer, with traits more likely subject to exploitation by one possessing ulterior motives than to harboring any such motives of his own.

It was after two in the morning when the last wave of military left the taverna offering a farewell nod to Petro and an effusive, hugging session of goodbyes to Sappho.

Sappho dropped into a chair next to Petro and said to the waiter clearing the tables, "I think I deserve part of your tip."

"You earned it," he said without looking up from the plates. "Maybe you should consider going someplace where you won't bump into your customers on your night off." He looked at her. "Do you act like this every night?"

Petro answered for her. "Every moment of every night."

Pointing at Petro she said, "I didn't pick the place, he did." She leaned toward Petro and whispered, "Besides, you really can't say that until you've spent every moment of a night with me."

"Promises, promises."

Sappho jerked her hand in the air. "Check, please.'"

"Are you kidding?" said the waiter. "Your friends not only paid the check but tipped me three times what I expected. You're welcome to come back any time you want, Sappho, and if the boss won't comp your meal, I'll pay for it out of my own pocket."

"I'll keep your offer in mind," she said, pulling Petro out of his chair toward the door, "but right now I have another one to deal with."

"Thanks and good night," said Petro to the waiter.

As they walked out the front door, Sappho said, "Enough with being nice to everyone else. It's time to start paying attention to me."

"What are you talking about?" he said as they headed toward his motorcycle.

"I thought you and that colonel were going to elope."

Petro smiled. "He did give me his card."

"Stop making me jealous."

Sappho stopped and turned to face him head-on. "One question."

"Sure."

"What was the real reason you asked me to dinner in this place?"

He hoped there wasn't enough light to make out the color change he felt rush across his face.

"I told you, my friend recommended it."

"Yeah, yeah, I heard all that. But I also heard the two of you going at it. It sure seemed to me as if the colonel was the only one in the room you had any interest in talking to. It was as if I wasn't there."

"Uh, let's be real here. Once you get into your restaurateur mode, it's bye-bye to anyone having a one-on-one conversation with you. You're off entertaining the entire room and nothing else matters."

She reached up and clutched the front of his jacket. "Are you suggesting we find a room for just the two of us?"

Petro smiled. "If you can find one, that works for me."

She let go of his jacket and waggled a beckoning finger at him. "Follow me."

For no reason in particular, Petro thought Sappho lived with her parents. She'd never said she did, but he assumed from how closely they worked together she'd simply moved in with them after her breakup with her husband. Another wrong assumption he'd made about her. And one that made it more likely this evening would end up in her bed.

Though virtually alone on the road, with Sappho mounted snugly behind him on his bike, her arms squeezed tightly around him, and her lips pressed hard against his ear whispering directions, it took far more concentration than he'd like in his too-much-to-drink condition to keep them smoothly on the road. The process became even more difficult when Sappho's whispers turned to nibbles at his ear. Another reason for wearing a helmet, but that wouldn't have helped him once her hands turned to gliding along the insides of his thighs.

She lived southwest of Exo Gonia at the heart of the island's wine production country in the relatively out-of-the-way village of Megalochori. Her room was on the top floor of a nineteenth-century neoclassical mansion, a popular style in Greece back then among the rich, but one that hadn't really taken root on Santorini. Historically, whether built in or out of town, Santorini houses came in three basic forms: those dug out of the volcanic earth and lived in as caves, those built partially dug out and partially built in the normal way, and those built completely above ground, virtually all designed with vaulted roofs of one form or another. As the island's residents became more affluent, the mansions that evolved from those forms fell more under the Italian influence of the Renaissance than any other style. According to Sappho, architectural considerations had played no part in her choice of where to live. She loved her place for its southern view toward the island's fabled black sand beaches.

It being the middle of the night, Petro took her at her word about the view. He also believed her when she said the neighbor below was deaf.

He parked in the shadows close by the front door, turned off the motor, and waited for Sappho to slide off behind him. But she didn't move. Instead her hands moved higher up on his thighs and stopped just below his belt. He pulled her hands away and swung himself off the bike.

"Inside," he said, pointing at the front door.

She didn't say a word, just slid off the bike, walked to the door, and opened it with a key. He stepped in behind her and closed the door. She spun around to face him. Neither reached to turn on a light. They had no reason to. LEDs clustered by a nearby giant TV threw off a faint green, blue, and orange glow sufficient to make out all the shapes they needed to see.

He held her in his arms and kissed her. She pressed back hard and bit at his lower lip before probing for his tongue with hers. His hands ran up and down her back, coming to rest tightly and gripping the well-formed ass he'd watched so many times in the past forty-eight hours. They paused only long enough to wrestle their coats off onto the floor.

She raised her arms for him to pull off her blouse, and then undid her bra before undoing his pants and yanking everything down around his ankles. She ripped off his shirt as he kicked off his shoes and stepped out of his pants. Naked, he reached out for her, but she stepped back a pace to drop her skirt and panties.

Neither moved, each looking at the other's body. She stood only slightly shorter than he, a broad, sturdily built woman, with all parts in distinct proportion to the whole.

"I have more of a belly than you."

He stepped forward and touched her belly. "I like it."

She ran her hands along his chest. "I like that you like it."

He pressed his chest against hers.

Neither moved for a moment. Petro reached down with one hand and touched the small triangle of dark brown hair between her legs.

She shut her eyes as he stroked his way through to her most sensitive spot.

Sappho moaned, and pulled his hand away. "This way." She led him off to a bedroom at the rear of the house.

She pulled back the covers and pushed him down onto the bed. Before he could move she'd dropped her head to below his waist and kept it there until he forced himself to roll away from her mouth. He pressed her onto her back, holding her there with his hands firmly on her belly and his head buried farther down. She struggled to resist, but not with much conviction, and as her moaning and his movements achieved crescendo, he wondered just how deaf her neighbor might be.

He kept gently moving as he had until he felt her tugging at him to stop.

He slid up next to her and they kissed.

"It's your turn." She squeezed at what pressed hard against her side.

He kissed her again. "I don't know how to ask you this, but do you have a condom?"

"It's a little late for that don't you think?"

"Humor me."

She rolled over, opened a drawer in the nightstand and handed him an unopened box of condoms. "And before you ask, I bought them yesterday after you asked me out. Just in case."

"I'm flattered. They're magnum size."

"A girl can hope."

Petro laughed. "Let's try to stay serious for just a bit longer," as he rolled the condom snugly on.

"God, I certainly hope so."

And they did. And they did. And they did.

When Petro awoke, Sappho lay on her side staring at him.

"I don't want you to leave."

He rolled over and kissed her. "Me either."

"Stop saying all the right things."

"Okay, but at least tell me if I did the right things."

She reached under the sheet and stroked below his bare belly. "For sure."

Petro pressed against her and ran the fingertips of his right hand over the shape of her breasts pushing up beneath the sheet.

"Are we going for a second encore?" she shifted slightly closer to him.

"Third. But only if you'd like."

"I can't believe you're giving me the choice. Do horny men actually do that? Or are you just not for real?"

"At the moment I'm definitely feeling a lot more like the former."

Sappho sat up in bed, allowing the sheet to fall away. "The sun's up."

"I can tell from the fact I can see you." He reached across and lightly touched one of her breasts. "I love feeling you pressed bare up against my chest."

"Sweet talker." She pulled the sheet up to her neck. "I still don't have an answer to my question from last night."

"And what question is that?"

"What was the real reason you took me to dinner there?"

"Are we going over that again?"

"Only because I don't want to feel used."

Petro's face hardened and he sat up in bed, not looking at her. "Why do you say that?"

"Don't get angry. I'm just worried about being hurt. Is that unfair?"

Petro sighed. "No, it's not unfair, but what makes you think I'm using you?"

"Call it women's intuition, but when I offered to help make an introduction for that colonel, you said, 'It's better for you to stay out of this.' You made it sound as if you knew more about what the colonel had in mind than he'd told you. And *that* made me think it wasn't a coincidence you met up with him there."

Damn, she's smart. Petro kept his eyes from meeting hers. "I can see where you might have thought that, but you misunderstood what I meant."

Sappho reached up with both hands and turned Petro's face toward hers. "So, what did you mean?"

He focused on her eyes. Her dark brown eyes. "The part of the conversation where the colonel said he needed an introduction to that guy from the other night grew out of his telling me I should ask you to introduce me to potential backers. I was afraid that if the two of you got into talking about making an introduction for him, he'd suggest you do the same for me. I didn't want you thinking I needed or wanted your help with any of my business."

"But why wouldn't you ask me? You must know I'd be glad to help."

"Of course I do, and that's just the point. I didn't want you thinking the very thing that's obsessing you now." He paused. "That I might be using you."

Now Sappho sighed. "I guess I really screwed that up."

"Not at all. But that's my reason. I never want you to think I'm using you." *And that's the God's honest truth.*

"Well, permit me to add a qualification to that concern on your part."

"Being?"

"When it comes to this, feel free to use away," and she ripped the sheet away from their naked bodies.

Chapter Sixteen

Petro wasn't particularly religious, but he did wonder whether his early morning ride and hike up the hill to Dimos and Francesco formed some sort of penance for his evening with Sappho. At practically the moment he'd said goodbye, a harsh drenching rain blew in along a raw north wind, bringing rivulets to the roads and chills to the bones of anyone caught in the downpour. To make matters worse, the bike held no rain gear in its tiny storage compartment, leaving Petro to borrow a rain parka and hood from Sappho—in bright lavender.

Super Grape, as Sappho called him while she zipped him into her parka, decided to take the westerly high ground route into Fira. He figured that to be the safer, less likely flooded road, and taking care on a motorcycle was a serious concern in weather like this. The rain hadn't yet washed away the oil buildup left by exhausts on dry pavements, but had dampened the residue sufficiently to treacherously slick up the roadways. The water had also turned painted lines into ice rinks, metal plates into banana peels, and crater-size pits into camouflaged puddles. Plus, since Petro wore no helmet and had no visor to protect him from the pelting rain, the faster he drove the more painful the beating he took to his face. At least there wasn't any lightning.

Despite his caution, as he headed up onto the caldera, Petro couldn't help but glance out across the lagoon. Even with its brilliant azure blue and sapphire green waters now as gunmetal gray as the sky, the view still took his breath away.

The rain now came in fits and starts, at its fiercest masking everything beyond the near edge of the caldera so completely that Santorini's four other archipelago islands simply disappeared. No Thirasia, Aspronisi, Palea Kameni, or Nea Kameni. Only the bit of road in front of Petro's bike remained in sight. A chill ran down Petro's back. He tried to shake it off, not sure if the cause was rain soaking through to his skin, or thoughts of how much of this magnificent island and its resilient people had so often vanished on the random brutal whim of Mother Nature.

It took him nearly twice as long to cover the same ground he'd covered in dry weather, and still his face felt as if it had served as target practice for a swarm of bees. He parked where he always did, and jogged up the path to the church while trying to shake the bone-soaking chill he knew this time came from the rain.

He reached the door and tried the handle. Locked.

He banged on the door. "Open up, it's Petro."

"Who?"

"Stop screwing with me, Francesco, I'm soaked and freezing. Open up."

"The only Petro we know is serving as a male concubine to a Santorini chieftess who's demanded six Spartan warrior slaves in exchange for his safe return from her harem."

"On second thought, you better not open up. Because I might just kick your ass off the top of this volcano if you do."

"Okay, now I know it's you."

The lock clicked and the door opened. "Damn, Petro, you really do look like part of a harem. Purple just isn't your color."

"Screw you, Francesco. And it's lavender."

"Excuse me," said Francesco tossing him a towel. "Truth is you better get out of those wet clothes fast. This weather's not getting any better."

"That's the good news," yelled Dimos from the other side of the iconostasis. "The boys down at the hotel are calling it quits early. Everyone wants to get out of here as soon as they can."

"Is that all you got since I left?" said Petro taking off the parka.

"Yep," said Dimos peeking out from behind the iconostasis. "Unless you want to count endless hours listening to generals, air marshals, and admirals trying to out-*macho* each other with war stories. Trust me, your night was far more interesting."

"For sure on that score," said Francesco taking the parka from Petro and waving it at Dimos.

"It's lavender," said Dimos.

"Thank you," said Petro flashing an open palm at Francesco. "So, any word from the chief?"

Dimos gestured no. "He said he got your SMS on what you learned from Colonel Retsos, and to say you made the right decision not to push things further with him."

"Anything else?"

"Let me read it to you. I want to get this right." Dimos tinkered with his cellphone. "He wrote, 'Tell him I hope he enjoys the rest of his evening.'"

Francesco burst out laughing. "Don't forget to file a full report."

"She happens to be a very nice girl." Petro's voice had lost its lightness.

Francesco held up his hands, "No argument there. Dimos and I are just teasing you. All we've had to look forward to since you took off last night is razzing you when you got back."

Petro drew in and let out a breath. "I get it. I'm just tired, wet and, to be honest, feeling a bit down at how I've been lying to that girl. How am I ever going to tell her the truth?"

Francesco glanced at Dimos.

Dimos stepped into the room and pointed at Petro's bag. "The first thing you do is get out of those clothes, the second is take a nap. That way you'll only have the third point to worry about, and if there is something real between the two of you, you'll find the right way to tell her at the right time."

Francesco stared at Dimos. "Wow, that was really profound."

"Go to hell," said Dimos.

Petro smiled, picked up his bag, took out dry clothes, and changed.

No one bothered to mention the scratches on his back.

◇◇◇

Andreas hadn't planned on spending his Sunday morning at home. He'd promised his son they'd spend the day together exploring Athens at Christmastime while Lila shopped. Serious Christmas decorations first came to Greece after World War II, but once they caught on, the fashion took off with a vengeance in the traditional big way of Greek celebration everywhere.

He'd wanted to start their day off amid the brightly decorated Christmas Village displays occupying Syntagma Square, a surefire wondrous sight for any five-year-old. For the rest of the year Syntagma might be the focal point of mass demonstrations directed at the doings within the abutting Parliament building, but during the Christmas season—from the last week of November through the Feast of Theophany on January sixth—Parliament Square found itself transformed into a festive holiday wonderland, the tree annually erected in the midst of it all claimed to be the tallest in Europe, albeit artificial.

Sadly, not even Christmas stood immune to Greece's political realities. In 2008 demonstrators burned the Christmas tree to the ground. Although ensuing austerity had surely taken its toll, the annual Christmas tree lighting ceremony remained a popular draw for crowds eager to hear orchestras, bands, choirs, and popular singing idols performing traditional holiday favorites in many different languages.

Andreas swore he would not break his promise to his son, but nor would he risk talking coup possibilities on a mobile phone in the middle of a crowd of would-be eavesdroppers in Syntagma. That's why he sat alone in his kitchen, drumming his fingers, impatiently waiting to hear from his team on Santorini.

For over an hour he'd been calling Santorini every twenty minutes for an update. He knew he was getting on their nerves. He also knew there wasn't a thing any of them could do to prod their surveillance subjects into adding something of value to the investigation. Still, pestering made him feel somewhat better when he had to confront the little boy with the ever-sadder expression peeking into the kitchen to ask when they would leave.

Andreas stared at the clock on the wall. Almost one in the afternoon. Time to say bye-bye to their shot at monitoring the private thoughts of Greece's most likely pool of coup candidates. Once they'd left the hotel, Andreas doubted there'd be another opportunity. Career military officers at their level took great care to avoid precisely that sort of spying upon them.

"When can we go, Daddy?"

Andreas' heart sank. "I'm hoping soon, son."

"You said that the last time."

"I know."

"And the time before that."

Andreas bit his lip. "I'm trying my best."

As Tassaki drooped his head and walked away, Andreas' phone rang.

"Talk to me."

"Chief, it's Petro. You're on the speakerphone. We picked this sound bite up a couple of minutes ago. Colonel Retsos stopped by an Air Force group captain's room to say goodbye and a Navy captain joined them."

"That's it? What about the generals, admirals, and air marshals?"

"They all checked out without mentioning a word having to do with Prada."

"Or anything else of interest," said Dimos.

"Okay," said Petro. "The first voice is the Navy captain, the second is Colonel Retsos."

Hey, guys, it's late, we've got to get moving if we want to get off the island today. Everyone but us has checked out.

I stopped by to speak to Philippos about what you and I talked about last night on the drive back from the restaurant. I wanted to catch him before he gets back into the wild blue yonder and loses touch with the rest of us.

No such luck this week, fellows. I'll be in Athens at the Pentagon for meetings. We'll be neighbors.

Terrific, because our friend Retsos here would like your support in a little ASAP project he has in mind.

What sort of project?

I can speak for myself, thank you. It's a plan for addressing this insane idea the Prime Minister has for undermining our national defense.

Haven't we beaten that horse to death? Our brass won't touch it.

But they said we could if we wanted. I'm in for the Navy, Retsos is in for the Army. We need you for the Air Force.

In for what?

Tomorrow I'm aiming to set up an appointment with our surprise dinner guest from the other night.

Why?

To get him to convince the Prime Minister to change his mind.

Am I sensing you still haven't sobered up from last night?

Stop busting my balls, Philippos. You know I'm right. We're a country of only eleven million, with historic enemies many times our size at our borders. We can't afford to appear weak to them. Have you forgotten what's happened to us going back thousands of years whenever we let down our guard?

You sound like the Israelis.

For good reason. They're right.

I just don't see that guy helping us. He's a politician and politicians don't go head-to-head with their benefactors just because it's the right thing to do. Besides, he's a smart guy and if he agrees with you, don't you think he's already made your arguments to the Prime Minister and lost?

You could be right. But the Prime Minister is so misguided and wrong on this, we owe it to our countrymen to do what we can to stop it.

Inspirational words. But, as I said, what politician is going to listen?

Let me repeat what I said just in case you missed it. We have the support of our brass. There's no way I'd be involved in this meeting effort if my admiral hadn't said it was okay for us to try.

And don't forget that the person most upset at what we heard from him that night was your air marshal.

Silence.

If we get nowhere with this, your air marshal won't likely care that you didn't join in, but if we succeed, how do you think he's going to react when he learns you ducked out on the opportunity of involving his branch in the battle that brought the Prime Minister around to changing his mind on the future of our nation's military?

Retsos, sometimes you can be a real pain in the ass.

Should I take that as a yes?

A loud sigh.

Just tell me when and where.

Terrific.

Gentlemen, now that we have the Air Force on board, may I suggest we get the hell off this island? The weather's only getting worse.

"Okay, Chief, that's it," said Dimos.

Andreas fluttered his lips.

"Chief?"

"Just thinking, give me a minute."

"Too bad we didn't have the equipment we need to pick up what the two of them talked about on their ride back to the hotel last night," said Dimos.

"Hey, that reminds me," said Francesco. "We still need to get into the hotel and pull out our equipment."

"Tassos' nephew Christos will be back first thing tomorrow morning. It will be on a follow-up inspection, and we'll pull it out then," said Petro.

"That hotel guy's going to be pissed," said Dimos.

"Nah," said Petro. "He'll be in heaven, because he'll be told the hotel's getting a boosted rating, as long as the follow-up inspection confirms the original findings."

"Only one problem with that, guys," said Francesco. "No boats or planes will be coming here tomorrow. Forget about Christos getting to Santorini in this weather. And if we don't get off the island now, we'll be stuck here for days waiting for him."

"He's right," said Dimos. "Can't we yank the equipment out now? All the military guys are gone."

"There's no way to pull that off without Tassos' nephew setting up the cover story," said Petro. "And even if we could somehow get him here today, can you imagine the suspicions it will raise having three public servants show up in this lousy weather on a Sunday and *not* be looking for a payoff?"

"My wife's going to kill me," said Francesco.

Petro cleared his throat. "If it's okay with the chief, I'll take Francesco's place and work with Dimos, assuming it doesn't require any special skills."

Francesco stifled a strange-sounding cough. "Uh, no it doesn't." More coughing. "And I can teach you what you need to know in five minutes. A piece of cake." More coughing. "If it's okay with the chief."

"Are you feeling okay, Francesco?" said Andreas.

"Yes, just giddy at the thought of getting back to my wife."

"You're so full of shit your eyes are brown, but whatever's going on is fine with me as long as it's okay with Dimos."

"Okay by me, Chief."

"Now that we have that settled, Petro, what's your take on Retsos' intentions?" Andreas looked at a pad he'd been scribbling on during the recording. "He used the words, 'insane,' 'undermining our national defense,' 'misguided and wrong,' and 'do what we can to stop it,' in talking about the national policy of our Prime Minister."

"If you're asking whether I see it as *coup d'état* talk, I don't. He's just trying to convince a buddy to support him. They're all of similar rank, so he couldn't intimidate him, which left him to firing him up with words, by comparing the meeting with Prada to a 'battle.' It's how military types talk."

"And they know how to play on each other's ambitions," said Dimos. "To me the clincher came when he pointed out the potential downside to the Air Force guy's career, should his superior learn that his indecision cost his branch a share in the glory of a successful operation."

"Let's hope your read on the colonel is right," said Andreas, "because I sure as hell wouldn't want to wake up some morning to learn a coup had been growing right under our noses and we missed it."

"Maybe we could eavesdrop on the meeting with Prada," said Petro.

"Depends on where they meet," said Dimos. "But I doubt we'll be able to do it."

"Besides, he's too savvy a politician to say anything to them he wouldn't want repeated across the military," said Andreas.

"My guess is the three of them don't stand a chance of changing Prada's mind," said Petro.

"Or, rather, helping us figure out what's really on Prada's mind," said Andreas. "But you guys gave it your best shot and got us whatever info was out there."

"Does that mean it's okay for me to leave now?"

"Only if Petro is still firm on staying."

"Firm?" laughed Dimos.

"Fuck you," said Petro.

Dimos and Francesco laughed.

"You guys have been locked up together for way too long," said Andreas. He caught a glimpse of his son in the doorway and waved for him to come over. "As a matter of fact, so have I."

Tassaki's face lit up in a smile as his father hung up the phone.

"Christmastime, here we come!"

Andreas held Tassaki's hand as they crossed the street in front of their apartment building headed toward a break in the light-colored, low stone wall bordering the eastern edge of the National Gardens. Andreas thought a peaceful stroll to Syntagma along the Gardens' pastoral central serpentine paths had a better chance of resurrecting his holiday mood than a crowded march along the Gardens' northern border at busy Avenue Vasilisis Sofias.

Tassaki let go of his father's hand as soon as they entered the Gardens. Andreas let him run ahead knowing that his son came here practically every day with his mother or Marietta and likely knew this part of the Gardens better than he did. Andreas called out "left" or "right" when a path required a decision, and Tassaki promptly made the appropriate turn.

Tassaki skirted by a well-dressed older woman walking in their direction. She smiled as she approached Andreas. "A handsome young man you have there."

Andreas smiled back. "Thank you."

Had Andreas' mother heard the woman's compliment, she'd be doing her puh-puh-puh spitting routine to ward off the evil eye that so many Greeks believed accompanied such praise to their children. He could see his father now, shaking his head and telling her to stop acting like a superstitious, village peasant woman. Her response was always the same. "I won't because I am."

Andreas smiled again. He remembered his father and mother bringing him and his sister to Syntagma to see the Christmas Village. That was when he was about Tassaki's age or possibly a couple of years older. His mother never brought them there after their father died.

His father would have loved Tassaki. Family meant everything to him. It's why he took his own life, thinking he was protecting his family. How he could have thought leaving his children fatherless….Andreas shook his head and let the thought drift away. He'd chased that rabbit for much of his life but no longer felt the need. There was nothing he could do about the past, and for damn sure he didn't see martyrdom for himself as bettering his son's life.

Andreas first heard the shouting as they approached a grove of palm trees near the Gardens' western entrance closest to Parliament. Just beyond the palm trees, a broad rectangular garden space punctuated by a sundial on a pedestal, stood surrounded by a marble-paved square abutting the entrance.

No formal demonstrations had been announced for that afternoon in Syntagma, but with so many desperate people frustrated for so long, protestors of one persuasion or another could always be expected somewhere in the vicinity.

Andreas yelled for Tassaki to stop and stepped up his pace to catch up with him. Just as Andreas did, a thin swarthy man dressed in dark pants and a light blue jacket came limping into the square carrying someone in his arms and looking frantically back over his shoulder.

Andreas gripped Tassaki's arm and pulled him behind him.

"Dad, what—?"

"Shhh. Be quiet and just do as I say."

"But, Daddy—"

Tassaki's protest was drowned out by the shouts of five black-clad men wielding axe handles storming into the square behind the limping man. "Keep away from our Christmas, you fucking *mavro* Muslims."

One began beating his axe handle against the marble paving slabs in rhythm with the pace of their pursuit. The others joined in, beaters flushing a wild animal.

"Miserable cowardly sons of bitches," muttered Andreas.

"What?"

Andreas pointed. "Get behind that big palm tree and don't move until I come for you." He watched Tassaki run to the tree.

"Please, please, someone please help us."

Andreas turned to see the man limping as fast as he could straight for him. "Please help us. Please…my son." The terrified boy he held out in his arms looked to be about a year younger than Tassaki.

The axe handles' beat of *clack, clack, clack* against the marble grew louder. "We're coming for you, *mavros*."

Andreas knew what he faced. Get involved and risk himself and his son, or let the beatings go on and explain to his son why he did nothing to help. Not really a choice.

Andreas stepped forward to meet the limping man. "Get back to those palm trees."

"Get out of our way, asshole," said the pursuer closest to Andreas.

Andreas pulled his ID out from under his shirt and held it up. "Police. Now back away."

The man laughed, "I'm a cop too, so fuck off and get out of our way."

Andreas shook his finger at the man. "That's not going to happen."

The first man stopped about a meter in front of Andreas, an axe handle dangling by his right side. "No problem," and he whipped the handle up and around in an arc aimed at Andreas' head.

Andreas dove headfirst at his attacker, butting him hard in the face with his forehead as his hand latched on to the man's wrist and wrenched away the axe handle, followed by a nearly three-hundred-sixty-degree spin that ended with Andreas cracking the handle hard against the outside of the man's knee, dropping him to the ground screaming in pain.

A second man charged at Andreas wildly swinging another axe handle. Andreas used the one he'd taken from the first to block three predictable swings, execute a hard thrust of the handle butt to the center of the man's chest, and deliver a golf-pro worthy drive to his balls, dropping him screaming next to his buddy.

"Enough of this shit," said Andreas, pulling out his gun. "The next fucker who comes at me is dead." He pointed the gun at the man closest to him.

"Hey, I'm a cop, too. No reason to get like this."

"Then you know the fucking drill," said Andreas. "Drop your weapons and hit the ground, arms spread wide."

"Come on, we're just doing what the people want us to do but the politicians won't let us."

"I said, *drop*."

"Fine, we'll let you and your *mavro* boyfriend go."

"This time," added the man behind him.

"Permit me to put this to you more directly. Either you drop to the ground *now*, or I start putting bullets in your knees that will have you down there crying alongside your buddies." Andreas pointed his gun at the knee of the first man.

The man dropped his axe handle and followed it to the ground.

"Good, we're making progress." Andreas moved his aim to the knee of the man who'd chimed in. "What will it be, wiseass?"

The man fell to the ground without saying a word, and the last would-be attacker spread-eagled on the stone without waiting to be told.

"Good, now nobody moves until I tell you to." Andreas pulled out his phone and called for backup, identifying himself as head of special crimes, and that he was holding five assailants at gunpoint. With that introduction it took less than than five minutes for riot police stationed at Parliament to get there.

Andreas watched as the police handcuffed the five men on the ground. He told the squad leader, "I want copies of their IDs," nodding at the prisoners. "Spread the word I'm taking this prosecution very personally, and make damn sure none of your prisoners gets lost on the way back to lockup. Understand, Sergeant…" he looked at the sergeant's ID, "Apostolou?"

"Yes, sir."

Andreas patted him on the shoulder. "Good."

Andreas walked over to the man who'd taken the first swing at him. He crouched down. "I bet your knee hurts a lot."

"Fuck you, asshole."

"My, my, you Golden Dawn guys are all such talkers. But remember this the next time you think about joining your buddies in picking on some other defenseless soul. There just might be someone out there like me waiting to bust up your other knee." Andreas pressed hard against the man's injured knee as he pushed to his feet.

The man screamed.

Andreas turned and walked toward the grove of palm trees to find Tassaki. Andreas had no idea what he was going to say to his son. How could he possibly explain to a five-year-old what he'd just seen his father do?

Andreas hadn't looked toward the palm trees since he'd watched Tassaki race there to hide. Now, with the adrenaline fading, and thoughts of what could have happened taking over, all he wanted to do was find and hug his son. But he couldn't see him. He saw the man he'd saved sitting on the ground staring at the rear of the big palm tree where his son should be, but no one else.

Andreas burst into a run. "Where's my son?"

The man on the ground pointed at the tree.

As Andreas drew closer he saw a foot protruding from the back of the trunk. But it wasn't his son's foot.

Andreas heart skipped a beat. "Where is my son?" he shouted at the man.

Again the man pointed at the tree.

"Daddy, shh. You'll frighten Ibrahim."

Andreas stopped running just short of the tree. He walked around it and found his son sitting with his back up against the trunk, and his arm around the four-year-old boy.

"See, Ibrahim, I told you my daddy would protect us from those bad men. That's what my daddy does."

The other boy rested his head against Tassaki's shoulder and stared at Andreas.

Not sure what to say, Andreas simply smiled.

The boy looked at his father, who nodded and said, "Yes, we're safe, thanks to this man."

The boy smiled back at Andreas.

Andreas fought back tears.

"Sir," said the man as he stood up. "My son and I owe you our lives."

Andreas shook his head. "There's no need to say that."

"Yes there is. Especially these days. We live in fear."

Andreas wanted to change the subject. He already had more than enough to explain to his son, no need to get into the rampant racial tensions. "Where are you from?"

"Pakistan."

"You speak very good Greek. And obviously so does your son."

"He was born here. I have lived here since before the Olympics in 2004."

All at once, Andreas felt terribly ashamed. "I'm sorry for what happened."

"There is no reason for you to apologize. You stood up to those trying to harm us."

"But many of my countrymen do not."

"Yes, I know," said the man.

Andreas swallowed hard. "Are you okay? You were limping before."

"It is an old injury."

"I see."

"From another run-in with people of that sort."

"Do you need to see a doctor?"

The man smiled. "I am a doctor. But of Engineering. Or at least I was in Pakistan. Now I work nights in a hotel in Omonia."

Andreas stared at the ground, thinking about how rough an immigrant battleground that once elegant part of Athens had become.

The man shrugged. "At least it's a job."

Andreas nodded.

"Daddy, can we go see the tree now?"

Andreas had completely forgotten about Christmas. "I don't think your friend and his father are up for that right now."

"No, Daddy, Ibrahim wants to go. I was telling him stories about the *kallikantzaroi* and how we might find some in the Christmas Village."

"*Kallikantzaroi?*" said Ibrahim's father.

Andreas smiled. "They're kind of hard to explain but to the superstitious they're half-beast, half human, bad-spirited gremlins who slip into your house through a chimney during the twelve-day period from Christmas to Epiphany to wreak havoc and mischief in your home."

"Compared to what we've just been through that sounds like fun," said the father. "Would you like to see them, Ibrahim?"

Ibrahim nodded.

The father said softly to Andreas, "I think it's important to quickly put these sorts of traumatic experiences behind you. Otherwise you become afraid to live your life. And I don't want that for my son."

"You're a very brave man," said Andreas.

"I have to be, for him."

Neither man spoke for a moment.

"But it is your son who's made the difference in Ibrahim's life today. He sat with him the entire time you were fighting, keeping him from seeing any of it, reassuring him that you would keep us all safe."

Andreas was certain he was blushing, and at any moment would be crying.

"And he was right."

Andreas coughed. "Thank you, but we've got to hurry if we want to be able to spend time in Syntagma while it's still light out."

Tassaki and Ibrahim stood up and started walking toward the entrance.

Andreas and the other father hurried to catch up with their sons.

Andreas wondered how Lila would react to what happened. He felt he had no choice than to intervene, but as a mother, Lila might feel differently. Though he doubted it. For sure she'd be as proud as he was at how their son had comforted the frightened younger child, and likely even more relieved than Andreas that Tassaki hadn't seen his father fight.

"By the way," said the man, "I'm sure you've heard this before, but in addition to everything else, your son is a very handsome young man."

Andreas froze for an instant, recalling the woman they'd passed in the Gardens at what seemed an eternity ago. "Yes, thank you, I have heard that before." Andreas turned his head slightly away from the man and spit out under his breath, "Puh, puh, puh."

It couldn't hurt.

Chapter Seventeen

When Andreas entered his office the next morning he found Yianni sitting on his couch.

"Have you been booted out of your office?"

"No, Maggie told me to wait for you in here. Said she'll be back in a minute with coffee."

"So, what sort of plotting has the two of you lurking in my office first thing in the morning?"

"There's no plot," said Maggie, coming through the doorway with three mugs of coffee on a plastic tray. "We just wanted to tell you that we're ready to get to work on building a case against those goons who tried to take you out yesterday afternoon." She handed a mug to Andreas.

"So, you heard about my little walk in the park?"

"How could we not?" said Yianni. "You scared that sergeant shitless. He's spread the word to practically every cop in Athens that Chief Inspector Andreas Kaldis is taking a personal interest in prosecuting those five assholes."

"I'm glad he got the message."

"How bad was it?" said Maggie handing a mug to Yianni and sitting down next to him on the couch with a cup for herself.

Andreas shrugged. "It's as I told Lila, high anxiety until I got into it and realized just how inept those guys were. Then I took the first opportunity of ending it with words before one of them might have got lucky with his axe handle."

"Words?" said Yianni.

"And a nine millimeter."

"You told all that to Lila?" said Maggie.

"What choice did I have? Tassaki would have told her if I hadn't."

"And?"

"And nothing. She just nodded and hasn't said another word about it."

Maggie stared at him.

"Why are you staring at me?"

"Why are men so dumb?"

"I think she's about to tell us, Chief."

"You better believe I am. The poor woman is frightened to death. She doesn't know what to say. You have to talk to her about it ASAP."

"Doesn't this fall into the category of letting sleeping dogs lie?" said Andreas.

"Definitely *not,*" said Maggie in a raised voice. "Get her to let it out. She's too frightened to tell you just how frightened she really is. No matter how nonchalantly you told her your story, in Lila's mind both her husband and son were in mortal danger."

"Not to mention she's eight months pregnant," said Yianni.

Maggie swung her head around to look at Yianni. "I'm impressed that you actually do have some insight into women."

Yianni shrugged. "Thank you."

Andreas raised his hands. "Okay, okay, I get it. Enough already. I'll talk to Lila as soon as I have the chance."

"Now would be a good time," said Maggie.

"I'll call, I promise, but since you're both psyched up to get info on bad guys, let me tell you what's really been gnawing at me since my run-in with those five Golden Dawn *malakas.*" Andreas took a long slug of coffee before putting the mug down on his desk. "At least two of them were cops."

"It can't surprise you that cops are part of Golden Dawn?" said Yianni. "Hell, a lot of the ones I know voted those Nazi bastards into Parliament."

Andreas gestured no. "That's not my point. The two cops I tangled with were no more talented at hand-to-hand combat than your average street bad guy. Which is about the way most cops are. That got me to thinking about the two dirtbags who killed the Brigadier's daughter. Reminded me they're better marksmen than any cops we know, and likely better than all but the best of the military's top shooters."

Andreas looked at Yianni. "How many times have we watched the videos of those two killing the girl? Fifty, seventy-five?"

"At least."

"And every time we see them, we say the same thing. 'They're obviously doing this to put the blame on cops or military.' And why do we say that? Because they're highly trained and don't give a damn about being identified as such. What we haven't focused on is *whose* cops or military are they?"

"Whose?"

"Yes. I'm willing to bet there aren't that many current or former Greek military and police personnel capable of doing what those two did. Which brings me around to the task I have in mind for you two this morning." Andreas reached for his coffee. "We've been distracted from the basics for far too long, chasing after dry-hole conversations on Santorini. I want you to use every contact you have or can develop to get the names and descriptions of anyone under the age of forty-five capable of running the distance at the speed those two killers did and executing pinpoint handgun accuracy on a moving target. Once you have that info, eliminate the ones who don't fit the images on the video and let's see who's left."

"That sounds like a lot of possibilities," said Maggie.

"Could be, but I think not. I'm guessing such highly conditioned and talented marksmen are rare, and therefore relatively easily discoverable. If I'm right, using Greek personnel would be a dangerously risky proposition for whoever's running them. Which is why my instincts are telling me we're going to find that our shooters are foreign."

Andreas stretched out his arms. "But if I'm wrong, and there's a lot of names, at least we'll have a list of suspects to run down."

"And what do you want us to do about the axe handle-swingers from yesterday afternoon?" said Maggie.

"I think that sergeant's doing a pretty good job for now. As long as we have the names of the five bad guys, I'll make sure the prosecutor gives them every consideration they deserve."

"Lucky them," said Yianni, "winning the 'what happens if you cross Kaldis' lottery."

"Funny, I feel sort of like we just won the same lottery," said Maggie pushing up from the couch.

"Don't fret," said Yianni, "I'll take the military, you take the cops, and we'll be done in no time."

Maggie headed toward the door. "That's precisely my problem. I have no time."

Andreas smiled. "As the old adage goes, 'If you want something done, give it to a busy person.'"

As she went through the doorway Andreas heard Maggie say, "Well, here's another nugget to add to your adage list. 'If you want something typed or need coffee this morning, don't look for your secretary.'"

Yianni headed out the door right behind her. "I'm not even going to try to top that one, Chief."

Andreas shook his head. Then he reached for the phone to call his wife. Just as Maggie had told him he should do.

◇◇◇

"So where are you now?" Sappho asked.

"Working."

"That's what you told me last night when you said you couldn't see me."

"Okay, so I'm not creative with my excuses. But I'm honest."

"I'm beginning to wonder."

"Just don't frown. It will give you wrinkles."

"Don't worry, the cobwebs I'm developing waiting to see you will cover them."

Petro laughed.

"So when will I see you?"

"After the guy gets here from Athens and tells me what I have left to do, I should be done in a couple of hours. But no matter what, tonight for sure. I promise."

"What if he doesn't get here? The weather's horrible."

"He's on a boat headed this way, and if there's a break in the weather it'll dock. If not, I guess I'll just have to stay longer."

"I'll pray for a bigger storm."

"Me too."

"Hi, Darling, how are you feeling?"

"Fine." Lila's voice held a tentative tone.

"And Tassaki?"

"Fine."

"Has he said anything to you about yesterday?"

"No."

"Nothing?"

"Not to me."

"To anyone?"

Andreas heard his wife sigh. "I overheard him speaking with Marietta at breakfast."

Andreas waited for her to continue.

"She asked him what he thought about what happened yesterday."

Lila paused.

"He said it was scary at first, but the adults handled it and he made a new friend."

"That's terrific," said Andreas. "I don't know many adults who could sum up and accept such a frightening experience as simply and positively as he did."

"I know for sure I wish I could."

"Sometimes it's easier on those confronting a stressful situation than it is on those who can only imagine what their loved ones are going through."

"Is this Cop Family Counseling 101?"

"If not, it should be, because it's true. There's a reason so many cop families break up, and it's called worry."

"I wasn't worried for you, I was worried for Tassaki." Lila paused again. "And for our new baby."

"I was too. All that kept going through my mind from the moment I realized what was going down was *get home safe*. That thought is what kept me going. Kept me from hesitating."

"I know you did the right thing in protecting that man and his son, but that doesn't make me any more comfortable when I think of what might have happened."

"I understand completely, but we live in times where irrational acts can pop up anywhere, anytime. All we can do is stay alert, pray our time's not up when things go bump in the night, and keep living our lives as we want to live them. You might even say that, in the context of our world today, our household's lucky to have a cop in it."

"Nice try, Kaldis, but I'm still scared to death every time I think of those barbarian bigots with their clubs and you and Tassaki right in the middle of it all."

"That's how all bad guys want you to react. They win if you're scared. Yes, I take them seriously for the threats they present, but I also take my family seriously for the joy it brings to my life. If yesterday proves anything, it's that should the two ever cross paths, I'll do whatever it takes to eradicate the threat and protect the joy."

"I still get scared, Hero." Her voice sounded perkier.

"Understood. But may I suggest you accept a lesson from the teachings of Guru Tassaki who also admits to being scared on such occasions: *Have faith in the adults to handle it.* That's what I'm here for, and doing the best that I can while I'm at it."

Lila cleared her throat. "And a pretty good job of it too, Chief Inspector."

"Thank you, Ma'am."

"I feel a lot better now. Let's eat in tonight. Just the three of us."

"You mean three and eight-ninths."

Lila laughed. "Yes. All almost four of us. Now, if you'll excuse me, I'm going to find Tassaki and give him a big hug."

"Give him one from me, too."

"By the way, thanks for calling. It means a lot to me."

"As do you to me."

"Kisses."

Andreas stared at the phone for a few seconds after Lila hung up. *God bless you, Maggie, you did it again.*

Too bad the crisis protocols didn't allow him to give her a raise.

◇◇◇

Three uniformed military officers entered the Ministry of Public Order building and asked for the office of the Chief of State Security Police.

"We have an appointment," said Colonel Retsos.

As they waited for the elevator, the Navy captain shook his head, "I don't get it. You called this morning to schedule a meeting and his secretary said, 'Come right over.' As if he was expecting your call."

"Hey, I'm not in the habit of looking a gift horse in the mouth."

"Strange thing for a Greek to say," said Group Captain Philippos.

"Especially since this one could bite our heads off," said the Navy captain.

"Stop worrying and let me do the talking," said the colonel.

"Why does that not make me comfortable?" said Philippos with a smile.

"*Malaka.*"

Prada's office sat directly across the hall from the minister of public order's, and when the colonel introduced himself, Prada's secretary pointed them toward what had once been Andreas' office, "You'll be meeting over there in the minister's office."

The minister's secretary barely looked up from behind her desk. She simply waved the three men off in the general direction of a closed office door. They stopped at the door, and the colonel drew in a deep breath, let it out, and knocked.

"Come in."

As they went through the door, their eyes looked left toward a large desk commanding the office, but no one sat there.

"Over here, gentlemen," came a voice from the far right side of the office.

They turned to see Prada standing between two straight back chairs arranged across from a Chesterfield sofa.

"I thought it would be more comfortable for us to meet in the minister's office. He won't be back until the afternoon. Please sit." He waved at the sofa and one of the chairs.

Colonel Retsos moved briskly toward Prada and shook his hand. "Nice to see you again, sir. Thank you for agreeing to see us on such short notice."

"No reason to thank me," said Prada shaking hands with the others. "I assumed it must be important if our Army, Navy, and Air Force's brightest rising stars wanted to see me on such an urgent basis."

No one objected to the flattery.

Prada sat in one chair, the colonel in the other, the Navy and Air Force on the sofa.

"Would you like water or coffee?" said Prada.

"Nothing, thank you," said the colonel. His colleagues concurred.

"So, what can I do for you, gentlemen?"

The colonel cleared his throat. "Sir, we're here unofficially, but with the blessings of our respective general officers, to ask for your help."

"My help? What sort of help?"

"The other night at our dinner on Santorini, you shared with us the Prime Minister's views on a new order for Greece's national defense."

"Yes, one intended to put the needs of the people first."

"I understand that, sir, but we're here to express our unanimous concern that what the Prime Minister proposes is catastrophic for the nation."

"Catastrophic? That's a rather strong word, Colonel."

"But accurate. To put our security in the hands of NATO is to put the knives of the Turks to our throats. Do you recall when the Turks shot down that Russian warplane on the pretext of it violating Turkish airspace? We all knew why they did it, to protect their colleagues making billions smuggling terrorist oil in from Syria. Their sanctimonious claims of protecting Turkish airspace were laughable. Their jets penetrate Greek airspace all the time, and they've attacked our borders by channeling hundreds of thousands of refugees across their country and into ours—again enriching their colleagues making billions trading in human misery. And what does NATO do, or has it ever done, to control Turkish aggression? Nothing."

Prada, nodded. "I see your point, Colonel, but what is there that I can possibly do for you, or rather for our military?"

Retsos swallowed again. "You could convince the Prime Minister to change his mind."

Prada smiled. "I thought that might be where this was headed. Gentlemen, I respect your opinions, but you are grossly ill-informed if you think I could possibly convince the Prime Minister to change what he intends to serve as a basic tenet of the party's economic recovery program."

"Why not? We all know he's done it before. Indeed, several times."

"And those shifts have cost him dearly in the lost loyalties of some of his most powerful political supporters."

"So could pressing ahead with this badly misguided policy."

Prada paused. "The Prime Minister's earlier policy reversals brought violent demonstrations back to our streets. I don't think he wants to risk adding to that."

"The risk of *not* changing his policy is that he'll be adding Turkish soldiers to our streets."

"I think you're getting carried away, Colonel."

The two on the sofa looked decidedly uncomfortable.

"With all due respect, sir, I disagree. It's one thing to have domestic terrorists announcing a warning well ahead of time that a bomb will go off outside a specific symbolic building, and quite another to have Turks appropriating Greek territory because we're too weak to defend ourselves. And then there's FYROM and its ambitions toward us."

Prada shrugged. "What can I say? The Prime Minister will not agree with you. Lord knows I've tried."

"Then our nation is doomed. He must be stopped. You need to try again."

Prada rose up out of his chair. "I think not. Gentlemen, I thank you for coming but I really must prepare for another appointment. Sorry I couldn't be of more help."

"Thank you for your time, sir," said the Navy captain.

"Yes, thank you," said Philippos.

"I really wish you would reconsider," said the colonel as Prada shepherded them toward the door.

"I know that you do, Colonel." Prada patted him on the back. He opened the door. "Again, thank you all for coming."

When the last man left the office, Prada closed the door, turned around, and smiled. "*Gotcha.*"

Chapter Eighteen

December sunsets in Athens came around five, so when Maggie walked into Andreas' rapidly darkening office, he assumed it was to say goodnight or suggest he turn on a light.

"You look like a ghoul sitting in front of that computer screen. For God's sake turn on a light."

Andreas smiled. "I knew that's why you came in here. Just like my mother used to tell me: 'Turn on a light before you go blind.'"

"You should listen to your mother, but did she also tell you what your playmates have been doing without you?"

"What are you taking about?"

"Prada met with Colonel Retsos, a Navy captain, and an Air Force group captain this afternoon at the ministry."

"What? How could you know that?"

"Because I was doing what you'd asked me to do, chasing down potential police suspects in the girl's murder. I called a friend in personnel at the ministry. Her boss happens to have an office down the hall from the minister's, and when I told her I was looking for information on 'military-grade marksmen' she asked what's with all the sudden military action. Which led me to ask what she was talking about."

Maggie walked over to his desk and turned on a light.

"She said three officers had met earlier in the minister's office—"

"Babis' office?"

Maggie nodded.

"But I thought you said Prada met with them."

"If you let me finish, you'll get the whole story."

Andreas waved his hand. "Okay."

"So, I asked her for the names of the officers. She said she didn't know but she'd try to find out from the minister's secretary, one my friend described as a real bitch when it came to sharing information about her boss."

"Unlike some others?"

Maggie ignored him. "She called me back with the names. Apparently the secretary had come around to realizing it didn't pay to unnecessarily cross her co-workers. But just to let my friend know she wasn't telling tales out of school, she made a point of saying it wasn't a meeting involving her boss. Prada chose to meet there instead of using his own office, which by the way, is right across the hall from the minister's and has an even bigger bitch for a secretary."

"Did the secretary tell your friend why Prada hadn't used his own office?"

"She didn't bother to ask, but the secretary volunteered that the minister was out most days dealing with the demonstrations."

"Ah, yes, the daily demonstrations over Penelope's murder. From all reports Babis is handling them in his usual, inimitably inept fashion. At least they've kept him busy enough to stay off my back."

Andreas leaned back in his chair. "Thinking back to our brief stint in that office, I think I may have an answer to why Prada used the minister's office."

"Do you wish to share?"

"The ministry is paranoid about listening devices and sweeps all high-level offices regularly. In the case of Prada, my guess is he definitely wouldn't want what goes on in his office recorded."

"So what's that got to do with any of this?"

Andreas smiled. "Now it's my turn to say, 'hold your horses.'"

Maggie rolled her eyes.

"But Spiros, our former minister, was more paranoid about someone claiming he'd said things he hadn't—"

"How's he doing, by the way?"

"Fine, he's moved to Tripoli and is living in his ancestral family home. Lila and I visited him for the day a couple of weeks back. So far so good on the medical front. And his wife stayed in Athens."

"Which is probably why he's doing better."

Andreas waved his hand in the air. "Anyway, Spiros installed an elaborate system in his office to record whatever was said."

"Are you old enough to remember what happened to an American President who did the same thing?"

"No, but hopefully it was bad and the same thing will happen to Prada."

"You think he used the minister's office to record the conversation?"

Andreas nodded. "That's my guess. Babis certainly knows about the system, and I'd be surprised if Prada didn't. It's not on all the time, so he would have had to activate it." Andreas smiled. "And that's where we may have a shot at finding out what went on in that meeting."

"How's that?"

"I never used the system, and made it clear that no one else could use it during my time as minister. As a precaution against unauthorized use, I arranged with a technician in operations to put in a secure backup that made a duplicate recording anytime the system activated. That way I could access the backup to see who'd disobeyed my orders."

"Ever catch anyone?"

"No one ever tried."

"Do you think the new minister knows about the backup?"

"I never told him. And if no one told the techie about a change in operational rules, there just might be a duplicate copy of today's little get-together waiting to be heard."

"I can't believe you'd be so lucky."

"It's worth a try." Andreas stood up. "Now if you'll excuse me, I'm off to see a man about a recording."

"Music to your ears, I hope."

"For sure." Andreas headed toward the door.

"So, do you want to hear about the other thing?"

Andreas stopped and faced her. "What other thing?"

"That figures." She shook her head. "What you've had Yianni and me working on all day."

"You have an answer?"

"Sort of. On the police side, there were about a half-dozen possibles, but three were eliminated on the basis of comparing their descriptions to the images caught on video, one had a recent knee replacement operation making it impossible for him to do the running, and the other two are no longer in Greece."

"Where are they?"

"In the United States. Astoria and Pittsburgh."

"Any chance they came back to Greece for the hit?"

"Don't know yet. We'll check with immigration but they could have come in through a Schengen Agreement country, which would have allowed them to pass into Greece without going through our passport control. But as long as they travelled under their own names we'll be able to find out where and when they first entered a Schengen country."

"If nothing turns up, we'll have to verify whether they were in the U.S. when the assassination went down. That's going to take time. Anything on potential military candidates?"

"Yianni is still working on that. But your hunch is looking stronger. They just might be imported killers."

"As fun as it is to be right, I wish I understood what it all meant. Nothing adds up."

Maggie nodded. "There's a big picture we're missing."

"Yeah…a cinematic eureka moment would do quite nicely," said Andreas turning to head toward the door. "So, cross your fingers and pray I find that techie and he can get us the soundtrack."

Andreas didn't get to the ministry until after six and didn't expect to find his techie connection there at that hour. Public employees had earned a reputation for working as little as possible, and being gone by dark fit the job description for all but the most dedicated non-managerial types.

Andreas had to start somewhere, though, and so he went to the ministry building in the hopes that someone still there might know where to find the man after hours.

The guard in the lobby desk recognized Andreas and took the opportunity to say how much he missed him, and how different things were since he'd left. "Nobody at the top seems to know what they're doing."

Andreas could have said that he'd heard that same complaint from old-timers in several ministries, but instead said, "I hear you, friend. Wish I had an answer."

"Get rid of the fools who are ruining our country."

Andreas agreed, but didn't want to say so because he knew he'd be quoted by this guy at least a hundred times. On the other hand, he needed the man's help at finding the techie, and so he settled on saying, "Amen, brother, amen."

The guard nodded.

"Say, maybe you can help me, I've got a sticky technical problem and was trying to hook up with one of the technicians here who'd helped me out before. It's sort of urgent and I don't know how to find him at this hour. I thought someone here might be able to steer me in the right direction."

"Who are you looking for?"

"He's young, slim build, five-nine or so, brown goatee, always wearing a different band's tee-shirt—"

"That's Maxie. "He's crazy about his bands."

Andreas nodded, "Do you know where I can find him?"

The guard sidled up to Andreas. "Can you keep a secret?"

"Sure," said Andreas, having absolutely no idea what was coming.

"He's a good, hardworking kid, but in order to support his pensioner mother he works several nights a week as a substitute deejay at a disco, the midnight to seven a.m. shift."

"When does he sleep?"

"That's just the point. He lives about an hour from here and the disco is about as far away from here in the opposite direction."

Andreas shook his head. "Poor kid."

"That's what I thought, so I let him sleep in our break room. There's a cot in there and no one's ever around to disturb him."

"You mean he's here in the building now?"

The guard nodded, and pointed to a battered gray metal door marked EMPLOYEES ONLY. "It's one flight down. You can't miss it."

"Thank you," said Andreas.

"No problem. We're all in this mess together."

Andreas smiled and gave him a thumbs-up as he headed across the cloudy marble floor toward the door.

The door opened onto a landing between equivalently battered metal handrail staircases leading up and down. The paint looked gray, but it could have been green at one point. Even the graffiti complaints etched along the way were dull and colorless. He took the down staircase and at the bottom stopped at a door marked NO ADMITTANCE.

He knocked. No answer. He knocked again. Still no answer. "Maxie, it's Andreas Kaldis, I need to speak with you."

Andreas heard someone shuffling around inside. The door opened slightly, but enough for Andreas to make out Maxie's face.

"Minister? What are you doing here? Have I done something wrong?"

Andreas didn't correct Maxie's use of his former title. "Everything's cool, Maxie. I just need your help with something, and it's rather urgent."

The door opened wider. "It's a mess in here."

"No problem, we can talk standing here."

"Okay."

Andreas fixed his eyes on Maxie's. "Do you remember that backup recording system I had you install so I could tell if any unauthorized person used my office?"

For an instant all Andreas saw was a big blank stare, and then a smile broke across Maxie's face. "Oh, yeah. Man, I forgot all about it."

"Do you know if it's still working?"

"I've never checked, but it's simple enough to find out."

"It is?"

"Sure. I made it that way, since I knew you weren't into the tech side of things." He turned and disappeared for a moment before coming back holding an iPod.

Is this kid stoned, wondered Andreas. "So, can you check for me?"

"I'd love to help you, man, but I really need to get some sleep."

Andreas held his temper. "It's really important."

Maxie held out the iPod. "I understand, but so's my sleep. You'll just have to listen to it yourself."

Andreas stared at the iPod. "What's this?"

"It's what you asked me for. On it are all the recordings made in your office. I set it up as your backup storage. It's really a hard drive but, as I said, knowing you're not into the tech side of things, I figured giving it to you as an iPod would make it simple for you to figure out."

"You mean all I have to do is play it?"

"Use it the same as any other iPod." He smiled. "Or have your kid show you how to use it."

"Don't you want it back?"

"Nah, it's an old model, and the ministry paid for it. The only things on it are your recordings."

"Don't you want to keep a copy?"

Maxie smiled. "Whatever's on it is already copied," he pointed above his head, "up to my Apple iCloud account."

Andreas decided it best he leave now, rather than stay and demonstrate the true depth of his ignorance. "Thanks, Maxie. Sorry to have bothered you, but you were a big help."

Maxie gave a quick wave as he said, "Bye," and shut the door.

Andreas stared at the iPod, wondering what might be on it. That's when he decided to call Francesco and tell him to be in the office first thing in the morning for a rush job. No way Andreas was going to trust himself to fool around with this device.

Though the thought did cross his mind to ask Tassaki to play it for him.

◇◇◇

Sappho traced her finger along Petro's jawline. "You really do look like an ancient Spartan warrior."

"And precisely how old would that make me?"

"Old enough to have developed a better sense of humor."

Petro rolled onto his side and stared straight into her eyes. "I hope it never stops raining."

She pressed her head forward and kissed him lightly on the lips. "Then we better book our tickets on the ark."

He smiled.

"When do you have to go back to Athens?"

"I can't leave until that guy gets here."

"I don't understand why he can't just call and tell you what to do."

"He has to make arrangements with a third party, and that he can only do in person."

"It all sounds very mysterious to me, but hey, it's keeping you here so I'm not complaining."

"Me either."

"Maybe you'll be here for the big event?"

"What big event?"

"The mayor hit upon the idea of a big-time tree-lighting event to draw tourist attention to the island for Christmas. He wanted to do it at Akrotiri, but the Minister of Culture refused to go along, so he's putting it up in Pyrgos at the top of the hill by the castle ruins where it can be seen from almost any direction. Personally, I think he intended to put it there all along but he's from Pyrgos and didn't want to be accused of favoring his home village, so he suggested Akrotiri knowing the culture minister would never go along with it."

"Ah, the Byzantine ways of the Greeks."

"He's turned it into quite a big deal. Even the Prime Minister will be here for the lighting."

"When's this all supposed to happen?"

"In two days."

"If tomorrow's weather isn't any better, I just might still be around."

"Good, I'll keep lighting candles to Zeus to keep up the storms."

"I thought we only lit candles to the saints?"

"As long as it's working, I'm happy."

"Good point. Now where were we?"

"You were about to show me another god-like bolt of lightning."

"Oh, that old routine again."

She pressed her body tight against his under the sheet. "As I said, 'As long as it's working, I'm happy.'"

Francesco sat on the couch in Andreas' office wearing earphones connected to the iPod he held in his hand. "There's a lot of stuff on here, Chief. What is it precisely that you're looking for?"

"For starters, a conversation involving three of your old favorites from that hotel on Santorini—Colonel Retsos and his Navy and Air Force captain buddies."

"It took place yesterday afternoon," added Yianni from a chair in front of Andreas' desk.

Francesco tinkered with the face of the device. "I think this is what you want." He put it down next to a set of tiny speakers on a table in front of the couch, disconnected the jack to his earphones, and hooked the iPod up to the speakers. "Here goes," and he pushed a button.

The three men listened silently to the conversation. Then listened to it again. On the second run-through Andreas had Francesco stop it several times so he could take notes.

"Are you sure that's all there is?" said Andreas.

"Yeah. It ends on 'Gotcha,'" said Francesco. "There's nothing after that on the iPod. Only earlier conversations."

"He must have turned off the primary recording device," said Yianni.

"So, what's this all mean?" said Andreas.

"Got me," said Yianni. "It doesn't sound any different from what we've already heard, except this time they're bending Prada's ear instead of each other's. All of which makes me wonder what got Prada excited enough to say, 'Gotcha.'"

Andreas picked up a pencil and began tapping the eraser end on his desktop. "Francesco, how difficult would it be to doctor that recording?"

"Depends on how you want to doctor it and how close to perfect you want it to be. Are you talking about cutting, moving things around, adding new material? All that can be done, it's just a question of whether the job will pass professional scrutiny."

"Well, let's see what we've got here if we simply pull out a few lines and run them in sequence as a conversation." Andreas picked up his notes.

"Here's a little back and forth between the Retsos and Prada, starting with the colonel."

Thank you for agreeing to see us on such short notice.

No reason to thank me, I assumed it must be important if our Army, Navy, and Air Force's brightest rising stars wanted to see me on such an urgent basis.

Sir, we're here unofficially, but with the blessings of our respective general officers to ask for your help.

My help? What sort of help?

We're here to express our unanimous concern that what the Prime Minister proposes is catastrophic for the nation. Our nation is doomed. He must be stopped.

I think not.

"How's that for a gotcha sound bite? It plants the seed of a *coup d'état* storyline in our junta-wary public's mind. And once Prada's propaganda version hooks his target audience, anyone who happens to hear the full conversation will likely see it as consistent with Prada's editing job."

"Son of a bitch," said Yianni. "He's set those guys up to take a very big fall."

"A masterful job of ruining their careers," said Francesco. "And it all started with his dinner appearance on Santorini."

"This guy is really dangerous," said Yianni.

"But to whom?" said Andreas. "Why does he want to create the impression that the military is planning a coup, and who's in it with him? Until we have answers to those questions, we're no further along than we were before we heard the recording."

"Maybe there's something else on the iPod that can help with that," said Francesco. "If the minister or Prada thought it important enough to record a conversation, who knows what might be on it, especially since they thought they could erase whatever they didn't like?"

"Sounds like you have a project for yourself, my friend," said Andreas.

Francesco nodded. "Care to join in? Should be some fascinating listening."

Andreas smiled. "Love to, but Yianni and I have a call to make on a certain Brigadier."

"Oh, that sounds like fun," said Yianni.

"I was hoping for interesting, maybe even revelational answers."

"It's Christmastime, who knows? Santa might just grant your wish."

Andreas stood up. "From the way our luck's been running on this case, we're more likely to get trampled to death by his reindeer."

"As I said, sounds like fun."

Chapter Nineteen

The Hellenic Army General Staff headquartered at Papagou Camp in an eastern suburb of Athens slightly west of the Hymettus Mountains. From GADA, a straight shot east along Alexandras Avenue and a left onto Mesogeion Avenue brought them to Kiprou Street, a block beyond Athens General Hospital. A left there took them into the park-like grounds of the Ministry of Defense and up onto a blocks-long oval roadway encircling the massive Ministry of Defense building complex.

"We're meeting him in here?" said Yianni.

"I had Maggie call him so he couldn't press me for why it's urgent I see him, and he told her he's here tied up in meetings but will see us on a break."

They parked in a space as close to the main entrance as they could find. Inside, they asked for the Brigadier and were escorted down several long hallways, up an elevator to a sixth-floor wood-paneled office fitted with a rectangular mahogany conference table for twelve, and told to wait. They sat at the end of the table farthest from the door.

"Chief, have you ever given any thought to how easy it would be for us to simply disappear in here, should we happen to really piss this guy off?"

Andreas smiled as he put his finger to his lips and pointed at the ceiling. "Listening devices," he mouthed.

"I mean we're breaking in on his meetings with nothing but bullshit questions to which he can't possibly know the answers."

Andreas smiled again. "One person's bullshit is another's fertilizer, Grasshopper."

Yianni fought back a laugh.

The door swung open and in strode the Brigadier in full military dress. "Howdy, gentlemen. I've only got ten minutes, so let's get right to it." He sat at the far end of the table.

Andreas stared at him for a few seconds, stood, walked over, and sat down next to him.

"Thank you for agreeing to see us."

"Cut the bullshit, Kaldis, I've got serious work to do."

Andreas shook his head. "Man, you're a walking encyclopedia of contradictions, but frankly, I don't care about any of that any more. Just tell me how you knew about the Caesars' meeting on Santorini."

"I don't remember."

"Of course you do. And I want the truth."

"I don't have time for your crap."

"Okay, then, let me tell you what's on my schedule for the rest of the day if you don't start giving me honest answers. I'll be calling a press conference to announce that my unit's uncovered a criminal conspiracy to bring down our government, and I'll be putting you smack dab in the middle of it all."

"You're out of your mind."

"Really? Well, let's look at the facts. You sent us off on a wild goose chase to Santorini, knowing that your childhood buddy would be making a guest appearance to deliver a mega-downer of a message to a room full of top military brass, a message that would fire them up enough to want to beg your buddy to change the Prime Minister's mind and have them walking blindly into a trap set to shift all the blame to them for whatever you and your buddy have in mind. So, what's the deal? Prada unmasks a coup plot, a lot of senior heads roll, thanks to our recordings of their conversations, you get a big promotion, and Prada gets still more power?"

"You *are* out of your mind. You're forgetting that my daughter was murdered."

"Not at all. Your behavior is entirely consistent with someone who got the message her killers intended to deliver. Cooperate or watch more of your loved ones die. You've done *nothing* to help us with our investigation except to tell us precisely what Prada wanted you to." Andreas leaned to within a nose of the Brigadier's face. "Now's your chance to prove me wrong."

The blood drained from the Brigadier's face. "No one will believe any of that."

"Everyone will believe all of that. Remember your father?"

The Brigadier turned his head and stared out the window. His chin dropped down onto his chest. "None of what you said is true, except for one thing."

He lifted his head and turned to catch Andreas' eyes. "It was my old friend—your Prada—who told me about the Caesars meeting on Santorini. He called me after our meeting in the minister's office while I was on the way to meet you at that cafenion. He apologized for his behavior in the office and for not having spoken to Penelope when he had the chance. I told him to go fuck himself." The Brigadier sighed, his eyes now distant. "He said he understood I was angry with him, and that's why he felt obligated to share his suspicions that some of my military colleagues who were in the Caesars might be tied into Penelope's murder. He said he knew about their gathering on Santorini because the previous Friday he'd been invited to join them there for dinner on the following Friday. I'd just hung up with him when I met up with you, so when you pressed me for possible suspects, I passed on what he'd told me."

Andreas looked him in the eye. "This guy keeps screwing you and you keep swallowing his lines? No one's going to believe you could possibly be that gullible. It's far easier to see the two of you in cahoots."

The Brigadier nodded. "I see that now. But it's not just him who told me about that meeting on Santorini."

"Who else told you?"

"One of my buddies in the Army's A-branch. He deals with intelligence and security issues. He heard through a NATO intelligence contact that a group involved in advising the Greek government had something in the fire for Santorini."

"That sounds a bit vague."

"More like made up," said Yianni.

"What did they call the group?"

"All he said was that some private organization that's been advising our high-level government officials for years appeared likely involved in something about to happen on Santorini. So when Prada told me about the meeting on Santorini, I assumed they both were talking about the Caesars."

Andreas' eyes narrowed and his lips tightened. "I swear, Brigadier, if I find out this is more of your bullshit, I'll spend the rest of my life hunting for your head."

Yianni sat forward, tensed and ready to pounce.

The Brigadier leaned back in his chair. "You'll be wasting your life. There's nothing left to hunt. The reason I'm here today is I'm resigning from the Army. My wife can't stand the memories. And, frankly, neither can I. We're moving out of Athens. Maybe even out of Greece."

Andreas' expression didn't change. "Get me the name of that group."

"My friend won't tell me."

"I don't care what you have to do to him or for him, but *get me the name of that group.*" Andreas pounded his fist on the table.

"I'll try."

"You'll try right now, dammit. Get him on the phone and if he doesn't answer you go kick down his door. Don't you get it? We're trying to find your daughter's killers."

The Brigadier pulled a phone out of his pocket skimmed through a directory and pressed a number. "Believe me, I get it." He held the phone up to his ear.

"Hi Eleni, it's me. Is Nikos in?"

A long pause followed.

"Hi, Nikos. Yeah, all's fine but I need a favor. It has to do with Penelope."

Pause.

"No, her mother's not doing well, but what can one expect? We're both trying to find closure. In fact that's the reason for this call. Remember when we were talking a while back about a group involved in something going down on Santorini?

"Yes, the one you heard about through your NATO buddy, and, yes, I know you don't know the details. All I need is a name, and not your contact's, the organization's."

Pause.

"Stop being so melodramatic about protecting confidences, asshole. After all, you're talking to me, and it's not as if I'm threatening to tell your wife you're screwing Eleni on your office desk."

Pause.

He laughed. "Honestly, I knew nothing about that, but if you don't give me the group's name now, for sure I'm telling her."

Pause.

"Are you certain?"

Longer pause.

"Thanks, buddy, and don't worry. Your secret's safe with me." He laughed. "Same to you."

He hung up the phone. "Gentlemen, was I ever wrong. The organization is the Mayroon Group, a New York-based international consulting firm that relies upon a global network of divisions to support its role as advisor to a host of the world's government and industry leaders. Mayroon loomed behind every one of our current Prime Minister's election victories, and even told him to lose his first race, because in its judgment he wasn't ready yet, and whoever won that election would be fatally tarred by the inevitably worsening financial crisis. Mayroon proved to be right."

"You're saying a foreign-based think tank is our PM's political guru?" said Andreas.

"Not just political, but economic, societal, you name it. And not just his. They're advisors to whomever is willing to pay them."

"How does your friend know this Mayroon is into something on Santorini?"

"He said the night before he called to alert me, his NATO contact got it from a young lady he'd met at a dinner party. She worked for the head of Mayroon's political-intelligence division and thought it would impress the contact. She said she knew something 'big' was about to happen on Santorini because her boss had received direct orders from Mayroon's chairman that had her rushing around all afternoon finding detailed maps and photographs of the island."

Andreas shook his head. "Loose lips. They're everywhere these days."

"Sounds like someone's considering a real estate investment," said Yianni.

"That's the likely answer," said the Brigadier, "but you asked me why I thought the Caesars were involved in this, and that coincidence is my answer to your question."

"When did this conversation between the NATO contact and the young lady take place?" said Andreas.

The Brigadier shut his eyes. "We spoke two days before Penelope's murder. So the conversation would have been a day earlier."

Andreas nodded and turned to face Yianni. "Any questions?"

"Yeah," said Yianni spreading his arms. "Now what?"

Andreas handed Yianni the car keys and sat in the passenger seat, drumming the fingers of his left hand on the dashboard and staring out the side window as they passed along Mesogeion's wide boulevard of government buildings, private offices, residences, and shops.

Andreas didn't speak until they were almost back to Alexandras Avenue. "I hate coincidences. Especially when I sense there's another explanation."

"Are you doubting the Brigadier's story about NATO?"

"No. I'm thinking about all the other coincidences. Both the Caesars and Mayroon are in a position to give direct advice to our Prime Minister, yet we know the Caesars are looking to have Prada use his influence with the Prime Minister. I'd bet Mayroon does the same.

"Then there's the timing. On day one Prada receives an invitation to join the Caesars for dinner on Santorini. The next day Mayroon is running around gathering info on Santorini. On day five the Brigadier's daughter is murdered, on day eight the Caesars meet on Santorini, and on day eleven Prada is yelling '*gotcha*.'"

"But what's the tie-in to Mayroon," said Yianni, "or to the Caesars, for that matter?"

"That's what's driving me crazy. My mind keeps going back to something else the Brigadier told us in the cafenion. He said, 'Any military man giving serious thought to coup possibilities would know that a coup could not possibly succeed without *powerful outside benefactors*.'"

"Mayroon?"

"They certainly qualify."

"But the Caesars aren't talking coup, and Mayroon's client is already in charge of the government."

"As I said, it's driving me crazy. I'm certain all the pieces are right there in front of us, except for the one that makes sense of everything."

"Any idea on where we can find that bit of information?"

"If Francesco can't pull something helpful off the minister's recordings…" Andreas threw up his hands, "…we're nowhere."

"I guess that means we're heading straight back to the office."

"Do you have something better to do?"

"I was planning on buying you a Christmas present," said Yianni, deadpan.

"You have plenty of time. We exchange presents the old-fashioned way, on the first day of the year on Saint Basil's Day."

"It will melt by then."

"Huh?"

"There's a terrific ice cream place nearby."

"As a great man once said, 'On Dasher, on Dancer, on Prancer on Vixen, for a double chocolate fudge I'm a'fixin.'"

"And you have the balls to criticize what I think is funny?"

"Onward, onward, two scoops await."

◇◇◇

"Hello, oh master of all things dark and hidden," said Andreas into his mobile phone.

"It's a bit early in the day for you to be into that sort of drinking, don't you think?"

"It's not booze, it's gelato. Yianni took me to a place Tassaki's Uncle Tassos will just love."

"The one just off Mesageion?" said Tassos.

"You know about it?"

"You think I got this way eating carrots?"

Andreas laughed. "Where are you?"

"On Syros, dodging raindrops."

"I have something to get your mind off the weather. Did you ever hear of the Mayroon Group?"

"Maroon?"

"No, MAY-ROON. It's an international consulting firm the Brigadier told us helped get the Prime Minister elected."

"Never heard of it, but that's not the sort of thing our man-of-the-people, anti-establishment Prime Minister would likely brag about."

"What's the chance of your knowing somebody who might be able to give us a line on the Mayroon Group?"

"If it's true, pretty good. Let me make a few calls."

"Great."

"Anything I should know before I start chasing this rabbit?" said Tassos.

"My sense is Prada's somehow involved in whatever Mayroon's into. And Mayroon apparently is focused on something having to do with Santorini."

"As close as Prada is to the Prime Minister, I'd be surprised if he's not in with Mayroon. What do you think's going on?"

"No idea, but something bad. That much I'm sure of."

"Last I checked, something bad is always going on. It's why cops have jobs."

"Mine at the moment is to keep Detective Kouros from assaulting my double chocolate fudge with his spoon. Bye." Andreas glared at Yianni. "I meant what I said about guarding my ice cream. Pick on somebody else with your spoon."

"We're the only customers in here, and besides, all I wanted to do was taste it. Don't you teach Tassaki that sharing is good?"

"He doesn't believe that line when it comes to ice cream either."

Yianni laughed. "How long do you think it will take Tassos to come up with something?"

Andreas shrugged. "Don't know, but if we wait around here until we hear back I'd say there's a pretty good chance they'll have to roll us to the car." He waved his spoon at the dish in front of him. "This stuff is really—"

The sounds of the explosion and shattering glass had both men diving under their table for cover, and coming back up with guns drawn. First they looked for bad guys, next for any injured. A scream came rolling in through the blown-out storefront.

"Everyone looks to be okay in here," said Yianni. "The explosion came from next door."

"Call it in as a possible bomb." Andreas picked his way over broken glass and out through an opening that a minute before had been the gelato place's front window.

A young, dark skinned woman in a *hijab* headscarf stood screaming in front of the grocery store next door.

Instinctively, Andreas scanned the street before approaching the woman. "Miss, are you okay?"

She cringed and backed away.

"Miss, I'm here to help you, I'm with the police." He pulled out his ID with his left hand, his right still firmly holding his gun.

Her eyes fixed on the gun.

"Do you know if anyone is inside the store?"

She didn't speak.

"If you want me to help, you have to tell me. Do you know if anyone is inside?"

She mumbled something in a language Andreas did not understand.

"You'll have to tell me in Greek. Or English."

The woman hesitated, then said in Greek, "My husband and my daughter. It is our shop."

"Are you hurt?"

She shook her head, "No. I was there." She pointed at a kiosk twenty meters up the street.

"Stay here." Andreas turned to head into the store just as Yianni came out of the gelato place.

"Where are you going?"

"Inside," said Andreas. "There are at least two people still in there."

"Chief, our homegrown anarchists give advance warning of bombings. But there wasn't any, so this could be foreign terrorists, and that means there might be a second bomb rigged to kill first-responders. Like us."

"What are you trying to say?"

"We should wait for the bomb squad. They're trained for this. They'll be here any minute."

A cry came from inside the store.

"That sounds like a little girl," said Andreas.

"I know," said Yianni.

Both men turned and entered the store through what was left of the front doorway. Inside lay a jumble of broken glass, shattered cans, exploded cartons, and splintered wood. The distinctive odor of C-4 hung over all others scents.

"Let's find them and get the hell out of here, Yianni. It was definitely a bomb."

Another cry came up from the same voice.

"It's coming from behind that counter," said Yianni pointing toward the rear of the store at a metal display case filled with meats and shattered glass.

They found a girl who looked about six, sitting on the floor next to a prostrate, unmoving man, eyes open but fixed straight ahead on the ceiling, blood seeping out of one ear.

Andreas felt for a pulse. "He's alive, but we don't dare move him. Get the girl out of here. I'll stay with him until the medics arrive."

"Are you nuts?"

"Just get her out of here."

Yianni reached for the girl and she screamed. He took her by her arms to lift her up and she started kicking him.

"Take her to her mother."

Yianni clutched her to his chest with one arm and carried her away, holding her kicking legs tight to his body with the other.

Andreas crouched down by the man's head. "Everything's going to be okay. Your daughter is safe and an ambulance is on the way. Just hold on, buddy. You'll be fine."

Andreas looked up to where the man's eyes stayed focused. Nothing but an ugly, peeling yellow ceiling. *I wonder if he's thinking that might be the last thing he sees on Earth?* All cops wondered what their last thoughts might be, even if they didn't admit to it. Most imagined it would be their lives passing by them in a blur, but on the thankfully few occasions Andreas had come close to a life-ending experience, it wasn't anything like that. He'd thought only of how lucky he was to have friends and family to take care of his loved ones.

Andreas' eyes moved from the ceiling back onto the man. He reached out and stroked the side of the man's face. *I wonder if he's finding peace in similar thoughts.*

Andreas shook his head. Hard to imagine how he could with so many Greeks vilifying dark-skinned immigrants as scapegoats for the nation's hard times, and treating them as threats to what those same bigots believed to be Greek values. *Now they're being bombed.* A tear came to Andreas' eye. *I pray his last thoughts will not be of despair.*

Andreas sat in silence, his hand resting on the man's forehead, losing track of time. He listened for the sound of the ambulance. It should have been here by now; the hospital was practically next door.

What's taking so long?

Finally, a siren. It had probably been only a couple of minutes since Yianni called it in, but waiting with someone holding on for life makes time drag on. He heard Yianni shouting outside, and a moment later the sound of someone cursing as he drew closer to Andreas.

"What's going on?" said Andreas.

"He didn't want to come inside until the bomb squad gave the all clear. But I convinced him it was safe."

"I was just following procedures."

"You two can take this up later. But for now, take care of him." Andreas stood up and stepped back so the medic could get to the man.

He crouched down by the man's head. "Help is here, sir, you'll be fine." He turned to Yianni. "Tell my buddy to get in here with the bag. STAT."

Andreas' phone rang, causing the medic to duck away from his patient. "Are you crazy bringing a cellphone into a possible bomb site? Get out of here, now. PLEASE."

Andreas headed for the front door, his phone still ringing. He pressed answer. "Hello."

"It damn well took you long enough to answer. Are you still fighting with Yianni over claims to your ice cream?"

"Sadly, no. Things have got a little dicey since we last spoke. To be specific, we're now in the middle of recently detonated bomb site."

"*What?*"

"I'm sure you'll hear all about it on the news. There looks to be one critically injured man, but no other casualties, and my guess at who's behind it is some slime-bucket anti-immigrant group screaming 'Greece is for Greeks.'"

"Never fails to amaze me how little they know about the genetic makeup of most they call Greeks," said Tassos.

"If they're bombing with an intention to kill, they're really stepping up their game," said Andreas. "It's as if they're taking hints from the more insane of our Mediterranean neighbors on that score."

"Let me change the topic for a moment," said Tassos. "I'm calling about Mayroon."

The subject had completely dropped from Andreas' mind. "That was quick."

"I called the one person I knew who would definitely know about Mayroon if what you'd been told was true, and who would want to talk about it if he did."

"Who was that?"

"A longtime, dyed-in-the-red-wool communist I knew from my days watching over him in a Junta prison. He'd been with the Prime Minister since the very beginning, a member of his inner sanctum. But when the PM went back on his promises and did precisely what he'd been elected to change, he spoke out against the PM, who promptly purged him from the party in the next election."

"Hell hath no fury like an old-time communist purged."

"You have the picture."

"So what did he say?" asked Andreas.

"You were right about Mayroon. It's been in the Prime Minister's corner for about a decade. The rich socialite who's been backing him since those days introduced him to Mayroon's chairman. She likely paid Mayroon's charges, too, at least early on. They've done everything from teach him English to writing his speeches and outlining his policies."

"How's Prada fit in?"

"Back then the PM didn't speak much English so Prada acted as his interpreter. He used that opportunity to get in tight with the Mayroon boys, and now he's the primary link in Greece between Mayroon and the Prime Minister."

"That's terrific. You've been a big help. The bomb squad just arrived, I better go talk to them."

"I know you're pressed, but don't you want to hear the best part?"

"There's more?"

"According to my guy, Mayroon expects those it assists in gaining power to acknowledge that support by assisting other Mayroon clients looking to do business in the victor's country."

"What sort of assistance?"

"Cutting through red tape, getting an inside track on privatization opportunities like shipyards, airports, railroads, utilities, real estate…you get the picture."

"Yeah, the *quid pro quo* for gaining power is giving his benefactors a great deal on the nation's crown jewels. Sounds like the more things change—"

"Not really," interrupted Tassos. "Apparently the PM isn't following through on what he promised Mayroon he'd do once elected. Said it's not politically feasible."

"At least he's consistent in not treating Mayroon any differently than he has the two million Greeks who elected him."

"But Mayroon isn't as accepting as the Greek people are of ill treatment. At least that's what my communist friend told me. He said Mayroon's Chairman is very, very angry. And get this, Prada's been trying to get the PM to cooperate with Mayroon. It's Prada who convinced Mayroon that the group's long patience and deep-pocketed support would be rewarded once his friend was prime minister. Now he's the one set up to suffer for the Prime Minister's new agenda, new friends, and new promises. Prada's relationship with the Prime Minister has been badly strained over this."

"Very, very interesting. Sounds like Prada's thinking Mayroon won't take kindly to him if he can't get his principal to stick to his word. Anything else?"

"Isn't that enough?" said Tassos.

"Did he have anything on why Mayroon's interested in Santorini?"

"Not a clue. But from what I can tell, Mayroon was expecting to own Greece, and that's not happening."

"Well, thank you, you master wizard, you."

"You're welcome. I doubt there's anyone else I know who'd know more about Mayroon than he did, but I'll check around to see if there is anything else I might be able to come up with."

"Just be careful. We don't want Mayroon wondering what we're up to."

"Do *we* know what we're up to?"

"Good point," said Andreas. "Later, I've got to run. Thanks, buddy."

"Bye."

Andreas stood at the edge of the street and turned off his phone. Ambulances, fire trucks, police, news crews, and simply the curious all about him. Everywhere. Disasters drew attention.

The storekeeper's wife stood five meters away clutching her daughter tightly against her side, both staring unblinking into the shop. Disasters scar far more than just those attacked.

Terrorists knew all about that.

The sky had turned an ugly ominous gray. He drew in and let out a deep breath, hoping to change his mood with a whiff of fresh air, but too much C-4 still lingered to give him any relief.

He waved to the head of the bomb squad. The man must be busy these days. And likely to be busier. Had the country gone mad? He knew the world had…but Greece?

And if his country had, what could Andreas do about it? What could a lone soul railing against the madness expect to accomplish?

He watched the mother and daughter grip each other as the medics wheeled their husband and father out the doorway on a stretcher, Yianni holding an IV above the comatose man's body.

Andreas shut his eyes. That was the answer: Just do your job, whatever it is, the best that you can, and don't let the bastards get you down.

Andreas bit at his lower lip and opened his eyes. *Prada and Mayroon, I think it's time I welcomed you to my world.*

Chapter Twenty

The storm pummeling Santorini broke early enough that morning to allow a few boats to dock. Tassos' nephew Christos arrived on one of them and Dimos and Petro picked him up at the port. In the first moments of their serpentine drive along the road up from the harbor, Christos asked that they please do their absolute best to quickly finish up whatever they had to do at the hotel in order to get him to the airport in time to beat the predicted arrival of more bad weather that afternoon.

As hoped, the hotel manager turned ecstatic at the news of his property's status upgrade and gave Dimos and Petro undisturbed access to confirm the original findings. They finished in less than two hours and Tassos' nephew caught his flight back to Athens.

It took another couple of hours for Dimos and Petro to pack up and haul the equipment down from the church to the van. They planned on returning together in the vehicle on the next ferry back to Athens. Depending on the weather, that would likely be the following afternoon.

Dimos was tying down the equipment in the back of the van when Petro's mobile rang. He walked away from the van to answer it.

"Hi, Chief."

"Petro. So, how did it go with Tassos' nephew? Is everything out of the hotel?"

"Everything's cool. Dimos and I were just talking about

catching the ferry tomorrow back to Athens. It all depends on the weather."

"Good, because I need you here right away."

"What's up?"

"Not sure yet, but more than just the military appear interested in changing the Prime Minister's mind about things."

"What sorts of things?"

"Don't know yet, but something called the Mayroon Group helped get him elected and isn't happy at how he's treating them now that he's in power."

"Can't say I've heard of it, but how does it plan to change his mind?"

"That's what I need you here to help figure out. All we have so far is a rumor that Mayroon is angry with him, but my instincts are it ties into whatever Prada's up to."

"If all you want to know is what Mayroon's doing to try and change the Prime Minister's mind, I could simply stay here until tomorrow night and ask him."

Silence.

"What are you talking about?" said Andreas.

"The Prime Minister is coming here for a tree-lighting ceremony tomorrow night. Santorini's mayor has made it into quite a big deal. The PM's appearance is the centerpiece of the show."

"Petro, hold on. I'm putting you on the speaker so Yianni can hear this. We're in a car headed back to GADA. We just met with the Brigadier. He's who told us about Mayroom. He also said Mayroon's all wound up over something having to do with Santorini. They're studying maps of the island."

"Maps," said Petro. "Why maps?"

"I wondered that too." Andreas paused. "Can you possibly find out from your connections on Santorini when the Prime Minister committed to coming there, and whether Prada was involved in getting him the invitation?"

"I can try, but why?" said Petro.

"We've got a Greek general's daughter murdered for no apparent reason, her killers made to look like police or military specialists, a confidant of the Prime Minister winding up the military to come out hard against his boss' policies, and a powerful international organization very angry at their ungrateful Prime Minister protégé."

"What are you suggesting?" said Yianni.

"Something that's happened before."

"Kapodistrias?" said Yianni.

"Yes."

Kapodistrias was Greece's first elected head of state after its 1821 War of Independence. The equivalent of America's George Washington, the rule of Ioannis Kapodistrias came to a tragic end.

"*Assassinated,*" Petro murmured.

"Do you remember why?" said Andreas. "And what happened next?"

"I get your point, Chief," said Petro. "Kapodistrias went against a proud and powerful family that helped him gain power. The family had controlled patronage in their region of Greece, but Kapodistrias refused to allow them to continue conducting their business as usual. He said there was a new national political order that everyone had to follow if the bankrupt, sharply divided country were to heal. To make his point, Kapodistrias put the leader of the family in jail, and the man's brother and son assassinated him for the insult. The country went into chaos, ultimately leading foreign powers to install Bavarian Prince Otto as King, a ruler who deferred to the assassins' family's preferences."

"You got it," said Andreas.

"But do you actually think there's a plan to assassinate the Prime Minister?" said Yianni.

"I think there's enough to set off alarms, and I sure as hell don't want to be the one who ignored them."

"When are you going to tell the Prime Minister?" said Petro.

"Good question. No good answer. We've no hard facts to go on, only pure conjecture easily explained away by longstanding trusted friends and advisors of the PM. With what we have, they'll make mincemeat of us. Worse still, if there is a plot, telling the PM will likely tip off whoever's behind it to abandon this plan. They'll come up with something different, a plot we'll never know about until it succeeds. Our only chance of protecting the Prime Minister is if we don't tell him and catch the bastards in the act."

"And how do you propose we pull that off?" said Yianni.

"Let's get the PM's schedule and see where he's most likely to be targeted."

"That could be anywhere," said Petro.

"Theoretically, yes. But Prada's put a lot of effort into laying the groundwork for blaming whatever happens on the military. That makes me think it'll be done somewhere and somehow in a manner that screams 'military operation' to the public." Andreas paused for a moment. "Again."

"I have no idea where that could be. Do you?" said Petro.

"I sure don't," said Yianni.

"Petro, I think it's time you formally recruit your lady friend onto our side."

"You know about her?" said Petro.

"Of course I know about her. Who connected with this case doesn't? I just saw no reason to jump in on teasing you over someone I'm certain is a wonderful young lady."

Pause.

"What should I tell her?"

"Do you trust her?"

"Yes."

"Then tell her whatever you have to tell her in order to get her focused on picking the best available spot on Santorini for blaming an assassination on the military."

Petro exhaled. "Okay, but it's going to be tough."

"Telling her, or finding the site for the hit?"

"Both."

"Good, the first will prime you for finding the second."

"Maybe the weather will turn bad enough to call off the ceremony?"

"That's called wishful thinking for the best, but we've got to prepare to confront the worst. I know what I'm asking you to do will be uncomfortable for you, but look at it this way: If you really like the woman, sooner or later you're going to have to tell her the truth. Just consider me as giving you the impetus."

"I can think of some better words to describe what it feels like you're giving me."

Andreas laughed. "I'll let that one slide, Officer. We're counting on you. Just let me know if you need anything from us. Yianni and I will be on Santorini with you tomorrow, come hell or high water."

"We've already had the high water."

"Then get ready for the other, for it's a-comin'."

"Bye, Chief."

Petro hung up and looked up at the gray sky.

"Is everything okay?" said Dimos.

Petro gestured no. "Definitely not okay. You better plan on catching the ferry without me tomorrow."

Dimos smiled. "So that's who you were talking to, the girl-friend, and she's convinced you to stay." He shook his head. "Women sure do have a way of getting men to do what they want. Too bad we haven't quite figured out how to get them to do the same for us."

Petro sighed. "Yeah, too bad. Too bad for sure."

"Poor kid. You're putting him through relationship hell. I sense he really likes the girl," said Yianni.

"If it's meant to be, it's meant to be. He'll take some grief but it's not as if he's admitting to being a serial killer or something."

"To a lot of Greeks, Chief, cops rank pretty close to serial killers."

Andreas waved him off. "What choice did I have?"

"I agree, but it's going to be a hell of a tough sell, and with everything going down tomorrow…." Yianni shook his head.

"You know it, I know it, he knows it."

"Maybe you should reconsider speaking to the Prime Minister?"

Andreas gestured no. "It won't work. We have no hard facts."

"We have a murdered girl."

"Yes, but nothing linking her murder to Mayroon, Prada, or a conspiracy to take out the Prime Minister. Even if these Mayroon folks are the same sort of blood-vengeance zealots as the Maniots who murdered Kapodistrias for offending their family's honor, what possible reason would they have to kill the Brigadier's daughter?"

"Maybe she knew something?"

"Maybe, but no one we've spoken to suggests that she did."

"I thought you saw her murder as a message?"

Andreas nodded. "I still do, and believe if we can figure that out, everything else will fall into place. But a message to whom? It's not the sort of message that gets a parent to cooperate. Despite what I said to the Brigadier, what worse harm could you possibly do to parents than kill their only child?"

Andreas crossed himself three times, drew in and let out a deep breath, and slammed his fist on the dashboard. "But damnit, who has time to concentrate on any of that now? We've got a possible assassination plot about to go full boil, and barely a hint at the who, where, when, or how of any of it."

"At least we have Santorini."

Andreas cocked his head toward Yianni. "We're about to find out if it lives up to its old nickname."

"You mean, 'beautiful island?'"

"No," said Andreas looking back out the side window. "The Devil's Island."

◇◇◇

"Anything for us, Maggie?"

"Welcome back, boys, from what I heard has been a busy day, and there's still practically half of it left to go."

"I take it you spoke with Tassos," said Andreas.

"Right after you did. Almost made me jealous of all the excitement you two have in your lives, but I used it as inspiration for following up on Yianni's list of possible military hit men."

"Any luck?" said Yianni.

"Yep, but not sure if it's good or bad."

"Meaning?" said Andreas.

"There are a dozen possibilities, half of them still on active duty. Any one of them capable of pulling off the shooting."

Andreas shook his head. "I was hoping to eliminate home-grown possibilities."

"No such luck."

"Anything else?"

"Francesco said to give him a shout when you got back."

"Good, maybe he found something for us on the recordings from Babis' office. Yianni, wait with me in my office so we can hear the news together, and, Maggie, please tell Francesco to come in."

Yianni followed Andreas into his office and sat in a chair in front of Andreas' desk. "What do you think it'll be, good or bad?"

"Greeks are natural pessimists."

"With good reason."

Francesco knocked on the open door. "Is this a good time?"

Andreas nodded and pointed to the couch. Yianni angled his chair to see both men.

"So, what do you have for us?"

"You have no idea how boring a minister's life can be," said Francesco.

Andreas smiled. "As a matter of fact I do."

Francesco nodded. "True, but this hits new lows, I assure you."

Andreas waved his hand. "Just tell us what you found."

"On the conversations our distinguished minister of public order recorded, he spent most of his time trying to get those he recorded to say how much they liked him and respected his leadership capabilities."

"Must have been a hard sell," said Yianni.

"It was, but he probably got enough to edit down into a nice promotional piece about himself."

"Any indication of his reason for chasing compliments?" said Andreas.

"Not so far as I could tell. But no matter the subject, he steered the conversation around to how much better he could have handled it, and pressed whoever he was talking with to agree."

"Sounds like that U.S. presidential candidate, the billionaire guy," said Yianni.

'Yeah, the one with the hair."

"Guys, please," said Andreas. "Was Prada involved in the conversations?"

"Barely, and not another word mentioned about his time with the Caesars on Santorini."

"Damn," said Andreas. "You're sure absolutely nothing was said about the military or Santorini?"

"Well, yeah, Babis had a lot of tough words to say about the minister of defense."

"What sort of words?"

"As hard as he tried to get everybody to say great things about himself, he worked even harder to get them to shit all over the defense minister."

Andreas leaned back in his chair. "But no mention of Santorini?"

"Only when Prada talked about going there for dinner with the Caesars. But we already knew that."

"How did the subject come up?"

Francesco looked at his notes. "It was the day of the dinner. Prada walked in on the minister while he was recording a conversation with a member of parliament, and the minister didn't bother to turn off the system. Prada said he was leaving for Santorini for dinner with the Caesars, and the minister asked if he still thought it was a good idea."

"Still? As in they'd discussed it before?"

"Yes."

"What did Prada say?"

"That because of who was coming to Santorini, it was 'imperative.'"

Andreas sat up. "Did he elaborate on who was coming to Santorini?"

Francesco gestured no. "Both men dropped the subject. I assumed he was talking about the Caesars."

Andreas looked at Yianni. "Call Petro and tell him I don't care what it takes, I need to know ASAP *when* the Prime Minister received his invitation to attend that tree-lighting—and if Prada played any part in getting it for him."

"I think you already told him you wanted to know that," said Yianni.

"*Well, tell him again!*"

"Okay, no reason to yell." Yianni pulled out his phone.

"Uh, do you guys need me anymore?"

Andreas gestured no. "Sorry about raising my voice to Yianni."

"We're all under pressure, Chief. If you need me, just call. I'll be in the office." Francesco quickly left.

"Petro's not answering his phone. He's probably talking with the girlfriend."

"Then send him a text message. This is *critical*."

"I know. And by the way, didn't you just apologize for raising your voice at me? Not a direct apology to me, of course, but nevertheless an apology."

Andreas waved his hand at Yianni. "Okay, Mister Suddenly Super Sensitive. It's not anger, it's excitement. I couldn't put my finger on why a business-driven group like Mayroon would have an interest in assassinating a Prime Minister they helped elect, even if he wasn't doing all that they wanted. After all, he's still the most powerful person in Greece—and their creation. Sensible businessmen don't destroy their golden goose just because it isn't at the moment laying all the eggs they want. That's not good business."

"Unless there's another goose ready to take its place?"

Andreas nodded. "Our son of a bitch of a public order minister is auditioning for the role of Mayroon's new golden goose, and doing all that he can to spike the chances of his strongest competition, the minister of defense."

Yianni nodded thoughtfully. "So what's Prada's role in all this?"

"That cagey bastard? He's acting like the perfect theatrical agent." Andreas leaned forward in his chair. "Try Petro, again. *Please*."

Chapter Twenty-one

The Santorini of grand, enveloping sapphire vistas and blue-domed, brilliant white churches clinging to cliff sides was what drew the tourists, but much of the island looked nothing like that, ranging more from the downright homey to honky-tonk. Patchwork fields and vineyards dotted with occasional churches and well-used outbuildings, beaches lined by commercial hodgepodges of vacationer attractions, and random eclectic architecture straining to pay varying degrees of symbolic homage to the vaulted roofs of the famed caldera properties, all seemed driven more by a shared desire to profit off the tourist boom than to honor the island's history and traditions.

But no matter the varied styles or tastes of summer visitors that drew them to the island's differing locales, they came *en masse* from May through October. And that meant profit.

Petro thought Sappho would be at home, perhaps at the restaurant, but when he called to say he could stay another day or two, she told him to join her at a beachfront taverna on Perissa, Santorini's most popular beach. Perissa sat at the eastern edge of the island's southern coastline, on the southwest side of Mesa Vouno, the limestone mountaintop site of ancient Thira, named after late-twelfth-century BCE Spartan King Thiras, whose people Santorinians credited with creating Ancient Thira's ports, towns, and sanctuaries.

Santorini's second most popular beach, Kamari, once the port of ancient Thira, lay on the other side of Mesa Vouno, but the only practical way to drive between the two beaches involved a long circuitous route winding west, north, and east around Mesa Vouno and Mount Profitis Ilias, a journey that in the best of traffic took close to thirty minutes.

Kamari and Perissa beaches shared the same black volcanic sand, Kamari's running north to the airport, and Perissa's heading westerly through Perivolos Beach toward the town of Exomitis. Fifty years ago sleepy Perissa had been all fields, a big white church and a few scattered buildings. Today, the Perissa-Perivolos strip offered miles of summer action as hot as its sand, with restaurants, bars, hotels, and a panoply of tourist shops working feverishly to accommodate beach worshippers from around the world searching for fun in the sun.

It took Petro thirty relatively careful minutes on puddle-ridden two-lane roads, passing by dormant vineyards, closed hotels, shuttered summer homes, skeletons of unfinished buildings, quiet villages, and sleepy shops to reach Perissa. Gray, brown, and black—slightly tinged with green—served as the colors of the land, while shades of white, dirty beige, stone gray, and random splashes of primary colors dominated the low, local structures. Sparse trees—Petro recognized few beyond eucalyptus, tamarisk, and palm—stood randomly along the roadsides while fallow winter fields ran off toward the sea or mountain ridges.

Petro parked next to four thick wide-plank wooden steps leading up to an all-white, two-story stucco building of unmistakable modern design but indeterminate purpose. A row of unfinished plywood sheets ran across the building's first-floor front wall, likely protecting windows beneath from winter gales. Two white stucco pillars at the base of the steps bore the same single word mounted in black wrought iron script: MIAMI. Evidently this was someone's idea of bringing a bit of America's Miami to Santorini. Why anyone would want to do that was another story, though it undoubtedly tied into the entrepreneurial mania behind Santorini's extraordinary success at giving tourists what they wanted.

At the top of the steps a broad, white marble-tiled deck stretched across in front of the building, its stucco roadside wall just high enough to block from view—for anyone sitting on the deck—the two-lane tarmac separating the northern commercial side of the road from the expanse of ebony sand and deep blue sea to the south.

But he saw no one on the deck today, or on the beach.

What in the world is Sappho doing here?

Directly up and beyond the steps stood a set of solid dark-stained wooden doors partially ajar. He headed straight for them and poked his head inside. "Hello, anyone in here?"

"Yes, dear, I'm back in the kitchen."

So it's a restaurant.

Petro followed Sappho's voice past tables and chairs neatly stacked and covered in clear plastic sheeting. Beyond them, a mirror-backed bar area ran the length of the east wall, but with not a single bottle visible, undoubtedly all safely locked away for the winter. For sure booze thieves stood as a bigger threat on Santorini than table- and chair-snatchers.

Petro aimed for the left doorway on the back wall, the one not labeled WC.

Sappho met him as he stepped into the kitchen, giving him a quick hug and a cursory kiss on both cheeks.

"That's it?" said Petro. "I tell you I'm staying and you kiss me like I'm your brother."

"I don't have a brother, so I'll have to take your word on that." She grabbed his hand and pulled him deeper into the kitchen. "So, what do you think of it?"

"I think you're all wound up. As for 'it,' what's the 'it' I'm supposed to be thinking of?"

"This place, silly. What do you think of this restaurant?"

"You're thinking of opening here?"

"If I can make a deal, yes. The current owners put a hell of a lot of money into it," she waved at all the equipment, "and the portable stuff that might disappear in wintertime is locked up inside the walk-ins." She pointed at two huge coolers against the rear wall by a door marked EXIT. "It's a turnkey operation all set to go."

"Why are they selling?"

"Because they don't know how to run the business. They're a couple from Athens who thought it would be chic to have a place on Perissa. They spent more time hanging out with their customers than taking care of them. That's a big no-no in this business. You can never forget that your role is to serve your guests, not party with them."

"They're losing money?"

She gestured no. "Even in this economy it's hard to do that on Santorini, what with the constant turnover every few days of new customers with fresh cash. They simply lost interest in their fantasy when the island's regulars stopped coming and they found themselves having to wait on actual customers, instead of serving as kings controlling the entrance of supplicants to their castle."

"I get it. But why would you move *your* restaurant here? This is a place for a summer business."

"We're not moving the restaurant. This would be all my operation. My mother and father want me to do it. They know how much I've dreamed of having a place on this beach. They can get all the help they need during the summer and I know I can turn this into a goldmine."

"Just wear a bikini and the place will be packed twenty-four/seven."

Sappho batted her eyes. "You silver-tongued devil, you."

"How far along are you in negotiations?"

"Far enough that I'm about to make an offer. I want to do it while they're still dejected over their summer experience. Memories tend to get rosier the longer they endure an Athens winter, and I wouldn't want them toying with the idea of taking another run at it."

"You're a hard-nosed businesswoman."

"It's the only way to be on this island. Look out for yourself, because everyone else is."

Petro nodded. "Yep. Sure is."

"You still haven't answered my question, what do you think of the place?"

He forced a nervous smile. "I don't know the business."

Sappho nodded. "So you don't like it?"

"I didn't say that."

"You didn't have to.

"Okay, it's a bit too much over the top for my tastes. I like my Greek island places to look like Greek islands."

"Fair enough. I can assure you it won't be called 'Miami' if I get the place. The over-the-top glitzy touches will be gone, but the bones will remain because the island's attracting a lot of Chinese, Russians, and Indians, and those of them with money love that sort of glamour."

Petro smiled. "As I said, I don't know the business."

Sappho caught his eye. "Would you like to learn?"

Petro looked away.

"Sorry, I didn't mean to be so pushy. Damn it, I'm always chasing away the men I like."

"Is that why the island's so empty?"

She poked her finger in his chest. "Don't push it, wise guy, or I might withdraw the offer."

"I already have a job."

"Please. Don't tell me you're in the hotel business. You know about as much about that as I do about brain surgery. Sure, you can try to make some money putting people together in the business, but you're not a hotelier. And I doubt you ever will be. That's not your skill set."

"So, what is my skill set?"

"I'd prefer we not get into that here, as there's no telling who might walk in on us."

Petro grinned. "Follow me."

Sappho grabbed her purse off a counter top. "This should be interesting."

He walked into to the dining room, and took down a table and two chairs from under the plastic.

"Sit, please."

Sappho put her handbag on the table and sat down staring at him grim-faced. "Is this the part where you tell me you really do have a wife?"

"That would be easy." He sat down and faced her head-on.

"Don't tell me you're gay. I won't believe you."

Petro drew in and let out a deep breath. "I'm a cop."

"Please, tell me you're gay. Anything but a cop."

Petro blinked. "That's all you have to say?"

"Darling, I knew you weren't what you said, and that you were into something suspicious. I just hoped it wasn't something bad. Now you turn out to be a cop. So much for my hopes." She smiled and reached out for his hand. "Let's get to the part where you tell me you're sworn to secrecy and can't tell me any more."

"You're watching too many movies."

"Because I haven't had anyone to keep me company for quite a while."

Petro looked down and squeezed her hand. "As a matter of fact, not only can I tell you what I'm doing, I need to ask for your help." He looked straight at her. "Which I know sounds right out of a movie."

"Any number of bad ones."

"This one could get particularly bad."

"Uh, do you happen to have any identification you could show me?"

He looked at her for a long moment. "Yeah, sure." He reached for his wallet and pulled out his ID card.

"I thought you guys carried them around your neck…under your shirt." She looked at it, then at him, straight-faced. "Okay."

"Do you want to hear the rest?"

"Why not? Break my heart completely."

She leaned back in her chair, pulling her hand away from him as she did, and crossing her arms.

Petro swallowed. "I was assigned here to supervise an operation intended to determine if there was a military plot against the government. Just by coincidence, the targets of our surveillance decided on meeting in your restaurant."

"So, you spied on our customers?"

"Yes."

Sappho shifted in her seat. "Using me for access."

"I didn't think of it that way."

"I bet you didn't."

"This isn't easy," said Petro.

"I'm certain not nearly as easy as I was."

Petro raised his hands. "Stop. There's no reason to go that way with this. I'm here because I want to be with you."

"No, you're here because you need my help. You just admitted that."

Petro rubbed at his eyes. "Do you really want to believe that?"

She jumped to her feet. "No, I definitely don't *want* to believe that. But what else can I believe?"

"Let's not turn this into some very bad movie dialogue."

"It can get worse?"

"I'm going to tell you what I know and what I need to know from you, and after I do, if you still believe I'm here just to use you, you'll be in a position to do me some very serious harm. In other words, I'm prepared to trust you with my career."

Sappho walked around in a twenty-step circle three times before stopping abruptly in front of him. "Fine, tell me."

"Sit down, please." He pointed at the chair and waited until she sat.

"We believe there may be a plot to assassinate the Prime Minister."

She stared at him for ten seconds. "Let me see that ID again."

He reached for his wallet.

She raised her hand. "No, that was just my way of saying to myself you must be insane."

"I wish I were."

"Who do you think is trying to kill him?"

"Not sure, but we think it involves that civilian who turned up late at the military dinner in your restaurant."

"Him? Hard to imagine. I thought he was a friend of the Prime Minister."

Petro shrugged. "What can I say?"

"No need to say anything. Cain and Abel says it all." She sighed. "So what do you want from me?"

"Two things. First, we need to know when the mayor invited the Prime Minister to participate in the tree-lighting ceremony tomorrow night, and what part the Prime Minister's slick friend played in that invitation."

"No problem, I'll call Nikolaos right away."

"Nikolaos?"

"He's Santorini's mayor."

"Oh."

"That's the benefit of having a local girl as your operative. So what else do you need to know?"

"Where would you pick as the best place on Santorini for an assassination if you wanted to make it look like a Greek military conspiracy?"

"I see we're done with the easy questions."

"Any ideas?"

"Assuming the Prime Minister uses the military's part of the airport, that's a possibility."

"Yes, but it's controlled by the military, so that would make it hard to pull off unless the military actually is involved. We're looking for a place that will make it seem like the military's behind it, even though it's not."

She shrugged. "Sorry, but I'm in the restaurant business, not the cloak and dagger. I can't think of anything else."

Petro nodded. "Okay, so tell me about the top of Pyrgos where the tree-lighting ceremony will take place."

"What's there to tell? It's set up next to what's left of the old castle. The villages of Skaros, Emborio, Oia, Akrotiri, and Pyrgos all have ancient castle ruins, but even the best-preserved suffered severe damage in the earthquake of 1956. They're made of volcanic rock and pumice mortar, the same as virtually everything else on this island. I think they date back to the Middle Ages."

"Any military significance?"

"Today? Not that I know of."

Petro sighed. "That's it?"

"As I said, this sort of thing isn't my bag."

Petro stared at her without saying a word.

Sappho stared back.

"So?" said Petro.

"I assume 'so' is your way of asking whether I believe you?"

Petro nodded.

She shrugged again. "I don't think it really matters at this moment. Unless you're a lunatic or serial killer who's come here to have your way with me, something very serious could go down on Santorini in the next twenty-four hours or so."

"Yes, it could."

"So, whether or not I ever want to see you again, *if* what you said has even the slightest bit of possible truth to it, an assassination of our Prime Minister on Santorini would be very bad PR for our business. And, after all, above all else I am a 'hard-nosed businesswoman.'" Sappho emphasized her words with finger quotes.

Petro nodded. "I deserved that."

"No, you deserve a lot more, or a lot less, but that's for me to decide when my mind's in a different place."

"Fair enough."

She pulled out her phone and punched in a number. "Time to call the mayor. By the way, since I'm doing all this secret agent stuff do I at least get a code name or something?"

Petro's face turned deadly serious. "Absolutely. Would you prefer Crockett or Tubbs?

"Huh?"

"Miami?" Petro waved his hands in a broad gesture around the room. "*Miami Vice?*"

She wrinkled her forehead and gave him a blank stare.

"An old American cop show. Crockett and Tubbs are the lead cops."

Sappho rolled her eyes. "You know, up to this point I thought we at least had a sense of humor in common." She pressed buttons on her phone. "Another disappointment."

Andreas recognized the caller ID coming through on his office line as Petro's, and picked up before Maggie could answer. "I hope you're calling with good news."

"All I can say is I'm calling with answers."

"That'll work."

"My friend spoke to the mayor and he told her that an invitation to the Prime Minister to attend the tree-lighting ceremony went out a month ago."

"A month ago? Dammit. So much for my theory. I'd have bet just about anything that Prada somehow was behind getting the PM his invitation *after* Prada had been invited to dinner with the Caesars. We're back to square one."

"Not so fast, Chief. You'd have won your bet."

"But the invitation was a month ago and Prada was invited to dinner with the Caesars two Fridays ago."

"Yes, but guess when the Prime Minister *accepted* the invitation."

Andreas sat bolt upright in his chair. "I almost wish you're not about to tell me what I know you're going to tell me."

"Yep, two Fridays ago."

"My God, it *is* an assassination plot."

"The mayor said he'd been pushing the Prime Minister to come but was getting nowhere. Then out of the blue Prada called him that Friday to say the PM would love to come, but he needed to know the precise details of when and where he was expected to be on the island."

Andreas felt goose bumps running up his arm. "Did your friend get the details?"

"My friend's very good. She dragged everything out of him with promises of a big dinner at her restaurant."

"Is she with you now?"

"Yes."

"Let me speak to her."

"Chief—"

"Don't worry, just put her on the phone."

Andreas heard a muffled back and forth."

"Hello?"

"Is this Sappho?"

"Yes, and how did you know my name?"

"I'm Chief of Special Crimes. I'm supposed to know those sorts of things. But in case you're wondering, Petro didn't tell me. He's been very protective of you. Even fought with me over getting you involved in this. I want to thank you for making me look good in front of him. Your help's been invaluable and proven me right."

"Anything I can do to make him look bad is fine with me."

Andreas stifled a laugh. "Well, as I said, you've been a very big help to me, if that helps you any."

"I just wish I could have got you a better line on where the attempt might take place. All the mayor could tell me was that it's going to be a quick in and out trip. Straight from the airport to Pyrgos for the ceremony, and immediately back to the airport."

"How are they getting from the bottom of Pyrgos to the top?"

"The mayor didn't know, but my guess is our Prime Minister would like to be seen as a vigorous young leader and will likely hike up the hill through the village streets greeting everyone who comes out to see him along the way."

Andreas nodded at the phone. "I'm sorry to say that sounds about right." He paused. "That's all very helpful, thank you, but the primary reason I wanted to speak to you was to tell you that you've done a great service for your country."

Pause.

"Did you hear me?"

"Uh, yes, but do you mind if I call you back?"

"Call me back?"

"Yes. You see, Petro placed this call and for all I know—"

Andreas burst out laughing. "I get it, you want to make sure I'm who I say I am. I wish everyone were as cautious as you.

Sure, feel free, but I won't give you my number. That would defeat the purpose. May I speak to Petro again?"

Pause.

"Yes, Chief."

"She's a winner."

"I know."

Andreas swallowed. "We've got a serious problem. I've no doubt there'll be an attempt on the PM's life, and most likely in Pyrgos. I want you up there right away. Check to see if anything strikes you as unusual, different, or out of line."

"It'll be dark by the time I get there."

"Trust me, whoever plans on assassinating our Prime Minister will be working through the night."

"That's not what I meant." There was a slight bristle to Petro's voice. "I've never been to Pyrgos. I have no idea what's 'unusual, different, or out of line.'"

"So, find a local you can trust to help you. And let me know when you get there. Any questions?"

Pause. "No."

"Good. And you're doing great work. Keep it up."

"I'll try my best. Bye."

Andreas put down the phone. He knew he'd been tough on the kid, so much so that had his conversation with Petro been face-to-face he might have had to duck a few times. His efforts to do some repair work on the inevitable damage his demands surely wreaked on Petro's relationship with Sappho probably wouldn't help much, but the bottom line was Andreas had no choice. The Prime Minister's life was on the line.

Everyone else's life would just have to wait.

Petro put his phone back in his pocket and rubbed at his chin.

"Are you thinking of an appropriate thing to say?"

"More like how do I tell you that I have to leave?"

"I heard. For Pyrgos."

He nodded. "Not sure what I'm looking for, but I've got to start on it right away."

"Is it dangerous?"

"Could be. The chief wants me looking for anything abnormal, but if there really is a plot to assassinate the Prime Minister tomorrow, the bad guys must be up there making sure everything looks just the opposite. My wandering around on a rainy night might just be the bit of abnormal that tips *them* off, and who knows how they'll react to that?"

"I think you need a local to give you cover."

"The chief said sort of the same thing."

"Which reminds me. I'm debating whether I should call to verify if he's who you said he is."

Petro waved a hand in the air. "Go ahead, knock yourself out. They're your message units."

"Okay, I've made up my mind." Sappho lifted her purse off the table as she stood up. "Let's go," and headed toward the door.

"Go where?"

"To Pyrgos."

"You're not coming with me. I just said it could be dangerous."

She stopped and turned around. "What other local can you call for help who you can trust with what you're up to? Do you even know another local?"

Petro looked at his feet.

"Besides, I like your boss. He actually tried to make you sound as if you cared for me."

"I do."

She waved one hand in the air. "Enough already with the *kamaki* lines."

"Whoa, I'm not a *kamaki*."

"As I understand the meaning of *kamaki,* and I'm not talking about the little trident that fishermen use to spear the innocent octopus, any man who does whatever it takes to seduce the woman of his interest at the moment is a *kamaki*."

Petro shut his eyes.

"Counting to ten are we?"

"Don't you ever let up?"

"I will once we get to work. I don't want our Prime Minister assassinated, and as I said before, certainly not on Santorini."

Petro set his jaw. "You'll have to do whatever I say."

"Don't I always?" Sappho fluttered her eyelashes.

Petro rubbed at his eyes with his fingertips and shook his head. "Why do I just know I'm going to regret this?"

Chapter Twenty-two

Andreas told Yianni to pick him up at home the next morning in time for them to make the first flight out of Venizelos International Airport to Santorini. He'd decided against requisitioning ministry aircraft for the trip as that presented too big a risk of word getting back to Prada. No way he'd see Andreas flying to Santorini that morning as anything other than a warning to call off whatever was on for that night.

Now came the most dangerous part of his plan: telling his more than eight-months-pregnant wife that he was leaving town. He wasn't looking forward to what he expected to follow her inevitable words, "For how long?" so he made a tactical decision to stop along the way for flowers.

He floated, "Hi, honey, I'm home," out into the apartment as soon as he walked through the front door.

No answer.

He walked through the rooms looking for any sign of life. "Hello?"

Marietta met him just outside the kitchen. "Mr. Kaldis, Mrs. Kaldis is sleeping."

"Was trying to," came from the living room.

"Oops," said Andreas, handing the flowers to Marietta and heading on toward Lila lying on the sofa in a cream silk bathrobe.

"Sorry about that, my love." Andreas bent down and kissed her on the forehead.

"You're home early."

"How are you feeling?" He sat on a chair next to the sofa up by her head.

"Just perfect. Feet swollen to where I have no ankles, battery acid popping into my throat every time I lie down, and don't even ask what it's like when I need the loo."

Andreas smiled. "Hope I'm not catching too much blame."

"Blame? For this?" Lila pointed at her belly. "No." She sighed. "Though at times I must admit there's a bit of resentment at how men get to go on living their lives without any of the physical restrictions we have to put up with."

"Really?"

"Uh-huh, but it's all worth it in the end."

She reached out her hand and Andreas took it. "So, why are you home early?"

"To spend time with you," he swallowed. "Before I have to leave for Santorini in the morning." He braced for her to drop her hand.

She didn't. "I rest my case."

"That's not what I thought you'd say."

"For how long?"

"That's better."

Marietta came into the room carrying Andreas' flowers in a vase. "Mrs. Kaldis, look at the beautiful flowers Mr. Kaldis brought for you."

Lila used Andreas' hand to pull herself up to a sitting position. "Oh, so you'll be away for *that* long."

Marietta put the flowers on a table next to the sofa and quickly left the room.

Andreas waited until Lila seemed to have found a comfortable sitting position. "At least one night."

"At least?"

Andreas looked back toward the kitchen then leaned forward and whispered. "I think we've uncovered a plot to assassinate the Prime Minister. We think it's planned to go down tomorrow night."

Lila crossed herself. "My God, who's behind it?"

Andreas swung over onto the sofa beside her. "We don't have a scrap of hard evidence. It's all speculation at this point."

"Names, please."

"As I see it, Prada for sure, and likely Babis. A lot of effort has gone in to setting it up to look like a military operation so that the military takes the fall, but to me it's all pointing to a foreign-run organization."

"What foreigners?"

"An international consulting firm called the Mayroon Group."

Lila shook her head. "That sounds crazy. Like a James Bond film."

"Until it happens, then the entire world says it was so obvious, how could the authorities have missed it?"

"But what do they have to gain?"

"Power and first claim on our nation's assets. They helped get the Prime Minister where he is, but he's no longer playing ball with them."

"Then I take it their purpose is not to create a more perfect socialist state."

"I don't think the label matters. All they want is a more perfect puppet government to control."

"They want to seize power so that the seizers can rule?"

Andreas nodded.

Lila shook her head and slapped her hands on the sofa. "Is there anyone anywhere in our government who actually cares about our country? Our families? I'm sick and tired of one politician after another, one party after another, all focused only on what puts money in their pockets and nothing else. *They're* the reason we've got this Mayroon Group, and who knows how many others like them, believing they can direct our future. We're just numbers to them." She smacked the sofa again and sighed. "I'm worried."

"About what?"

Lila rubbed her belly. "I fear for our children's future if we remain in Greece."

Andreas put his arm around his wife. "You're really wound up."

Lila rested her head upon his shoulder as tears welled up in her eyes. "I'm more worried about you. If these people are willing to assassinate our Prime Minister and they think you might be able to stop them...."

Andreas kissed her on the forehead. "Don't worry, nothing's going to happen to me. There's no way for Mayroon to know I'm on to them."

"You can't be sure."

"You have to trust me on that."

"But why does it have to be you? We can live anywhere in the world."

He squeezed her shoulder. "Good question. Every day I go to work at a job that at times seems hopeless. And, yes, I've asked myself, 'Why do I care when so many others seem not to?' 'Why don't I quit?' 'Why don't we move out of Greece as so many we know already have?' For me the answer is simple. *I don't want the bastards to win.*"

Andreas paused. "Greece came this close," pinching his thumb and index finger nearly together, "to getting booted off the euro, possibly falling out of the European Union.

Andreas bit at his lip. "If Mayroon succeeds, we face the same fate as if we'd exited the EU. Our country run by profiteers, where the strong rule as unchecked as feudal lords, taking whatever they can from the weak. And those lords will not all be Greeks, certainly not in places where foreigners come with great wealth to spend on great vices. We'll all suffer, especially our children. Or we'll join the stream of migrants passing through Greece on their way to hoped-for better lives in other lands." Andreas shook his head. "I can't allow that to happen."

Lila lifted her head from his shoulder. "You can't stop it alone."

"I can try."

"How?"

Andreas stared toward the Acropolis. "I wish I knew. I really wish I knew."

Lila reached over and turned his face toward hers. "The flowers are lovely. And a wise decision on how to deal with a cranky wife."

"You're not—"

Lila put a finger to his lips. "Of course I am." She kissed him.

"Okay, I know when not to disagree with you."

Lila smacked him lightly across the chest. "I'm glad your sense of humor is back."

"Why?"

"Because I've changed the color in the baby's room again."

I guess that means we're staying.

Sappho parked her car at the edge of a roundabout close by a taverna and next to a long series of ascending, pebble-inlaid, deep-tread steps, set off on the left by a blue double-pipe railing, and on the right by a white masonry wall bearing a sign in the shape of an arrow marked CASTLE pointing up the steps.

She stepped out of the car and stood next to the driver side door. Not a bit of sunshine, starlight, or moonbeams made it through the cloud cover, but at least it wasn't raining; the sky held a dull milky-gray glow in its clouds. She watched Petro pull up and park his motorcycle next to her. "I thought I'd lost you."

"Nope, not a chance. I just decided you needed space." He smiled.

Sappho forced a grin on an otherwise grim face. "My guess is this is the entrance they'll use if the Prime Minister plans on walking up to the top. The main square is a bit farther down the road, but this gives him options on the route to the top."

"It's as good a place as any to start. We can check out the other possibilities later."

"You really don't plan on sleeping tonight, do you?"

"Just lead the way," he waved his hand toward the steps, but abruptly held it up for her to stop. "What about that?" He pointed to a sign warning that vehicles parked where they'd parked would be towed.

"I'm local. They know my car. No one will tow me."

"What about me?"

She shrugged. "Who cares? Let's go." She started toward the steps.

Petro followed, shaking his head. "Hey, show some mercy. I might get shot at before this is over."

"I can't wait."

The name Pyrgos meant tower or castle, and much of the village's modern-day attraction remained rooted in the diligent preservation of its medieval configuration and atmosphere, despite having grown far beyond its original castle walls. What remained of Pyrgos' roughly fifteenth-century castle sat atop the highest village on the island, silhouetted against the slopes of Mount Profitis Ilias. The village once boasted a citadel ringed by the solid outer walls of abutting houses built as a protective perimeter for an enclosed community of churches, houses, stables, assorted hiding places, and a labyrinth of passageways. The citadel's narrow roads followed the contours of the hillside, leading up to a single entrance into the castle, one guarded from above by a place where boiling oil would rain down upon invaders successful enough to overcome its other defenses. If all else failed, the village relied upon a system of underground tunnels for its ultimate escape plan.

Petro followed Sappho's lefts and rights, twists and turns, up dimly lit stone steps and stretches of paths, past one church after another.

"How many churches are in this village?" he asked.

"Last I heard, around forty-five. You should see them during the day. Some of them look like they belong on top of a wedding cake."

They entered a small square. More steps on the far side led up to yet another church.

"Let's stop here for a minute," said Petro.

"Tired already?"

"No, we need to talk about a plan."

She pointed to a wall without windows over by the steps. "Over there. Too many eavesdroppers in this town."

"In every town." Petro leaned in and whispered to her, "I sense we're almost at the top."

She nodded. "Up the steps is the Church of Agios Nikolaos. From there it's not far to what remains of the castle and Theotokaki, a tenth-century church inside the castle walls."

"But where's the tree?"

"In the square in front of the entrance to the castle. Aristocrats used to gather there in what was called The Coffee Shop High Up."

"Catchy name," said Petro.

"So much for the history lesson. What's your plan on figuring out where the bad guys are?"

Petro let out a breath and leaned his back against the wall. "It's all closely packed buildings with doorways, windows, rooftops, and a million other places to hide, plus church bell towers that give a potential shooter an angle on practically every part of the village...." He waved his hand in the air. "We're in a literal assassin's paradise."

"That doesn't sound promising."

"It isn't."

Sappho walked toward the steps. "Well, let's head on up for a look at the tree."

"Whoa. Two people wandering about in the dark in lousy weather in front of an unlit Christmas tree is about as obvious a tip-off as I can think of for anyone on the lookout for something out of the ordinary."

"So, hold my hand and act as if you're hoping to get lucky."

Petro bit his tongue and took her hand. The best play at the moment for improving his situation seemed to be no retort, witty or otherwise.

They took their time reaching the square, pausing every so often along the way to enhance the image of two lovers strolling aimlessly in the dark. The square looked smaller than he imagined, only thirty meters long by less than half that in width, but the unlit tree stood out in bold silhouette against the clouds.

"Impressive-looking tree," said Petro.

"Usually there's more light up here. I guess they're keeping it dark so that when the tree goes live tomorrow night it'll make a big impression. I've been thinking," whispered Sappho in his ear, "there are a lot of places to hide, but unless your assassins are suicidal, they don't want to be caught."

Petro nodded. "I agree with that."

"Which means they need to find a place with a clear escape route."

"Do you know of any?"

"Regrettably, a lot. This village was built with escaping from pirates in mind. But they'd have to be a local to know the secrets."

"I doubt they're local. But who knows what they know?"

"My grandfather used to play in a tunnel under the castle as a kid. It ran from here to Exo Gonia. It would have been perfect for what you have in mind, but it was destroyed in the earthquake of 1956."

"Anyone ever try to repair it?"

"The town tried in 1996 but stopped because it wasn't technically feasible."

"Do you know where the old tunnel entrances are?"

She gestured no. "Are you thinking your assassins dug out a tunnel?"

Petro gestured no back. "They wouldn't have had time. I just want to make sure no one else might have done the repair work and our bad guys know about it."

"I'll ask my father."

Both stood staring at the tree outlined against the sky.

"Where to now?" she asked.

"Let's check out the other routes the Prime Minister might take to get up here."

"I doubt they'll make you any more comfortable."

"I know," said Petro. "But at least I get to hold your hand."

Sappho didn't say a word. Nor did she let go of his hand.

Andreas and Yianni arrived shortly after sunrise, and Petro met them outside the airport arrivals building.

"Nice ride," said Andreas pulling forward the passenger side front seat so Yianni could squeeze into the back.

"I particularly like the neon green," said Yianni. "So understated."

"It's Sappho's. You guys didn't give me much notice on picking you up. I had to make do with what was available."

"Ignore him," said Andreas. "Just tell me what you've got for us."

"A lot of potential hiding places, and nothing more than that. We covered what seemed every centimeter of Pyrgos and spent the rest of the night up by the square where the ceremony's taking place sitting in the living room of Sappho's aunt's house staring out a window looking for anything suspicious."

"Did you see anything?"

"Yeah, her aunt. Sappho told her we'd come to the village for dinner, had car trouble, and needed a place to stay until morning. I don't think she believed us. She kept peeking in to see what we were up to."

"Smart lady," said Yianni.

Andreas drummed his fingers on the dash. "Maybe something will pop out at us in the daylight."

"I thought the old tunnels under the castle might be the way they planned on doing it," said Petro. "It would be the perfect escape route, because even though there are a lot of places to hide in Pyrgos, there aren't a lot of ways out. We could choke off the exits and trap them in here rather easily."

"And they'd know that," said Andreas.

"But the tunnels aren't passable. Sappho's father checked with his friends in construction."

"Couldn't they just blend in among the crowd and disappear?" asked Yianni.

"Yes, but let's remember one very important thing." Andreas paused his drumming on the dashboard. "In order for the plan to work, they can't be anonymous killers. There can be no doubt left in anyone's mind that the military orchestrated it all. They want the whole world to think that Greece's military assassinated its Prime Minister."

"But the killers still have to get away," said Yianni.

"Unless they actually are Greek military," said Petros.

"Even if they are, whoever's behind it won't want them caught," said Andreas. "At least not alive."

"Maybe they'll use a bomb?" said Yianni. "Take out the assassin and the target at the same time"

Andreas gestured no. "I don't see Mayroon inspiring that sort of suicidal dedication in its assassins. If the killers who took out the Brigadier's daughter are any indication of the kind of talent Mayroon employs, they're not the sort willing to die for a cause. Professionals who get paid to kill for a living want to survive to spend their money. Besides, a bomb of any sort runs the risk of being confused with the non-lethal type of bombings our homegrown terrorists love to do. It muddies the blame-it-on-the-military message this whole operation is about."

Andreas stared out the side window as they entered the outskirts of Pyrgos. "There has to be a plan that screams military and gets the assassins out alive. We just have to figure out what it is."

Petro peeked at the clock on the dash. It read eight a.m. "We've got nine hours left to do it. The ceremony's set to take place at Santorini's signature moment of sunset."

Andreas rubbed his forehead. "Great. Let's find a good place for breakfast, because it looks like we'll be skipping lunch."

"Hopefully not dinner," said Yianni.

"I know the perfect place," said Petro.

"Have you eaten there?" said Yianni.

"No, but I spent much of last night staring out a window in its direction fantasizing over what breakfast must be like there."

"Between the aunt peeking in on you all night, and your fantasizing over the perfect breakfast, it sounds like your girlfriend had a really great time," said Yianni.

"You can ask her when you see her. I'm inviting her to breakfast. We'll need her to find our way around the village." Petro glanced over at Andreas. "If that's okay with you, Chief."

"Why not? She might even get Yianni to behave."

"Don't bet on it."

Petro smiled. "This could get bloody."

Chapter Twenty-three

Breakfast on the enclosed balcony looking down over the town went well. Yianni behaved, Petro looked anxious, and Sappho acted her usual self, keeping Andreas laughing most of the time.

"I don't understand why Petro is always complaining about you, Chief. You seem like such a nice guy."

"I'm happy Petro invited you to join us. I'm learning so much I never knew."

"I'm here to help. Did he ever show you the little voodoo pin cushion doll he has of you?" Sappho turned to Petro. "Go ahead, honey, show him little Andy-baby."

Yianni burst out laughing. "Andy-baby?"

"What can I say, he ordered it from America."

"Where's that road lead?" said Petro pointing south.

"Trying to change the subject, are we?" She followed the direction of his finger. "It's the road leading to the three-hundred-year-old monastery of Profitis Ilias on the top of the mountain of the same name"

"How far is it from here?"

"Thinking of joining, are we?"

Petro's face tightened.

"About four kilometers, depending on how you measure."

"Any other way down once you get up there?"

"Nothing like a road. There's a hiking trail down the other side of Mount Profitis Ilias that splits at Ancient Thira, with one branch going east to Kamari and the other west to Perissa."

"What are you thinking?" asked Andreas.

"Escape routes. Like you said, it's all about escaping."

Yianni nodded.

Andreas slapped his hand on the table. "Okay, folks, time to get to work."

◇◇◇

Much of what loomed as mysterious in the dark no longer bore a threat in daytime. The hidden corner, ominous passageway, and perfect sniper position of the night before proved to be a vendor's stall, an entryway to a tiny quiet square, and a grandmother's window for gazing down on passersby.

What also became starkly apparent in daylight was the historic beauty of this medieval village: square white- and sand-colored homes of mostly red, green, or blue doors and shutters, and bright white churches of Byzantine and cubist influence bearing a Renaissance touch here and there, all domed in Aegean blue or white. One ornate bell tower followed another, as if each were trying to outdo the other.

They'd walked up every pathway to the top, and down the same pathways to the bottom. They'd checked out every known entrance to the old tunnels, and every building or bell tower with a line on the tree-lighting ceremony. Doing just the things one would expect security to do in advance of a visit by the Prime Minister.

It was nearly three in the afternoon. The three cops and Sappho sat drinking coffee at a taverna off the main road and watching the media trek by on their way to set up for the ceremony. From the snatches of overheard conversations Andreas picked up from the crews passing by, the TV networks were doing someone a mighty big favor by putting so many of their people through so much work to cover such a soft news story.

"Anyone have any new thoughts?" said Andreas, looking into his coffee cup.

Silence.

"Me either." Andreas lifted his head. "I have to tell the Prime Minister."

"But if he pulls out now, we blow what's likely our only chance at catching the plotters," said Yianni.

"From what we've come up with so far, there's a better chance that if we don't tell him he'll be dead." Andreas shook his head. "That's not a decision for me to make. It's up to him to decide whether to take the gamble."

"What's the chance of him believing you?" said Petro.

"Or thinking you're crazy and deciding to give in to those pressuring him to replace you?" said Yianni.

Andreas shook his head. "I won't know until I try. But for sure I'm going to try."

Andreas took out his phone and called Maggie. "Hi, my love." Pause.

"Yes we're all having a wonderful holiday on Santorini while you slave away in the office. Listen, I need you to somehow patch me through to the Prime Minister without word getting to Prada that I'm trying to reach him. When you get ahold of him, I'll be available on this line."

Pause.

"Yep, you got it. A matter of life and death."

Andreas hung up the phone. "God bless, Maggie." He paused. "In fact, surrounded as we are by so many magnificent churches, I think this might be a good time for all of us to pray for Greece."

"Amen."

More than fifteen minutes had passed with no word from Maggie. Andreas left the others in the taverna and walked up to the square. A half-dozen people stood talking with a blond, thirtyish male TV reporter who'd evidently told them the Prime Minister would be coming soon. Anything to generate a crowd.

Andreas' phone rang. "Maggie?"

"I can't get to him, Chief. He'd already taken off in the helicopter when I reached his secretary. I told her it was urgent and to put me through on his mobile, but she refused. She said he was on a conference call at the moment with the Chancellor of

Germany and President of France. There was no way she would interrupt that call."

"Fuck," said Andreas.

"My sentiments exactly. I called back every five minutes but he's still on the call. I just hung up with her after giving it my best 'it's a matter of life and death pitch,' but that didn't work either. Her answer was, 'This financial crisis will be the death of us all.' At least she promised to tell him you called the moment he's done with Germany and France."

Andreas gripped the phone tightly. "Somehow that doesn't sound promising. I'll have to catch him here."

"He's supposed to land around four."

Andreas looked at his watch. "About thirty minutes to go. Patch him through to me if you should happen to hear from him."

"Don't hold your breath."

"One can hope. Bye."

He stared at the unlit tree before shifting his attention to a young, dark-haired female TV reporter speaking in English with a tourist couple. Possibly the only tourists in Pyrgos in December. She looked new to the TV news game, and he guessed not likely to recognize him. He walked toward her. "Excuse me, Miss?"

"Yes, sir?" she smiled.

"What's happening?"

"Our nation's Prime Minister will be here to join Santorini's mayor in lighting this magnificent tree."

"Sounds exciting. When's that?"

"Sunset, at precisely five."

"Will there be a procession up the hill?"

She gestured no. "At least certainly nothing formal like at Easter time when thousands of fire lanterns light up the hillside."

"How's he getting up here?"

"He'll have to walk most of the way unless he uses a donkey or motorbike." She waved her mike hand at the crews. "The guys who carry our equipment drove their vans as far in as they could, which wasn't very far."

"At least he'll get some exercise."

"The Prime Minister won't mind. It gives us the chance to show him walking through the village, mingling with the people." She nodded at Andreas. "Such as with you, sir, if you decide to stay around for just another hour."

"Do you know what route he's taking to the top?"

"Not yet. His security won't tell us until the last minute. But don't worry, we'll catch up with him and if you can't stay, you can still watch it tonight right here." She pointed at the symbol on her mike.

"Thank you, you've been most helpful."

She nodded and went back to her conversation in English with the tourists.

Andreas walked back down to the taverna, sat with his crew, and shook his head. "No luck. Maggie can't reach him and security hasn't decided yet how or from where they're getting him up to the tree. Though it looks like he'll be walking."

"I still go with my original guess," said Sappho. "It gives them choices for getting up the hill and is away from all the congestion where most will park."

"Do you really think there'll be a crowd? The village is dead," said Yianni.

"Of course it's dead, it's December. But the mayor is not going to be embarrassed. If you work for the island today, and want to still be working for it tomorrow, you and your entire family better be up in that square tonight, applauding like mad."

"Anyone with any other suggestions?" said Andreas.

Petro and Yianni gestured no.

Andreas looked at his watch. "Well, it's four o'clock. The Prime Minister should just be landing at the airport. If we're right about the plot, let's hope we're also right that it's not going to happen there."

He looked directly into Sappho's eyes. "You've been a terrific help, but when we start up the hill with the Prime Minister I don't want you coming with us." He tapped his index finger on the tabletop. "We have no idea what's going to happen or where, but whatever it is, there's nothing more you can do to help us."

"But—"

Andreas held up his hand. "No buts. We can't be distracted worrying about your safety. Period."

Petro looked down.

"Okay, I get it. So let's go." She stood up and waited for Petro to stand. She smiled at him, took his hand, and led him out the door.

Andreas and Yianni followed behind them, not saying a word.

When they reached the place picked by Sappho, it was obvious to Andreas that a lot of folks agreed with her, even the mayor, for he stood at the bottom of the steps amid a crowd of dignitaries. No media yet, though. They must be waiting for official word on where the entourage would stop with the Prime Minister, who should have been coming any minute.

Andreas doubted there'd be more than a few police motorcycles, followed by whatever number of SUVs were needed for the Prime Minister, his aids, and security detail. Greece hadn't yet fallen into the security gear-up frenzy plaguing other western leaders. Andreas wondered if today would change all that.

Three minutes later, the motorcade came into view as it headed south along the main road into Pyrgos. When the motorcycles reached the roundabout and turned in to park, Sappho leaned over and said to Petro. "Told you so."

Petro smiled.

"This is it, folks. From here on out it's IDs showing and a condition red alert." Andreas pulled his ID out from under his shirt so that it hung around his neck.

The first people out of the SUVs were the Prime Minister's security agents, the second his official photographer. The Prime Minister stepped out and waved to the crowd as he made his way over to the mayor. Cameramen came bursting around the corner, pushing through the crowds and shouting. "TV. Let us through. TV."

"Are they always that pushy?" said Sappho.

"Yes," said Andreas. "Now remember. Stay here. Find someplace to wait until this is over."

Sappho nodded.

Andreas worked his way through the throng toward the Prime Minister, holding up his ID as he did. He was about six deep in the crowd away when the PM and the mayor turned and started up the steps toward the top.

No way Andreas could catch up to him through this pack. He circled left around the crowd pushing to get on the stairs and made his way along the outside of the stair railing to where he could pull himself up and over it ahead of the Prime Minister. His entrance did not go unnoticed, and two security agents stopped him before he could reach the Prime Minister.

Andreas held up his ID. They were not impressed. "I've got to speak to the Prime Minister."

"Not now, sir."

Andreas waved his hand at the Prime Minster, and shouted, "Prime Minister."

One of the security agents grabbed Andreas' hand in an effort to apply a wristlock. Instead, the agent found himself doubled over in pain through the judicious application of a bit of small circle jiu-jitsu to his own hand by Andreas and thrust backwards into the Prime Minister. The second agent reached for his gun. Andreas put up his hands and said, "Play nice now in front of the cameras."

"Andreas," said the Prime Minister. "What's going on?"

"I must speak with you, sir. It's urgent."

"It must be. My secretary told me your secretary had virtually camped out in my office trying to get me to speak to you. I planned on calling you as soon as this is over. I've got to run. Sunset won't wait, even for the Prime Minister of Greece."

"It can't wait, Minister." Andreas leaned in and whispered in his ear. "I believe there's a plan to assassinate you here."

The Minister's trademark smile vanished and he froze in place. "What?"

"It's complicated. But everything points to it."

"Who's behind it?"

"People close to you."

"What people?"

The mayor tapped Andreas on the shoulder. "Sir, would you please allow the Prime Minister to move along? We'll be late for the ceremony."

"I won't be long."

The Prime Minister regained his composure. "Come, walk with me, Andreas. Is this your way of telling me you've reached that 'instinct borne of facts' moment we spoke of when we last met?"

"Still no facts, sir. But instinct, yes. And there are too many people and not enough time for me to explain it all now. Just please take my word for it that if you go through with this I believe there will be an attempt on your life."

"And if I don't, will the threat go away?"

"Likely not. If I'm right, they'll find another way to try."

"One you won't know about."

"Correct."

"You do know I've taken to wearing a bulletproof vest to these events?"

"Smart, but we don't know how they plan on doing it, and they're likely terrific marksmen who expect you to be wearing one."

"And you have no evidence of who's behind this plot?"

"Not a shred. Only conjecture."

The Prime Minister looked ahead at the police leading the way up the hill, smiled and waved at people shouting his name. He waved again for a TV camera up ahead.

"Sounds like I don't really have much of a choice. If there's no way to prove there's a plot or conspiracy, either I take the risk here today where we have a bit of warning or I take the risk every day for the rest of my life when we don't."

"That's about how I see it. But obviously the call's up to you, not me."

"Well, I guess you better run ahead. I'll tell my security chief to take orders from you. And by the way, I hope you don't mind me saying this, but deep down inside I'm praying you're insane."

"Not at all," Andreas said. "I hope so too."

Chapter Twenty-four

About the only bit of luck Andreas felt he'd found so far was that one of the security agents possessed a sharpshooter's rifle and said he knew how to use it. Andreas sent him off to the top of the bell tower closest to the square with the best view of the ceremony. The square ran lengthwise roughly north-south, with its northern edge parallel to the southern wall of the old castle. The unlit tree stood in the middle of the square. Barely had the agent reached the tower when the crowd accompanying the Prime Minister up a cobbled path began pouring in from the east to an already packed square. Some folks climbed up onto the castle's southern wall, others moved to the western edge of the square along its drop-off to the hillside below. The Prime Minister soon stood surrounded on all sides.

Andreas had posted Petro and Yianni two meters on either side of where the Prime Minister now stood at the northern end of the square, facing the TV cameras, the tree beyond them, and hundreds of people gathered around it. Andreas stood directly behind the Prime Minister with his back to the castle's south wall and those perched on the wall behind him.

"Can you hear me?" Andreas said into his wrist mike. He pressed his other hand against his earpiece, waiting for a reply.

"Clear as a bell," said Yianni.

"Me too," said Petro.

"This is a pretty tight crowd for taking a long sniper shot," said Andreas.

"Unless you don't care about taking out a few more in the process," said Yianni.

"Then why not use a bomb?" said Petro. "There must be some misguided soul out there that those wealthy bastards could buy to die in exchange for a guaranteed better life for his family."

"Let's hope that if there is, he or she is not here tonight," said Andreas. "But as I said before, we have to stick with what brought us here, the assumption this will be a precision, military-style operation and not some sloppy bombing." *Please, God.*

He looked up at the tower at his sharpshooter. He had the best position of anyone. *Good.* Suddenly, Andreas swallowed hard. *What if* he's *the assassin?* It could be anyone. Petro was right. These people could reach anyone. And if he were the one, then the Chief of Special Crimes had just put him in position to assassinate the Prime Minister.

Terrific. A joint police and military conspiracy.

"Get a grip," he said aloud to himself and looked west. The sun stood cued to set right on time.

The mayor launched into his speech, generously thanking the Prime Minster for turning an event meant to shine the Christmas spirit across Santorini into a beacon of good cheer for all of Greece. The mayor got on a roll and by the time he'd turned the mike over to the Prime Minister, only a bare slice of the sun remained visible.

Halfway through the mayor's speech, all but one TV crew had turned from filming the mayor to catch the sunset. Now all cameras swung back to focus on the Prime Minister.

The bit of tension in the Prime Minister's voice might have been taken by some to be displeasure at the little time the mayor had left for him to speak. Andreas saw it differently. Bravado was fine until you're in the actual line of fire. Then you sweat.

The Prime Minister's speech lasted less than three minutes, consisting mostly of thank-yous to local dignitaries, but even that took longer than he seemed to want. He finished with a grand flourish of his arm toward the tree, "Santorini, *let there be light.*"

All but the same lone camera swung around to catch the moment the tree would burst into light. The blond male reporter's camera remained fixed on the Prime Minister.

It flashed across Andreas' mind in a blur: the cameras, the reporters, the vans, all expected, all wanted, all invisible. He screamed into his wrist mike. "It's the TV crew. The blond and his cameraman."

Andreas leaped forward, seized the Prime Minister by the back of his collar, and yanked him back into the crowd behind them just as a blinding array of colored lights exploded from the tree in all directions. He'd pulled the PM to the bottom of the castle wall when Andreas heard the first sharp crack of pistol rounds, followed by screaming people. More pistol shots. More screaming. Andreas realized the assassins were firing in the air, trying to scatter the crowd away from the Prime Minister. He pushed a now-sprinting Prime Minister along the base of the castle wall toward its western end. They'd have to jump off the hilltop edge of the square. And they did, an instant before the first shots whizzed over their heads.

Yianni and Petro, with guns drawn, rushed west toward the sound of gunfire through a panicked crowd pressing at them in the opposite direction. As they neared the northwest corner of the square, the crowd opened up and Yianni saw the reporter crouched by the end of the castle wall, taking aim downward off the edge of the square at a wide ledge running three meters or so below that part of the square. Andreas and the Prime Minister must have fled there. Petro fired first, but missed. The reporter swung around, fired, and did not miss, catching Petro in the middle of his chest, then fired an immediate second round hitting Yianni squarely in a similar fatal spot. The reporter calmly returned his aim to what lay below as a distinctly higher-pitched crack came ringing down from above.

The bullet caught the side of the reporter's head, driving him sideways into the castle wall, bouncing him off the rock, and over the edge.

◇◇◇

Andreas heard the body crash onto the ledge. He peeked out from behind the mess of building materials he and the Prime Minster huddled behind on the far north end of the same ledge. Andreas kept his gun focused on the downed assassin as he shouted into his wrist mike. "Yianni, Petro, where are you?"

No answer.

"*Yianni, Petro*," he screamed.

Still no answer.

He pulled the Prime Minister closer. "There's still at least one assassin out there. And I can't reach my men."

Out the corner of his eye, Andreas caught two men staring down at them from where the reporter's body had fallen. He raised his gun and fixed his aim on them.

"Prime Minister, are you okay?" yelled one of the men.

The Prime Minister touched Andreas' arm. "It's okay, they're from my security detail." He stood up and yelled back, "Yes, I'm fine."

Andreas stood, holstered his pistol, led the PM to the three-meter high cliff-face directly below the agents, and boosted him up into their waiting arms. Andreas backed up to the edge of the ledge, then ran for the cliff-face, vaulting himself high enough up the rock face to grab its top edge. The PM's agents took hold of Andreas' arms and pulled him up.

"Thanks. Have you seen—?" Andreas didn't move, just stared at the two bodies lying by the base of the castle wall. "*Get an ambulance!*" he shouted to the agents and ran to his men. He dropped to his knees, saw the bullet holes, and felt for a pulse.

He found one. Then he felt for another. Found that one too. They'd both been knocked out, either by the impact of the bullets or by striking their heads on the ground. No matter, they were alive.

Andreas shut his eyes, said a prayer, and crossed himself. "And thank you, too, Dear Lord, for ballistic vests."

"Chief."

Andreas looked up. It was the agent from the bell tower. "I got one of them, but the other one took off before I could get a bead on him."

"Which way did he go?"

"Down toward where the vans are parked."

"Do me a favor and stay with my men until the medics get here."

"Will do."

Andreas turned to leave, but stopped and looked at the agent. "That was great shooting. I owe you one. A big one." And Andreas was off and running.

Andreas didn't have to know the way down; all he had to do was follow the stream of people still racing down the hill. When he came to the first of the media vans, he saw someone in the driver seat.

"Hey, buddy, did anyone from a media crew just go by here?"

"You mean leaving? Are you kidding me? This is a once-in-a-lifetime opportunity for every reporter up there. I don't know if they'll ever leave."

Andreas showed him his ID. "Think harder."

"Well, come to think of it, a cameraman from an independent went by here in a hurry a few minutes ago."

"Independent?"

"Yeah, they're the sort that do freelance work trying to sell whatever they come up with to anybody who'll take it. He might have left. They parked a rented green-and-white van by the main road. Never even tried to cut some distance off their hike to the top."

For an easy getaway. "Thanks." Andreas ran down the hill to the main road. No green-and-white van.

The survivor had escaped.

He called Santorini's police chief, who was still up at the site of the ceremony, and told him about the van. The police chief said he'd already shut every road leading out of Pyrgos toward the ports and airport, and with Andreas' description of the van, they should have no trouble finding it, hopefully with the would-be assassin still in it.

Andreas had a gnawing feeling, though, that catching the suspect wouldn't be that easy. "How are my men?"

"A little groggy, but they'll be okay. They got hit with some powerful loads for a nine millimeter. You guys ought to get better vests. Those shooters came loaded for bear. Literally."

"Thanks." Andreas hung up, shut his eyes, and said another prayer.

A mustached old man in a Greek fisherman's hat and frayed denim work shirt sat smoking a cigarette in the doorway of a tiny white house across from where Andreas stood praying. "The missus doesn't let me smoke inside."

Andreas nodded, forced a smile.

"Say, aren't you Sappho's friend?"

Andreas nodded again.

"I thought I recognized you. I watched you and two other guys walking up and down here with her most of the day."

The last thing Andreas wanted now was to chit-chat. He had to figure out the assassin's next move.

"If it's Sappho you're looking for, she's in that taverna over there." He pointed across the road.

"Thanks, but I'm looking for a green-and-white van."

"Oh, that guy. He took off. Almost ran over my neighbor he was in such a hurry. Crazy driver. Doesn't even know where he's going."

"Why do you say that?"

"Because unless he's interested in checking out our southern beaches in December in the dark, or in some moonlight sightseeing down in the village of Emborio, he should have turned right. That's what gets you to the ports and airport. But he went left."

"What's to the left?"

"The Monastery of Profitis Ilias."

Andreas nodded.

The old man puffed on his cigarette. "And that military radar station the monks keep praying for God to kick off their mountaintop."

Andreas' mouth dropped open. "Did you say a military radar station? Are you sure?"

Nod. "Lived here all my life—"

"Thank you." Andreas sprinted across the road and into the taverna. Sappho sat with a group of men huddle around a table staring up at TV coverage of what had just gone down at the top of the village.

He grabbed Sappho by her arm. "Is your car here?"

"What's going on? *Is Petro okay?*" The news says people have been shot, but they're not giving details beyond saying the Prime Minister is safe and unharmed."

"Yes, he's fine. I'll tell you everything on the way. Let's go."

She stumbled out behind him, as he led her by her arm. "Go where?"

"The radar station up by the monastery."

Sappho drove as Andreas called the Santorini police chief and every ministry official he could think of who could alert the radar station that an assassin was headed their way. But no one could get through.

That's when he called for backup.

The first minutes of the usual nine-minute drive from Pyrgos to the monastery ran through the village's modern outskirts along a broad two-lane road passing by closely spaced one- and two-story traditional homes. That abruptly changed when the road turned serpentine climbing up the mountain toward the monastery. The two lanes shrank to barely more than one, presenting only a bit of dirt shoulder to the side of the road pressed against the mountain, while the opposite side offered a cliffside drop. But traffic still buzzed along in both directions.

The sky held enough light for Andreas to make out the broad details of the mountain. Gray, beige, and green splotches of unrecognizable vegetation along the hillsides, wind-battered slim green trees clinging haphazardly to the edges of the road, the odd stone wall holding back erosion, and a rare building strategically placed to take advantage of the stunning views.

He kept assuring Sappho that Petro was fine, and asked what she knew about the radar station.

"There's an entrance close to the one for the monastery. It has an up-and-down, single-pole gate, sliding metal gates, and a guard posted twenty-four/seven. A road leads around from there to radio towers and dishes twenty meters or so from some monastery buildings. It was built in the 1960s and the Greek military operates it for NATO. The monks hate it, but can't get the Greek government to remove it. They like NATO money too much."

"What's the layout past the front gate?"

"I haven't been in there since my father took me when I was a kid. He had a friend who worked there and he wanted me to see what it was like so I wouldn't be curious and go exploring on my own. He said it's dangerous up there. Too much radiation."

"Do you remember anything about what you saw?"

"Just look at the mountain and you'll see the towers. They're the island's biggest eyesore."

Andreas waved his hand. "Anything more than that?"

"Square, concrete buildings, some painted in camouflage, some not. They looked like bunkers from old war movies."

"What about an airstrip?"

"On the top of that mountain? Not a chance." She turned to him for a moment then looked ahead.

"What is it?"

"I remember seeing a helicopter pad on top of one of the bunker buildings. I've never seen anyone actually use it, but it's there."

"*That's it.*" He slammed his hand on the dashboard.

"Easy, Chief, the car's not paid for yet."

"Remind me to tell Petro he owes you a big kiss from me."

Andreas called the Santorini police chief and told him that their suspect was trying to escape by helicopter from the radar base. The chief said he'd alert the Air Force and warned Andreas to be careful, because still no one had been able to contact anyone at the radar station.

"When we see the guard," he told Sappho, "I want you to tell me if you recognize him. Something's not right. No one can get through to the station."

"That's convenient if you're trying to make the military look like it's behind the operation."

The entrance appeared just as Sappho had described, plus a whole lot of signs making it clear this was not a place that welcomed tourists. The pole gate was up, so Sappho pulled her neon green car right up to the sliding metal gates.

A soldier stepped toward her window.

"I don't know him," she whispered to Andreas.

"May I help you, Miss? This is a restricted area, only authorized personnel are allowed in."

Andreas leaned over so he could see the soldier's face. "Soldier, are you aware that an assassination attempt on our Prime Minister's life just took place in Pyrgos?"

The soldier put his hand on his sidearm. "No, and who are you, sir?"

"Let's all stay calm, soldier. I'm going to reach inside my shirt and pull out my ID." Andreas reached for his ID with his left hand as the soldier squeezed the grip on his sidearm. Andreas held his ID out for the soldier.

"Sorry, sir, but this is a military installation."

"I'm Chief Inspector Andreas Kaldis, head of the Greek police's Special Crimes Unit, and we have reason to believe one of the suspects has escaped onto this installation."

"Sorry, sir, but I can't allow anyone in without military permission."

Andreas smiled. "That's a little difficult to arrange when no one answers your phone."

"I know, sir. All communications have been shut down for repairs, but only for an hour. It should be up and running by eighteen-hundred hours."

"And the cellphones?"

"Everything here is shut down."

"That sounds strange don't you think? A radar base without communication to the outside world?" said Andreas.

"All I know is we've had nothing but grief with our communications systems for about a week, and orders came down from the Ministry of Defense to do what the telecom folks told us to do. They promised they'd figure out the problem and fix it within an hour."

"By then the assassin will have escaped. You know who I'm talking about, don't you?"

"No, I don't." His hand still gripped his sidearm.

"The fellow in that green-and-white van you just let in here."

The soldier's expression lost its military starch. "But he had written permission from the Ministry of Defense to be here. Some sort of filming."

"Soldier, can you see down the hill from here to the road back to Pyrgos?"

"Yes."

"Well, then, how about if you take a look down that way, and tell me whether you see a hell of a long line of red and blue lights screaming along in this direction. Because when they get here, and see you haven't let me in, I can assure you that you'll be arrested as an accessory to the attempted murder of our Prime Minister. After all, if you're going to let the real bad guy get away, they're going to have to nail somebody to make the press happy."

The soldier took a step back.

"Go ahead, walk over, take a look."

He hesitated but backed away farther to get a line of sight down the mountain to Pyrgos.

"Oh shit," was what Andreas heard as the soldier came running up past the front of the car and yanked open the gates. "Come on, come on," he yelled waving for Sappho to drive ahead.

"Thank you." She smiled to the soldier as she drove through, then gave Andreas a glance. "Always pays to be nice. He might just turn out to be a customer."

Andreas lifted his right hand from the side of the seat and placed his gun in his lap.

"You had that in your hand the whole time?"

"Yep, always pays to be prepared. He might just turn out to be a bad guy. Now, please just get me to that helipad."

"It's back around over there."

Fifty meters farther in, they found the green-and-white van. It sat diagonally across the road making it impossible for them to pass.

Andreas opened his door. "You stay here and when the cavalry gets here tell them to get as much light as possible on the building with the helipad and to cover it from every angle they can." He swung his legs out the door, and turned his head to Sappho just before getting out. "Thanks."

He'd not gone five meters when he heard the helicopter coming in from the south. He started running along the rough road but had to concentrate more than he liked on not tripping in the dark. By the time he reached the first set of structures the helicopter was only a hundred meters away and beginning its approach to the rooftop. He couldn't make out the markings but it looked like a military-style AB-205 copter. Another nice touch.

He made it to the near corner of the building adjacent to the one with the helipad without seeing or hearing a soul, then crept along the side of the building, looking for any sign of the cameraman. He had to be nearby, most likely already up on the rooftop. Probably expecting company. That meant a likely sniper rifle, possibly with a night-vision scope. And these guys didn't miss.

Andreas' thoughts ran to his wife, his son, and his soon-to-be born second child. He hadn't thought about any of that up until now. Only his duty to protect the Prime Minister and catch the would-be assassin. But now the Prime Minister was safe, and if Andreas tried to storm the building to capture the man on the roof, the most likely outcome would be Andreas' death.

Cornered rats were dangerous, and this one most definitely was cornered. The cameraman's only escape was from that roof, a position he'd protect at all costs.

It was a Charge of the Light Brigade decision for Andreas. The copter now hovered about thirty meters over the roof. With so many towers so close by, the landing would be tricky. It would take a talented pilot exercising serious concentration, which was precisely why Andreas began shooting at the cockpit.

He could tell he'd got the pilot's attention when the copter suddenly lurched back and pulled away. He'd also drawn the cameraman's attention. Bullets started flying from the rooftop, all sailing over his head because he'd left the shooter no angle on him from above.

With the rat now trapped, the next move depended on whether the pilot had the balls to try again for the roof.

That's when virtually every cop on Santorini, plus MPs from the Air Force base, arrived with sirens blaring and lights flashing, sending a clear message to the pilot that his welcome would be anything but warm and fuzzy. The helicopter hovered for a few seconds, then angled off into the night.

More brains than balls.

Andreas liked the pilot's thinking. Now he had to make sure the charging cavalry didn't mistake Andreas for one of the bad guys. So he hunkered down and waited.

Within five minutes every official gun and light on the mountain pointed at that rooftop, covering it from all angles. The cameraman had no place to go. The question was, what would he do now? The answer came moments later. A rifle and two handguns flew from the roof and clattered to the ground near Andreas, followed by the English words, "I surrender."

Chapter Twenty-five

The interrogation of the cameraman yielded precisely what Andreas thought. Nothing. After eight straight hours of hearing nothing more than, "I want a lawyer," he was transferred to Athens' Korydallos maximum security prison. Europol identified him as a Greek-speaking Scottish citizen dishonorably discharged from British SAS, but they had no relevant information beyond that. His dead partner shared a similar resumé but with the U.S.'s Navy Seals. Andreas held the faint hope that he might soften up and talk once the prosecutor made clear that he faced a life sentence, but probably not, because in Greece every sentence was negotiable if you had the right contacts.

The pilot proved to be a different story. He wouldn't stop talking. He'd never made it off the island. A Greek F-16 Fighting Falcon scrambled out of Souda Air Force Base on Crete had only to buzz the helicopter once for the pilot to set the chopper down. He landed in the Santorini Airport and identified himself as a captain in the Hellenic Coast Guard who moonlighted for a private charter service flying military-style helicopters. All he knew about tonight's flight was that a news film crew with Ministry of Defense authorization to use the radar station's helipad had requested an active-duty military pilot to take them from there to Athens. The owner of the charter service confirmed the pilot's story and showed a letter on official Ministry of Defense stationery authorizing the "news crew's" request.

The telecom company had a similar story. Someone possessing great technical expertise and identifying himself as from the Ministry of Defense had scheduled a repair of chronic communications problems at the radar site—a repair that would require a temporary but complete shutdown of all systems. The supposed Ministry of Defense expert had told the telecom that the shutdown presented no problem and the radar installation would be expecting it. When Andreas asked if that seemed unusual, the telcom representative said the only unusual aspect was the military agreeing to pay up front in exchange for expedited service.

More nails in the military's intended coffin.

But not a hint of Mayroon's or Prada's involvement.

The next morning, Prada received a personal telephone call from the Prime Minister asking that he join him for coffee at his office in the Maximos Mansion. Prada arrived early, but he did not have to wait. The Prime Minister's secretary showed him straight into her boss' conference room. The Prime Minister sat waiting at the far end of a rectangular conference table surrounded by paneled walls, built-in bookcases, heavily draped windows, and Kaldis on one side of him, the Brigadier on the other.

"Ah, my friend, welcome," said the Prime Minister. "Please sit. Or if you want a coffee, please help yourself." He pointed to a credenza by the door.

"No, thank you." Prada sat at the end of the table farthest away from the others, his eyes darting from one face to another.

The Prime Minister nodded. "I believe you know my other guests."

"Yes, but why are they here?"

"Ah, good question. Let's have the Chief Inspector answer that."

Andreas leaned forward. "Good morning. Sleep well?"

Prada gave him a dismissive look.

"No matter, none of us did. In fact, I haven't been to sleep yet. Spent the whole night talking to witnesses. Trying to catch those responsible for attempting to assassinate the leader of our nation is tiring work."

"Get to the point, Kaldis," growled Prada. "If you have a point."

"Relax. There's plenty of time. The Prime Minister graciously cleared his calendar for this meeting. Do you have someplace more important to be?"

Prada glared, but said nothing.

"Good. Oh, by the way, I should tell you not to worry about us recording any of this. It's all off the record. Though I must say I did appreciate the opportunity we had to listen to those hours of recordings you and our distinguished public order minister made in his office. Very informative."

"I know of no such recordings."

Andreas laughed. "You're showing fear. Look, we all know you're lying." He held up a digital player for Prada to see. "So, let's cut to the chase. Yesterday two highly-trained, ex-military commandos attempted to assassinate our Prime Minister in an elaborate plan involving Greek military installations, personnel, and assets. The hired assassins carefully avoided doing anything that might cause harm to anyone other than our Prime Minister. Crowds were scattered by shots in the air, police attempting to intervene were purposely immobilized with shots to their ballistic vests rather than killed by shots to the head, all to create the impression of a carefully executed Greek military operation."

"Thank God you were there to protect our Prime Minister." Prada's voice showed no sign of strain at making the words sound sincere.

Andreas smiled. "That's very kind of you to say, but for that I really have to thank you."

"Me?"

"Yes, it was your little speech some days back at your dinner on Santorini with the Caesars that got me on the road to figuring it all out."

"Figuring what out?"

"Do you want to listen to the recordings?" said Andreas.

The Prime Minister leaned forward. "I found them very interesting."

Prada's left eye began to twitch.

"What really put us on track was how quickly your invitation to the dinner led to such a sudden, intense interest in Santorini by some of your longtime friends."

The Prime Minister nodded. "Mayroon."

Prada visibly blanched.

"Yes," said Andreas. "The very next day Mayroon started running around, gathering info on Santorini. On day five, the Brigadier's daughter died. On day eight you met the Caesars for dinner on Santorini. And on day eleven you're heard saying '*gotcha*' after a recorded meeting between you and three military personnel from that Santorini dinner." Andreas held up the player. "Would you like to hear it?"

Not a word from Prada.

"I didn't think you would." Andreas put down the player. "Nice plan. Arrange to have all the bread crumbs lead straight back to the military and the minister of defense, and make your toady buddy the minister of public order a national hero in the process by having him ride in on a white horse, the hero who'd uncovered the military perpetrators of a great treason."

Andreas leaned forward. "Did I say 'nice' plan? I meant 'brilliant,' because the only ones involved in executing the plan knowing anything about its real purpose were the foreign assassins, and I'd bet even they didn't have a clue of who stood behind it." Andreas shook his head. "Nope, there's only one person on earth who knows that."

Andreas let the thought linger.

"That one person must be feeling mighty anxious this morning. With one assassin dead, the other in prison, and both identified as foreigners, that pretty much gets the Greek military off the hook. So the plan failed."

Andreas looked over at the Prime Minister. "I forget who said, 'If you're going to shoot the king, don't miss,'" and turned his attention back on Prada. "But that's the problem. The killers missed. Now everyone having anything to do with the plot is racing around covering tracks and eliminating loose ends."

Prada blinked.

"Which should make you very, very uncomfortable."

"You're crazy, Kaldis. I had nothing to do with this. The Prime Minister is my closest friend and has had my unqualified support his entire political life."

"It's the end-of-life part that has us here today. Notably yours," said Andreas.

"I don't understand," said Prada.

"Sure you do." Andreas leaned back in his chair. "Something I've never been able to figure out is how the death of the Brigadier's daughter tied into all of this. Even today, he remains convinced you had absolutely nothing to do with her assassination."

Prada's eyes met the Brigadier's.

"I always thought of her murder as some sort of a message to the Brigadier. But I was wrong. I missed the obvious. Why don't you tell us why she died? You owe the Brigadier and his wife at least that much."

Prada stared down at the tabletop. He cleared his throat, but didn't look up. "They knew Penelope was my goddaughter. I used to talk about her with pride. When I told them of the opportunity for putting their business plan back on track—"

"Replacing me with the minister of public order?" said the Prime Minister.

Prada nodded but still didn't look up. "They told me that they were tired of 'Greek promises' and needed guarantees. I said I could give no guarantees." He drew in and let out a breath. "That's when they murdered Penelope and told me to take it as their guarantee of what would happen to me should I fail to deliver on my promises."

"You miserable bastard." The Brigadier sprang out of his chair but caught himself a pace toward Prada. He paused, straightened his jacket, and returned to his seat next to the Prime Minister.

"There is nothing I'm more ashamed of in my entire life." Prada looked up. "But there's also nothing more I can do about it."

"Yes, there is," said Andreas. "You can give us the people at Mayroon who are to blame."

"They'll kill me."

Andreas shook his head. "You're an intelligent man. Are you going to make me state the obvious?"

Prada gestured no. "I'm dead anyway."

"Yep, you're loose end number one," said Andreas. "But if you give me the names, we might be able to get to them first."

"You'll never be able to prove a thing."

"Let us worry about that," said the Prime Minister

"Then what happens?"

"I wouldn't worry about then, I'd worry about you and now," said Andreas.

"That's what I meant."

Andreas started to speak but the Prime Minister put out his hand to stop him, and leaned forward. "It's simple. I'll let you live. They will not be as generous. The decision is yours. But if you don't cooperate, I may change my mind."

Andreas blinked. So did the Brigadier.

Prada stuttered, "But, but—"

"No buts, only a decision. Give us the names," the Prime Minister slammed his hand on the tabletop, "*now*!"

And he did.

The three names Prada gave up had the Prime Minister biting at his lower lip. He'd been betrayed by his closest confidents at the highest level of Mayroon. He didn't say a word for about a minute after Prada finished, then simply told him to leave. No one seemed more surprised than Prada, but he left immediately.

No one spoke for another minute.

The Prime Minister sighed. "I know you're wondering why I did what I just did."

"I expected to be arresting him."

"He will be. But if we arrest him now, before I've decided on how best to proceed, it will alert Mayroon. And I doubt Prada will tell them on his own."

"Won't he flee?" asked the Brigadier.

"To where? From whom? No, for now he can walk around free as a bird. But carefully observed. And without power. He is stripped of all authority as of this moment, and I've accepted the immediate resignation of the minister of public order, for failing to discover a terrorist plot against me."

"What terrorists?" asked Andreas.

He smiled. "I don't know, I'll make some up. But it will be announced as the same terrorists who murdered your daughter, Brigadier. Let us hope that puts an end to these painful demonstrations." He shook his head. "They must be extraordinarily difficult for you and your wife to watch, so brutally exploiting your daughter's memory for selfish political purposes."

Wow, he's smooth, thought Andreas. *Precisely the sort of tactic on which he rose to power.*

"Thank you, Prime Minister," said the Brigadier.

"Did Babis actually resign?" said Andreas.

"He had no choice. All my ministers signed an undated letter of resignation when I appointed them. That way they can't resist me if I want to dismiss them. All I have to do is date it."

"What about the actual killers of my daughter?" said the Brigadier.

"I think the two who went after the Prime Minister are the ones who pulled the trigger," said Andreas, "but there's no way of knowing for sure unless the assassin we captured admits to it, which is unlikely."

"Brigadier, I'd like to talk to you a bit more about your concerns, but could you please excuse us for a few moments? I want to discuss something else with the Chief Inspector."

The Brigadier nodded and left.

The Prime Minister swung his chair around to face Andreas. "I've not yet had the chance to thank you for saving my life."

Andreas nodded. "What else could I do? And it wasn't just me."

"I know, I plan on honoring you and your men."

"Thank you. And there's a young woman who deserves to be honored as well."

He nodded. "We work pretty well as a team."

Andreas wondered where this was headed.

"I particularly like the part where you bluffed about the recordings."

"I guessed he'd said a lot of incriminating things in the minister's office and wasn't sure what Babis might have recorded."

"Ah, yes, trust among political friends, a wonderful thing to behold. Which brings me to the point of my wanting to talk to you privately. I never should have replaced you as minister of public order. I want you back there."

Andreas' face tightened. "That's a great honor, sir. But my wife would kill me if I took the post."

"Why?"

"She says I get all moody and anxious around politicians."

The Prime Minister laughed. "I can imagine."

"Besides, we're expecting a baby and I'd rather spend my free time at home, which I'll never have if I join your cabinet."

"Fair enough, but the offer's open anytime you change your mind."

"Thank you."

Both men stood and Andreas extended his hand. The Prime Minister took it and then hugged him. "Thanks again."

Andreas nodded and headed to the door.

"Uh, would you ask the Brigadier to come back in? I have an offer for him too. Hopefully one he can't refuse." The Prime Minister smiled at his *Godfather* reference.

Which made Andreas think of another quote, one he'd seen on full display today. *Don't fuck with ultimate power.*

True peace seemed to have come to pass over the following weeks, or at least in Andreas' life. Christmas Day came and went with Maggie and Tassos joining them for the holiday, and everyone, including Yianni, Sappho, and Petro, had agreed to come to their home for a true Saint Basil's Day feast on New Year's Day.

Petro and Sappho arrived early, and Lila immediately dragged her into the kitchen to put her professional skills to good use. Petro took the opportunity to speak privately to his boss.

"I'm not sure I'm fully myself yet, Chief."

"If you mean from the shooting, I understand."

"I mean…I looked the man square in the eye. I saw nothing but death. I was…dead. It was a real kick in the ass about the meaning of life."

Andreas nodded. "Scary."

"More than scary. I don't think I can do this anymore."

Andreas bit at his lip. "Yep, the pay's certainly not worth it."

"That's not why I do it."

"I know." He patted Petro on the shoulder.

"So what's your plan?"

"I'm thinking of helping Sappho set up and run her new restaurant on Perissa Beach."

Andreas' face brightened into a smile. "That's terrific news!" He patted Petro's cheek. "I'm so happy for you two."

"Thanks, Chief. I didn't know how you'd take it."

"You know I'll miss you. We'll all miss you. And your job's always open, but if you have a shot at a better life, go for it."

"Hey, what are you two doing over there?" came a rumbling voice from across the room.

"I guess Detective Kouros is here," said Andreas.

"Who else?"

"Honey, could you come in here and give us a hand," yelled Sappho from inside the kitchen.

Andreas whispered, "There's still time to reconsider resigning."

Petro smiled, but left for the kitchen.

Yianni walked over to Andreas as Petro headed into the kitchen. "So, he told you, huh?"

"Yeah."

"I sensed he might leave from the night we spent in the medical center after the shooting. I still don't know how you broke the news to Sappho about us taking bullets to the middle of our chests—"

"Very carefully."

"Once she got there she didn't leave his side for a minute. She kept rambling on that somehow she felt responsible for what happened because she'd said something to him about how she couldn't wait for him to be shot. Then, as soon as she heard he was okay, all she did was yell at how she'd kill him if he ever let someone else try to kill him."

"Makes sense," smiled Andreas.

"I sure as hell wasn't going to disagree with her. One near-death experience a night was enough for me."

Andreas laughed.

"Did you hear the other news?"

"Don't tell me you're resigning too?"

"Nah, never, you're stuck with me. I heard it on the radio on the way over. Our old buddy Prada was arrested earlier today and charged with treason."

"On Saint Basil's Day? That's a little heartless," said Andreas. "I wonder what prompted the Prime Minister to pull the trigger on that?"

"Well, one thing's for sure," said Yianni. "He won't be finding the gold coin in his slice of the *vasilopita*"—the round sweet bread specially baked for Saint Basil's Day promised sweetness for all and a year of good luck to the one whose piece held the buried gold coin.

"Maybe Sappho and Petro will find it?"

"Nah, that piece should go to you or Lila. After all, there's a new baby due any day now."

"The one who'll need the luck is Tassaki, what with a little sister on the way."

"Do you have a name for her yet?"

Andreas nodded. "It's—"

"Mr. Kaldis."

He turned around. "Yes, Marietta?"

"There's a call for you."

"Who is it?"

"All he'd say was 'Penelope's father.'"

Andreas looked at Yianni. "The Brigadier?"

"Maybe he's calling to wish you *xronia pola*?"

"We all could use many years. Many good years." Andreas headed to his study and picked up the phone. "Hello."

"It's me." The voice came across as clipped, but clearly the Brigadier's.

"*Xronia pola*," said Andreas.

"Same to you."

"Are you okay?" said Andreas.

"I think so." The voice gained strength. "It's done."

"What's done?"

"An offer I couldn't refuse."

Andreas felt the butterflies rise in his stomach. "Where are you?"

"Skiing in the United States. My wife and I won't be coming back. I just wanted to say thank you for caring about what happened to our daughter. You were the only one who did."

Andreas held his breath, waiting for what would come next.

"I owed it to you to let you know before you read about it in the papers. You're a good man. God bless, and goodbye."

The phone went dead.

What the hell was that all about?

Andreas turned on his computer and clicked a link to world headlines. Nothing caught his eye. He punched in United States news and found a slew of political headlines. He added the word skiing, and BREAKING NEWS jumped onto the screen about a tragic accident involving three families on a ski holiday in the American West. He read the article literally holding his breath. The chairman and two high-ranking senior executives of an international consulting firm on holiday with their families died in a freak accident when the cable of the gondola carrying them to the top of a mountain snapped, sending the car crashing down the mountain. There were no survivors.

Andreas crossed himself. He wondered if any members of the plotters' families perished with them. And if they had, did the Brigadier or the man who'd dispatched him as an avenging angel care?

He wondered if anyone cared.

Andreas did. He had to. Someone had to. Andreas bowed his head.

Xronia pola.

To receive a free catalog of Poisoned Pen Press titles, please provide your name, address, and e-mail address in one of the following ways:

Phone: 1-800-421-3976
Facsimile: 1-480-949-1707
Email: info@poisonedpenpress.com
Website: www.poisonedpenpress.com

Poisoned Pen Press
6962 E. First Ave. Ste 103
Scottsdale, AZ 85251